PRAISE FOR *BRA*

"Viets brings readers a treat with a new series featuring coroner's investigator Angela Richman . . . Viets, a stroke survivor herself, builds her unusual premise into a compelling thriller that moves quickly and builds suspense steadily."

—Booklist

"Devastating migraines send death investigator Angela Richman, the heroine of this well-paced, darkly humorous series launch from Viets (*The Art of Murder* and fourteen other Dead-End Job mysteries), to the emergency room . . . Angela's endearing, spirited, and resilient humanity resonates on the page. Viets takes an entertaining detour from her usual cozy territory."

—Publishers Weekly

"[Viets's] complicated heroine deserves a return outing."

—Kirkus Reviews

"Cozy veteran Viets (Dead-End Job mysteries), a stroke survivor, returns to her crime fiction roots with this intriguing tale that will attract forensic mystery buffs and fans of Max Allan Collins's *CSI* tie-in series."

—Library Journal

"*Brain Storm* soars as Viets shows Angela's painful recovery, buoyed by her strong spirit and will to live."

—South Florida Sun Sentinel

"[*Brain Storm*] is an affirmation of hope and recovery with bits of well-placed humor to enhance a murder mystery plot that also touches on insurance fraud and hospital politics. Fronted by a unique and winning protagonist, this new series promises to be as popular as Viets's others."
—Oline Cogdill, *Mystery Scene Magazine*

"In her thrilling new series debut, *Brain Storm*, Elaine Viets calls upon her own challenging life experience in introducing Angela Richman, a death investigator working for upper-class Chouteau County in Missouri. Like Viets, Angela suffered a series of strokes, and this death investigator is now struggling—in the midst of her recovery—to investigate a homicide that put her lifesaving neurosurgeon Dr. Jeb Travis Tritt in jail. Crisply written, with deft characterizations and action, Viets tells a tale that only she could have written."
—Brendan DuBois, author of *Fatal Harbor*, two-time Shamus Award winner, and three-time Edgar Award finalist

"A very powerful and unusual novel. I think you've got everything here that a reader loves—a hospital drama and thriller, a strong central character. Made much more interesting because the central character is a very unreliable narrator."
—Ann Cleeves, international bestselling author of the Vera Stanhope and Shetland series

"Elaine Viets has written the exciting first book in a multilayered crime novel series. Angela Richman is not only an investigator but a victim in this complex novel of crime, punishment, and medical malfeasance."
—Charlaine Harris, #1 *New York Times* bestselling author

"Elaine Viets's newest is both a timely medical drama and a compelling mystery. *Brain Storm* gives us a detailed look at the shattered life of a determined death investigator. Readers will want more of Angela Richman's adventures."

—Jeff Abbott, *New York Times* bestselling author of *The First Order*

"In *Brain Storm*, Elaine Viets takes a dangerous turn down a dark alley but manages it with panache and a touch of humor. Angela Marie Richman is a kick-ass protagonist who is victimized by the thing we all fear most—our own mortality. This is territory Viets knows well, and she does a nice job of showing the readers the terrain, all while entertaining them."

—Reed Farrel Coleman, *New York Times* bestselling author of Robert B. Parker's *The Devil Wins*

"Trapped in a nightmarish world after suffering six strokes, death investigator Angela Richman finds she can't trust anyone—including her own mind. A thrilling, suspenseful, twist-filled read that kept me up late into the night, *Brain Storm* marks a fascinating new direction for a wonderfully talented writer."

—Alison Gaylin, *USA Today* bestselling author of the Brenna Spector series

"Haunting and creepy, with a fast-paced, twisty plot, and a protagonist you will not soon forget—this is Elaine Viets at her most deliciously dark."

—David Ellis, Edgar Award winner and author of *Breach of Trust* and nine other novels

"I've been a fan of Elaine Viets's books since she debuted her leather-clad heroine Francesca Vierling. And now I am delighted to see her give us another strong female character we can root for—death investigator Angela Richman. I'm also stoked to see Elaine venture into darker territory with *Brain Storm*, a multilayered mystery that is rich in its sense of place and character and propelled with medical intrigue. *Brain Storm* has everything I love in crime fiction—complexity, intelligence, pretzel plotting, and a touch of dark humor."

—P. J. Parrish, *New York Times* bestselling author of Thomas & Mercer's *She's Not There* and the award-winning Louis Kincaid series

"With *Brain Storm*, Elaine Viets offers readers a rare gem: a mystery that not only engages the head but also compels the heart. Following a near-fatal stroke, death investigator Angela Richman must struggle to regain her physical and mental health while at the same time trying to solve the murder of the inept doctor she blames for her predicament. Drawing on her own experience, Viets chronicles the harrowing journey back from the brink of death. And perhaps the most amazing aspect of the novel is that in the midst of such terrible darkness, Viets manages to deliver hilarious one-liners any comedian would envy."

—William Kent Krueger, Edgar Award–winning author of the *New York Times* bestseller *Ordinary Grace*

"A huge welcome to Angela Marie Richman, an edgy death investigator with a rapier wit and even sharper powers of observation, who makes her debut in Elaine Viets's *Brain Storm*. I loved the deadpan humor from this character, a tough broad who's survived with a vengeance and has scores to settle."

—Hallie Ephron, *New York Times* bestselling author of *Night Night, Sleep Tight*

FIRE
AND
ASHES

OTHER TITLES BY ELAINE VIETS

Angela Richman, Death Investigator

Brain Storm

Dead-End Job Mysteries

Shop Till You Drop
Murder Between the Covers
Dying to Call You
Just Murdered
Murder Unleashed
Murder with Reservations
Clubbed to Death
Killer Cuts
Half-Price Homicide
Pumped for Murder
Final Sail
Board Stiff
Catnapped!
Checked Out
The Art of Murder
Killer Blonde: A Dead-End Job Novella

Josie Marcus Mystery Shopper Mysteries

Dying in Style
High Heels Are Murder
Accessory to Murder
Murder with All the Trimmings
The Fashion Hound Murders
An Uplifting Murder
Death on a Platter
Murder Is a Piece of Cake
Fixing to Die
A Dog Gone Murder

Francesca Vierling Mysteries

Backstab
Rubout
The Pink Flamingo Murders
Doc in the Box

FIRE AND ASHES

ANGELA RICHMAN, DEATH INVESTIGATOR

ELAINE VIETS

THOMAS & MERCER

Text copyright © 2017 Elaine Viets
All rights reserved.

Published by Thomas & Mercer, Seattle

www.apub.com

Amazon, the Amazon logo, and Thomas & Mercer are trademarks of Amazon.com, Inc., or its affiliates.

ISBN-13: 9781477848807
ISBN-10: 1477848800

Cover design by Damon Freeman

Printed in the United States of America

*For Dick Richmond, good friend and newspaper editor,
who taught me how to say more with less.*

CHAPTER 1

Day one

Five fire engines, two ladder trucks, a portable light truck, a battalion chief's van, and what looked like every cop car in Chouteau County were fighting this fire. Death investigator Angela Richman knew it was already too late—she was summoned only for death. Tonight, someone had died in that blazing building, choked by the smoke and seared by those flames. Angela oversaw the bodies at Chouteau County crime scenes or unattended deaths. The death investigator reported to the county medical examiner.

Who was it? Angela didn't know yet. The detective's call was cryptic: "Luther Ridley Delor's house is on fire. One body so far. They're bringing it out. Get over there now." Seventy-year-old Luther called himself a financier to take away the sting of how his family made a trainload of money: running a nationwide chain of payday loan companies. People—especially desperate ones—knew the slogan "You get more with Delor." Was the old man dead? Was the victim his young fiancée? Or did a friend or servant die in that hellish fire?

Angela prayed there was only one victim. She'd expected this death. This was the third major fire in the county in two weeks. Fear smoldered beneath the comfortable surface of Chouteau Forest, Missouri, the biggest town in the county. Chouteau County was a ten-square-mile preserve for the 1 percent and those who served them, about thirty miles west of Saint Louis.

The blaze was in Olympia Forest Estates, an exclusive development built five years ago. That made it brand-new compared with the county's extravagant old-money mansions: robber barons' Romanesque castles, English country houses, and Bavarian hunting lodges built at the turn of the last century. Olympia's brick-and-stone houses seemed subdued after those architectural fancies, but they were still luxurious. Thanks to relentless advertising, everyone knew their prices—three to five million—and their amenities.

Angela, still recovering from six strokes, brain surgery, and a coma at the fairly young age of forty-one, leaned on her cane behind the yellow caution-tape barrier while she tried to spot the best route through the shifting, smoking chaos. She'd trundled her death investigator kit—a black rolling suitcase—across the water-soaked street. Her plain black pantsuit kept her warm in the chilly May night, and her flat, black lace-up shoes helped her navigate the treacherous ground.

Hastily dressed gawkers had gathered in the cul-de-sac outside the burning house. Angela stood next to a scrawny-legged, bald man in blue boxers and sandals and tried not to look at his pale, flabby chest. She knew him: Ollie Champlain. Ollie lived on stale bar snacks and martinis at the Forest Country Club.

"Woo-eee!" Ollie said. "You can almost smell the money burning. That's Luther's house."

Dread seized Angela. Now that she heard Luther's name, the death was real. The Forest "financier" had created a major scandal at age seventy. He'd left his wife of forty years for Kendra Graciela Salvato, a twenty-year-old manicurist. Luther's wife was fighting the divorce, but he'd given Kendra an engagement ring with a diamond bigger than Delaware and swore they'd marry as soon as he was free.

"Don't be disgusting," said a worried woman clutching her long, baggy plaid bathrobe. "The smell is horrible."

Angela caught the toxic stink of melting plastic mixed with the stomach-turning stench of burned meat and hair. The flames were eating the victim's body.

Ollie refused to be shamed. He acted as if the fatal fire were staged for his entertainment. "Look at the firefighters taking axes to that bay window. I can hear the corks popping in that thousand-bottle wine room."

"Humph," Plaid Bathrobe said. "The way Luther drinks, I doubt he could keep a thousand bottles."

"He was definitely pissed tonight," Ollie said. "I watched him stagger home with his little Mexican cutie. Kendra had to help him inside the house. It was fun watching her in that tight white dress. Luther was too drunk to walk into his house, much less run out of it. Jeez, I hope that's not her burning in that house. What a waste of a fine p—" Plaid Bathrobe glared him into changing his crude words. "A fine young woman," he continued. "The Rhinestone Cowboy's a shriveled old coot. I hope she gets out alive."

The Forest residents secretly laughed at Luther's garish outfits. The liver-spotted financier dressed like a drugstore cowboy, from his black Stetson with the diamond hatband to his tight, western-cut jeans flared to fit over his handmade Lucchese boots. Luther's rhinestone-studded shirts sparkled. Angela rather liked his style.

"I hope they *both* get out alive," Plaid Bathrobe said, her tight gray curls bobbing in disapproval.

"The firefighters are going to have a hard time searching Luther's place to save him and Kendra," Ollie said. "It has four or five bedrooms."

"At least they don't have to search a thirty-room mansion," Plaid Bathrobe said. "A house in Olympia Forest is downsizing for Luther. He left the Delor estate that's been in his family since the 1890s to move in with that woman. They never entertain, and it's no big secret why. No decent person would visit or invite them. *She* may get lost in that big place. Her house was practically a shack."

"What time did you see Luther and Kendra come home?" Angela asked.

"About nine o'clock tonight," Plaid Bathrobe said. "I'm Elvira Smythe. I heard the sirens a little after midnight. My husband slept through it all. He's still asleep."

Angela took out her iPad. Both these people had information she might be able to use about the body she'd be examining.

"I wonder if he set his place on fire with one of his cigars," Mrs. Smythe said.

"No, it was the arsonist," Ollie said. "Had to be."

"Whoever he is, he's destroying only the best neighborhoods," Mrs. Smythe said. "There hasn't been a fire in Toonerville yet. That's where *she's* from."

Mike Peters, a blond cop who looked like a cute country boy, came out from behind the yellow tape barrier. "Okay, people, let's go home. The blaze is under control. It's safe to return to your houses."

"I think I will go back inside," Mrs. Smythe said, pulling her plaid bathrobe closer. "It's cool, even if it is May."

"Good idea, ma'am," the cop said.

"I see some friends over there." Scrawny Ollie practically sprinted toward a group across the street.

The cop turned to Angela. "Hey, Angela, are you working?"

"Afraid so. I got the call from Ray Greiman. I was waiting for the smoke to shift so I could see my way through."

"I'll escort you." He lifted the yellow tape, and Angela ducked her ponytailed head under it. "Watch your step—that's broken glass and slippery mud. Glad you're dressed for work. How are you feeling? You had quite a battle not too long ago."

"A year ago last March. Six strokes, brain surgery, and a coma. Three months in the hospital, including physical therapy."

"You've made an amazing recovery."

"It's been a long road back. I'm glad to be working again."

"And looking good, too." He smiled at her. "I don't suppose . . ." He stopped.

Uh-oh, she thought. The newly widowed Angela still wore her wedding ring, hoping it would ward off any potential dates—but even married women get hit on.

Mike seemed to gather his courage, and the words tumbled out in a rush. "I don't suppose you go out with cops?"

"I would, Mike, but I'm not ready to date yet. It's too soon."

"I understand. But when you're ready, I'm here."

"Thanks." She smiled and changed the subject. "Do you know who's dead? Is it Kendra or Luther? Is anyone else inside?"

"Don't know. I just got here, and they put me to work keeping out the ghouls. The firefighters found a body in the upstairs bedroom. I hope it's not Kendra. She's a pretty thing. They'll be bringing out the body shortly."

CHAPTER 2

Day one

Kendra was alive and kicking. Mike led Angela through the snake tangle of hoses, ladders, and equipment to the side of Luther's house, where three burly paramedics struggled to force Luther's screaming, wild-eyed fiancée into a waiting ambulance.

"What the fuck's wrong with you?" Kendra shrieked at the paramedics. "Cowards! If you won't save him, I will. Luther's still inside!" Her eyes were wide and glittery.

Angela was no expert, but it looked like the fire had been largely contained to the second floor. The roof had gaping holes, and glass shards sparkled under the broken windows. An aluminum extension ladder was propped against the front of the brick house under a window missing its glass and frame. Smoke still billowed out the front windows and door. The whole yard was taped off, and more uniformed police officers held back the half-dressed neighbors who pushed forward for a better view of Kendra's battle.

"Fuckers! Leave me alone." Kendra's frantic fight was straight from a porn video: her white lace crotchless bodysuit exposed her bouncing breasts and round bottom and gave a gynecological view Angela definitely didn't want to see.

Everyone else in the development was staring. Some were almost as scantily clad as Kendra, but nowhere near as provocatively. Even the predatory public insurance adjusters—gray-suited vultures hoping to snag a percentage of the claim money—stopped to stare. Some were slack-jawed. On the sidelines, a pack of men howled with laughter at Kendra's struggles. Angela saw Ray Greiman, the detective she was working with, in the pack. She was disgusted but not surprised.

A square-jawed, blond paramedic told Kendra, "You have to go to the hospital, miss," and moved to clamp a meaty hand on her arm. She dodged his grip and kicked him in the knee with a dirty bare foot.

Square Jaw backed away as a no-nonsense woman made a grab for Kendra, but she raked that unlucky paramedic's neck with her red nails. "Ouch! Damn, that hurt!" the paramedic swore, as blood ran down her neck onto her uniform shirt.

"Quit fucking with me and save Luther!"

"It's too late, miss," said a third muscle-bound paramedic with a military buzz. "I'm sorry." He seemed genuinely sad.

Kendra brushed away his sympathy and shrieked, "Damn you. I'll save him myself. Luther! Hang on, sweetie." Buzz tried to cut her off, but she lunged toward the house's smoke-filled front entrance. As he grabbed for her, Kendra gave him a swift kick in the crotch.

"Oof!" he said, and bent over.

"Right to the cojones," Greiman said to the uniform next to him.

"She's a little Mexican wildcat." The uniform leered.

"Hell, I'd pay money to watch this show," a firefighter said.

Angela was pretty sure he was being paid by Chouteau County to control the blaze.

"When we got here just before midnight, she didn't make any sense at all," the firefighter said. "She was hysterical. Couldn't understand a word she was saying. Now suddenly she's Wonder Woman and wants to run in and save him."

"Old Luther was right," Greiman said. "He said she had the best ass in Chouteau County."

"She's certainly the richest piece of ass in town," the uniform said. "I heard Luther gave her two million when they got engaged, and she'll get another two mil when they marry. She must be some spectacular fuck."

"At Luther's age, any fuck is spectacular," Greiman said. "Look at her go. She's running right toward the front door."

"The smoke will stop her in her tracks," the firefighter said. "Even those lungs can't breathe in that."

He was right. The thick smoke left Kendra coughing and choking. She backed down the walkway, wheezing and gasping as she tried to catch her breath.

The portable emergency lights gave Angela a clearer view of the frantic Kendra. Her glossy black hair seemed singed, at least around her face. Her light-brown skin and white bodysuit were smeared with soot, and the skimpy lace outfit had a ragged tear at the waist. Kendra's long red nails—a manicurist's advertisement—were broken, but Angela didn't know if Kendra had broken them when she attacked the paramedic or during her escape from the house. Her hands and feet were cut and bleeding, but it was hard to tell how bad her injuries were.

"Help him." Kendra's voice had a harsh rasp, and she started choking again. "Please." This time when the paramedics closed in on her, Kendra didn't fight them. She was almost doubled over from the racking coughs.

Angela saw three firefighters—no, two firefighters and maybe a man—at the smoky second-floor window with the aluminum ladder leaning against it. Both firefighters wore helmets and masks and had SCBA—self-contained breathing apparatus—tanks on their backs. One firefighter stood at the top of the ladder while the other rested the man on the window opening. Angela thought the sill was gone.

"Luther!" Kendra's scream was cut short by a choking fit. "You're alive."

Angela wasn't sure. The man appeared to be unconscious and badly burned. His hands were charred claws, and his face was a black-and-red crispy mass. Angela couldn't see any hair. If that was Luther and he was still alive, he was facing excruciating pain and little hope of survival.

"Jesus!" Greiman vomited into the bushes. "Is that thing alive?"

"I hope not. For his sake." Angela felt queasy and dizzy but kept her dinner down. She was glad she had her cork-handled Austrian walking cane to keep her upright.

The firefighter at the window gently pushed the man's legs out of the opening. Now the badly burned body was in the arms of the second firefighter, who guided it down the ladder to the bottom. The paramedics abandoned Kendra and grabbed an orange plastic backboard. Kendra rushed over, crying, "Luther, my poor Luther. Speak to me!"

Greiman squished across the wet, muddy lawn in his mud-caked dress shoes to Angela. "He's Kentucky fried. The paramedics can't even put a face mask on him. Skin's peeling off. She killed him."

"We don't know if Luther is dead yet," Angela said. "And why would Kendra kill him? Doesn't she get another two mil when they marry?"

"She already got two million when they got engaged. That's enough for a beaner like her. Now she won't have to screw that scrawny old geezer. And he's gonna die. You don't have to be a doctor to see that. She set him on fire, and he was too drunk to get out of there."

"How do you deduce that, Sherlock?" Angela asked.

"You didn't hear what happened tonight at Gringo Daze?"

"It's their bargain night—five dollars off the bill," Angela said. "I expect the whole Forest was there. No one's tighter than the old rich. You should see them at a pancake supper."

"They were, and they all saw what happened. That's where Luther had his last supper, although I don't think he ate much. He was in the bar, pounding down Dos Equis and grabbing Kendra's ass. Drunk as a skunk. Talked about what great sex he had with her. Popped Viagra with a beer and said he and his little 'greaser gal' were going home to screw and we should expect to see flames. Too bad they were the wrong kind."

"Poor Kendra. She must have been humiliated."

"Who knows what those people think? She was trying to drag him out of there while he kept pawing her. Finally, the owner had to help her get him in the car. So she had plenty of motive. See that fire investigator putting that half-melted gasoline container in an evidence box? The firefighters found it by Luther's door. That's her father's lawn-service logo on it. Her old man has the contract for most of Olympia Forest."

"So? The crew left it behind."

"On the night the house happens to go up in flames? I don't believe in coincidence. She had the means and the opportunity, and it added up to two million reasons to kill Luther."

CHAPTER 3

Day one

"It's official," Greiman said. "Pop Roast is dead as a doornail." He'd managed to talk to the paramedics before they raced away.

Pop Roast? That was his nickname for Luther? Angela hoped none of the bystanders heard him. She glanced at the nearest knot of spectators and was relieved to see them busy talking to one another.

"Who pronounced him dead?" she asked. Missouri had weird rules about who could pronounce someone dead. Most states required some medical training. Not the Show Me State. Anyone could do it, as long as whoever signed the death certificate believed the pronouncer could determine if the person was really dead. Never mind that the moment when death occurs has baffled the best medical minds. Angela had pronounced two people dead, but she'd had no doubt: One was an old woman in full rigor who'd died in bed. The other was a man who'd been dead so long, his body was decomposing. Both times were solemn, scary experiences.

"The paramedics." Greiman was trying to wipe mud streaks off his expensive slacks with his handkerchief. "They're taking Kendra to SOS."

An engine's roar, flashing lights, and siren's wail confirmed his words: the ambulance was rushing to Sisters of Sorrow Hospital.

"There goes the killer. I'm getting a warrant for her fingernail scrapings and blood samples at the hospital," Greiman said.

"Why do you think Kendra is the killer?" Angela asked.

"I already told you." Greiman sounded as if he were speaking to a child. "I talked to the neighbors. She ran out of Luther's house screaming her head off. She distracted the firemen from doing their jobs in that porn-movie getup—and before you start your feminist bullshit, they were fire*men*, and she was damn near naked. She had the perfect setup to commit murder: She has a public wrestling match with the old man when he is drunk and horny. He humiliates her. She pours gasoline on him and has herself a weenie roast." Now Greiman was almost shouting. "And remember, she never said Luther was inside until it was too late to save him. The old bastard was dead."

"Whoa. Anyone see her with gasoline?" Angela asked. "Any record that she bought a can of gas? All you have is that half-melted container. You can't get prints off that thing."

"You'd be surprised. Besides, it's from her father's lawn service. The wits say Jose was here tonight, right before the fire, and he had an ugly argument with Luther. Six people heard him. Then the neighbors heard Kendra and her old man jabbering away in Mexican. He was probably telling her how to kill Luther. Jose got out of there, and Kendra grilled the geezer."

Angela caught the defensive I-don't-have-to-justify-myself-to-you note in his voice. Greiman's last major investigation, the murder of Dr. Porter Gravois, was a debacle that had divided the Forest's old guard. The detective's friends—the Forest grandees—made sure he got a raise, but scuttlebutt said he'd also received an off-the-record reprimand for his careless investigation. Maybe the warning had worked. Even Angela had to admit he'd been more diligent this time around. And he was right to get a warrant for a suspect's blood and nail scrapings.

"Time for you to go to work. You can check the murder scene in the morning when the house is safe to enter. The crispy critter is on the backboard by that uniform," Greiman said.

He pointed toward a twentysomething uniform who looked fish-belly white in the high-powered lights, standing guard over Luther's body. Angela grabbed her DI kit and rolled the ordinary black suitcase across the wet asphalt and muddy grass, steadying herself on the slippery surfaces with her cane. This wasn't a typical death investigation. Luther had been moved from the place where he died, which might have yielded useful clues. The paramedics had abandoned him on an orange plastic backboard in a well-lit corner of his yard, then roared off to the hospital.

Luther looked even worse than Angela thought he would. The Rhinestone Cowboy hardly seemed human. Only part of his saggy buttock and pelvis on the right side were unburned, and that skin was red and seared. She knew this would be an especially difficult death investigation: she would have nightmares for weeks afterward, and it would be a while before she could stomach meat again. Burning deaths were far worse than badly decomposed bodies.

She approached Luther slowly, her nose now mercifully unable to smell his sickening burned hair and roast-meat stink. Some pros used masks or Vicks VapoRub, but Angela didn't notice foul odors after a short while. Her nose wouldn't take them in. But she could definitely see Luther. At one in the morning, Luther was a nightmare vision on his orange plastic bier.

As she unzipped her death investigator suitcase, Angela's hands shook slightly, and her knees felt as if they might give way. Inside, she had a tape recorder, thermometers for body and ambient—air—temperature, a measuring tape, vials, Ziploc bags, paper bags, and plastic containers normally used for leftovers. But these containers would end up in the morgue, not the microwave.

Like many corpses, Luther seemed smaller in death. But he really was smaller. Burn victims could lose up to 60 percent of their weight.

She brought out the tape measure to record his height (length, actually) at five feet eight. The ME would weigh him. A few hours ago, this charred hunk of humanity had been alive with lust and laughter and the envy of all his friends, thanks to his sexy fiancée. Now he was a pathetic sight.

Angela steeled herself for the body actualization—the examination— with her familiar rituals. First, she slipped on four pairs of latex gloves. She would strip off the gloves and put them in her pocket as the body actualization went on so she wouldn't contaminate the investigation with fluids or fibers from other areas. She photographed Luther from about a dozen feet away to capture the entire body, then did a medium shot and finally a series of close-ups. The fire investigator and the police had taken their own photos and videos. These were for the medical examiner. Angela didn't have a medical degree, but she was trained. Death investigators were sort of like paralegals for MEs. Seeing Luther through the camera's viewfinder helped calm her stomach, which was pitching and heaving like a stormy sea.

Angela called up the form she'd need on her iPad: Body of a Burn Victim. The first question was easy. Luther had been positively identified by Kendra. At the morgue, the medical examiner would take X-rays to rule out any foreign bodies—bullets, for instance, or knife tips—that she might not catch in her visual examination. The form's routine questions soothed her, restoring order to this hellish chaos.

Were there any thermal injuries present? Luther's arms were raised in the familiar "pugilistic stance" of a burn victim, as if he'd gone nine rounds with death and lost. His arm muscles had contracted in the heat. Normally she would note every cut ("cutlike defect") and bruise ("contusion") on the body. Now she measured the burns and blisters on his seared flesh, from his head to his blackened, twiglike finger bones. She carefully covered his fragile hands in paper bags secured with rubber bands. They might crumble when the body was transported to the morgue. She saw no jewelry, but then he had no finger left to hold a ring. The heat from a fire made bones brittle, and they could fracture when the body was moved. Angela didn't see any bones jutting through the skin and noted that.

Her stomach twisted, but she knew this scene could have been far worse. Sometimes, the burned skull burst, and the cooked brains spilled out. She'd never seen that and hoped she never would. She tore her eyes away from the horror and returned to the next question.

Hair color? Luther's magnificent mane of white hair had been burned away, but Angela knew the color and noted the absence of hair.

Eye color? She couldn't tell. The eyes were cooked and shriveled. She fought back her nausea. Focus, she told herself. You have a duty to help Luther. He was a rich, silly old fool led around by his libido, but now he needs your skill. The man who'd been powerful enough to give $2 million to his young mistress was now a brittle-boned mess of kindling.

Was the victim's clothing consumed by fire? Luther wore the remnants of white silk boxer shorts: a melted elastic waistband and enough cloth to cover his genitals. She saw no sign of other clothes. She didn't remove his underpants. That would be the ME's job.

Was there an odor of petroleum product on the clothing? Angela forced herself to lean in closer but couldn't smell either oil or gasoline.

Was the victim a known smoker? Were there smoking materials found in the pockets? Angela knew Luther smoked cigars, but she saw no smoking materials on the body. The fire investigator would have to find out later how many cigars he smoked a day and if he also smoked cigarettes, a pipe, weed, or something stronger. Angela knew many otherwise law-abiding senior citizens liked a toke. Families sometimes tried to hide any illegal substances before the death investigation, and Angela would have to gently explain that she wasn't with the DEA, but she did need accurate information for her investigation.

Did the victim use alcohol? Yes. The Forest knew he was a drunk. Greiman said Luther was chugging beer and popping Viagra earlier. The Forest's chief medical examiner, Dr. Evarts Evans, would have to confirm that.

Was the victim known to drink to excess? Yes. Angela had no idea how much he'd drunk tonight—or rather, last night—but it had to be a lot. If his body was too cooked for the ME to do a blood alcohol test, he would have to use a piece of brain.

List all the medications prescribed to the subject. Since this was a fire-and-police investigation, they would have to get that information from his doctor later. Most of the Forest went to Dr. Carmen Bartlett. She treated just about everyone. Greiman said Luther had gulped down one drug—Viagra—with a beer chaser. A dangerous combination. Did Doc Bartlett prescribe the Viagra, or did Luther get it from some illegal source? Even virile young men took Viagra, believing it enhanced their performance. During the royal wedding of William and Kate, Scots brewed a special limited-edition India pale ale—laced with Viagra, chocolate, horny goat weed, and "a healthy dose of sarcasm"—called Arise Prince Willy. *Why am I thinking of that?* Angela wondered, but she knew. She'd allowed herself to be distracted from the stomach-turning scene on the backboard. She shook her head, as if to clear her jumbled thoughts, and attacked the next question.

Could the victim's medical problems have contributed to the fire or to his/her inability to exit the fire scene? If yes, describe. Ollie Champlain said Luther was falling-down drunk when he came home. *Victim was extremely intoxicated when last seen alive,* she wrote. The neighbors told Greiman the old man was in a fighting mood—at least that's what Greiman said to her. Luther had argued with Kendra's father. Could twenty-year-old Kendra have carried a drunken Luther down the stairs? If he fought her, could she subdue him? Was he too drunk or confused by the smoke to follow her instructions to escape? Did she even try to save Luther? Forest gossip said she got two million bucks just for wearing his oversize rock. She could abandon him to his death and still keep the money. And how could Greiman and the fire investigator determine that? Were they smart and unbiased enough to find out what really happened? Based on Angela's past experience, the answer was no. She pulled herself back to the questionnaire.

Was resuscitation performed? Was oxygen given to the subject? No to both questions. Luther was too far gone.

Was the victim heard to cry out by any witnesses? That was the key question, Angela thought. She was glad this question was on her form. She could ask around after she finished the body actualization. She'd seen Greiman jump to conclusions before. It wasn't her job to investigate this death—in fact, it was in direct violation of the rules. That task belonged to the police and fire investigator.

But she did have to record the facts. And she'd do everything she could to make sure Kendra was fairly treated.

CHAPTER 4

Day one

Ollie Champlain was capering for the crowd across the street, a crook-backed demon spewing racist insults among the flashing red lights and choking smoke.

"Sh! Ollie, don't say that!" Angela recognized the shusher, a rail-thin blonde in designer jeans. Virginia Carondelet.

"I tell it like it is." Ollie thrust out his chicken chest. "That little chili choker killed my friend."

"Not so loud." Virginia looked uneasy. Forest residents saved those words for when they were cloistered with their own kind.

"I employ a lot of Mexicans. Most are hard workers and I like them personally. But get too many and the tone changes. They're not like us." That bored drawl belonged to Nick, Virginia's husband. The pair were part of the younger Forest elite. Nick had clean-cut frat-boy looks, but his face was a little too dull to be really handsome. Angela had gone to school with them.

"Daddy hires a lot of Mexicans, too. They're cheap," said Bebe Du Pres Bradford, a plump, pretty blonde with nearly translucent skin. Bebe, Nick, and Virginia were holding silver flasks. The alcohol must have been keeping them warm. No one was dressed for the 3:00 a.m. chill.

"Hi, Angela." Virginia waved her over as if they were at a party. No, not quite a party, Angela decided. They were too subdued. More like a memorial service. "You know Ollie, don't you? Come join us."

Virginia handed Ollie her silver vodka flask. Booze dribbled down Ollie's turkey neck as he gulped. "Thank you, darling." He planted a sloppy kiss on Virginia's smooth cheek. She winced. Serves you right, Angela thought. Your booze is fueling his burning hatred.

After she'd finished Luther's body actualization, Angela had moved carefully across the wet street, using her cane to avoid the puddles and fire hoses. She hoped to find out if anyone had heard Luther call for help before the fire.

"Want a drink, Angela?" Bebe asked. "I have Great-grandmama Du Pres's bathtub gin flask from the Roaring Twenties. We're drinking Belvedere, and Nick has Macallan's. We keep it in the freezer."

"No, thanks. I'm working."

"We're working, too," Virginia said. "On a couple of fifths!" Her giggle was cut off by Nick's disapproving frown. "We don't mean to be disrespectful, but the only way to handle this tragedy is with a couple of drinks. We saw the firemen carrying Luther out. At least I think that was him."

Angela remembered how the gaudy Rhinestone Cowboy used to look and felt sick.

"That Mexican gold digger's done it now," Virginia said.

Angela said nothing, and tipsy Virginia interpreted her silence as agreement. She took another swig from her silver flask. Its smooth surface glowed in the harsh portable lights.

Mexican gold digger? It's time to say something, Angela decided. "Kendra was born here in the Forest."

"Don't be boring, darling," Virginia said. "She killed our Luther."

Our Luther? Before the blaze, the Forest had condemned him as a drunken bed-hopper who'd betrayed a "good woman." The fire had burned away his sins.

"We have the most delicious gossip," Virginia said. "Bebe works with Luther's lawyer. She's been telling tales out of school."

"I have not!" Bebe was mock indignant. "Luther blabbed it everywhere." She took a long drink of icy vodka.

"I bet Angela doesn't know," Virginia said. "She's a working stiff. But not a stiff—right, sweetie?" She waved her flask and sloshed some on her thin cashmere sweatshirt. "Oopsie."

"Spill," said Angela, and she didn't mean Virginia's drink.

Virginia lowered her voice. "Luther offered Priscilla a million dollars for a quickie divorce. Missouri has a thirty-day minimum. But she turned him down. Priscilla has her own money, and she said she'd spend every nickel to keep Luther from marrying that little man-stealer. She never signed the divorce papers, so she's still next of kin. Wasn't she smart? Now she's an heiress as well as a widow."

"I heard Luther gave Kendra two million when they got engaged," Angela said.

"See?" Bebe said. "I told you this wasn't confidential. Luther wanted to give his daughter a million to change her mother's mind, but Eve told him to go to hell. She told us all this tonight—I guess that's yesterday—when we were barbecuing by the pool."

"Eve left there about nine, before the fire started," Virginia said. "I wonder if she's home watching it on TV. You know Luther screwed the Mexican in the pool here?"

"Luther tried," Bebe said. "She got away at the last minute and ran to her car. Luther followed her, grabbing his crotch and bellowing, 'Baby, I love you! Let me show you how much.'"

"Ick," Angela said.

"I can't believe my manicurist is a murderer," Virginia said. "I really liked Kendra."

20

"Do you honestly think Kendra killed him?" Angela asked.

"We all saw her run out the front door in that tacky lace thing about the time smoke started pouring from the bedroom window, but no one remembers Kendra trying to go back to save Luther—until there were lots of witnesses."

"Did you hear Luther call for help when the fire started?" Angela asked.

"Not a peep," Nick said. "He was dead by then. Crafty little creature made sure it was too late before she started screaming for help."

"Her prancing around half-naked kept the firefighters from doing their job," Bebe said. "She did it deliberately, to kill poor Luther."

Poor Luther? Angela wondered. The Forest pariah was now upgraded to "poor Luther." Once again, the Forest protected its own—even someone who didn't want to belong. She remembered her last sight of Kendra being loaded into the ambulance. Her hands and feet were bloody, and her hair was singed. Kendra had looked like a victim. But in this crowd, low-rent Kendra was a killer.

"She's the arsonist." Bebe's voice was shrill with excitement. "She's setting the fires."

Virginia nodded sagely and belched slightly. "She hates us. They all do. Look at the arson targets." She counted them off on her long, fire-tipped fingers—with nails that had been painted flame-red by the woman she was accusing. "The first fire was started in a historic barn, destroying our history. Next was the Hobarts' pool house. Burned to the ground."

"That family has had so much tragedy," Bebe said.

"It's too bad the pool house burned," Angela said. "But their daughter died in a car crash last year." Get some perspective, people.

"I heard the fire investigator found the arsonists had been partying at the Hobarts' fire. Beer. Cheap liquor." Bebe lowered her voice to a whisper. "Heroin. The Mexicans celebrated while the building burned."

"Mexicans?" Angela said. "There's more than one arsonist?"

"Her father's Mexican, isn't he?" Virginia said. "He's done so well in this country, and now he's turned on us."

"Her mother's no better," Bebe said. "She cleans houses and brings in more Mexicans."

"It's sad," Virginia said. "Kendra's a good manicurist. She always fits me in when I have an emergency and break a nail. But we have to put aside our personal feelings and look at the facts. This is the third fire. First, it's our property. Now they're burning us alive in our beds. They'll burn down the whole Forest, then bring in all their relatives."

"I agree," Nick said. The blond preppie talked as if he had a mouthful of marbles. "Like I said, one or two are okay. But now the balance has tilted and they're dangerous. Kendra used the other fires as a cover to kill our Luther."

"She's smart," Virginia said, "but she didn't do it alone. She had help, and not just her family. I saw a black man creeping around Luther's house before the fire. They're just as bad as the Mexicans."

"What did he look like?" Bebe's eyes were bright with interest.

"Big. Muscular shoulders. He wore"—Virginia paused for another drink—"gold chains. I saw them gleaming in the light."

The mysterious black male, Angela thought. He appears at every crime scene in white neighborhoods.

"If Jose killed Luther," Nick said, "his daughter wouldn't have to marry the old man. He has to be in on it."

The others nodded in agreement, except for one couple who'd joined the group, Ann Burris and Bryan Berry. Ann wore a bronze-sequined sheath, and Bryan, a dentist, had on a well-tailored dinner jacket.

"I don't believe Jose or Kendra started the fire." Ann's sequins glittered in the portable lights. She and Bryan were the Forest's glamour couple. Ann avoided the safe, dowdy dresses the elite preferred and hosted the most popular parties and charity events. Bryan performed complex dental procedures and raced Porsches. Only they could afford to buck the Forest's opinions.

"Kendra does my nails." Ann's nails were long, strong, and fashionably red.

"So she paints your nails and you're an expert?" Virginia had had enough vodka to challenge Ann.

"We talk while she works. Kendra is a sweet, hardworking girl."

"She works hard, all right." Bebe's pale face was flushed. "On her back."

"Luther wasn't the best choice for a fiancé," Ann said. "But she had her reasons."

"She had two million reasons," Nick said. "If you know so much, who is setting the fires?"

"Bored teenagers," Ann said.

"Reggie Du Pres asked the cops to keep an eye on the Toonerville kids," Bebe said. "He called a special meeting. Mother told me."

"Toonerville teens aren't setting the fires," Ann said. "It's the Forest kids. They're bored. Summer's coming, and they're looking at a dull internship or even duller work in the family firm."

The air around the golden couple grew icier. No one accused the Forest's sons and daughters of crimes. "Ridiculous," Virginia said. Bebe brayed a laugh.

Nick said, "You're beautiful, Lady Ann, but you're wrong. We don't damage our own community."

"You do look beautiful, darling." Bebe awkwardly tried to change the subject. "Were you at a party?"

"Cocktails for the Friends of the Library. Poor Priscilla was there, too. I'd finally coaxed her out, and then someone told her Luther had been misbehaving tonight, and suddenly she didn't feel well. Just as well she left the party about nine. She didn't see this circus."

CHAPTER 5

Day one

A short, round woman with crinkly gray hair materialized out of the smoke and chaos and tugged on the sleeve of Angela's black pantsuit. "Excuse me, are you Elise's daughter?"

Angela thought the woman looked like an off-duty fairy godmother. She was somewhere in her sixties, about the same age as Angela's late mother. The harsh lights showed every line and wrinkle in her face, along with her faded blue eyes, the dark smudges on her yellow polyester pantsuit, and the mud on her sturdy white nurse's shoes.

"I'm Minnie Lynn Dunbar." Angela could barely hear her over the roar of the fire trucks. This woman could help Angela answer the major question about Luther. The phrase "burning question" floated through her mind, and Angela shooed it away.

"You don't remember me, but I used to work with your mother at the Du Pres's. You were just a little bit of a thing."

Angela had a vague memory of a plump woman who smelled of lavender lotion and gave her cookies in the drafty old Du Pres kitchen. "You helped clean and gave me homemade snickerdoodles."

"You do remember me. Or at least my cookies."

Angela shook the old woman's strong, work-worn hand. Minnie Lynn's nails were clipped short and polish-free, reminding Angela of her mother's hands.

"I left the Forest to get married. I'm a widow now, and moved back here to work for the Hobarts. I live two doors down and keep house for Miss Eudora Hobart, a maiden lady in her nineties. You look just like your mother. You've got her pretty brown hair. That's how I recognized you. You're tall like your daddy, too. What are you? Five ten?" Minnie Lynn asked.

"Six feet."

"My." Minnie Lynn treated Angela's height like an achievement. "Why are you dressed for work at this hour?"

"I'm a death investigator for Chouteau County."

"A college job." Minnie sounded impressed. "This is a terrible night. Terrible."

She shook her head sadly, but Angela heard a slight note of glee.

"Are you investigating Luther's murder?"

Murder? "We don't know how he died," Angela said.

"I do. *She* killed him."

"Kendra?"

"A tramp if I ever saw one." Minnie's face was alight, and she was eager to condemn Kendra and Luther. "He left Miss Priscilla to go chasing after that . . ." Minnie's vocabulary failed her. "Hussy," she finished. "Dried-up old coot had no shame. He was stupid enough to think that young woman liked him. Only part she liked was the bulge in his pants, and I'm not talking about his thingamajig. She was after his wallet. We know that's big and hard."

"When was the last time you saw Luther tonight? Before the fire started?"

"He came home about nine or so, dressed in that silly cowboy outfit. She was driving the old boy's Mercedes. She wore a tight dress and his engagement ring. Gaudy thing with a diamond the size of a golf ball."

"Were they fighting?"

"Not exactly. He was drunk as a sailor on leave and pawing her, like he always does. Running his liver-spotted hands over her bosom. Right in public. And she let him, too. The woman sets the tone in a relationship." Minnie was puffed with righteousness, like an angry hen. She couldn't bring herself to say Kendra's name.

"He was so sozzled he could hardly stand. He kept telling her to put on her white-lace . . ." She hesitated, then said quickly, "Her white lace F-suit. He used the F-word a lot. It took her a while to get the old coot inside the house. I'd just settled down with my TV show and a cup of tea when her father came storming up to Luther's house and pounded on the front door. He's a Mexican, you know. Luther and Jose had a fight at the front door. Loud enough I could hear it."

Angela wondered if Minnie Lynn had turned off the TV and peered out the window to hear better.

"I thank the Lord Miss Eudora and her caregiver are spending the night at the Hobarts' house. They shouldn't be subjected to language like that—or this sideshow."

"What was the fight about?"

"Jose said she should break off her engagement and come home because Luther had no respect for her. Then Luther said he respected the way she . . ." She stopped and lowered her voice again, though none of the nearby firebugs could hear them. "He used the F-word again. Said she was better than a pro.

"Jose tried to punch Luther. Kendra shouted at her father to stop and tried to drag Luther inside. She was angry and crying. Jose said if she insisted on marrying Luther, she should live with her parents until the wedding. She said she was staying with her fiancé until he settled down, then she'd go to her apartment tonight. She lives in a nice place in Toonerville. After that, they switched to Mexican. I saw her shake her head no and try to shut the door.

"Luther was still riled up. He pushed her out of the way and shouted that Jose was fired. Screamed, 'I'll bankrupt you, you stupid beaner!'"

"Luther said that in front of Kendra?" Angela said.

"He did. And she said nothing. Luther was still shouting when she pushed him inside and slammed the door. Then it was quiet. Next thing I know, I smelled smoke and saw flames coming out of Luther's bedroom window. She was running around in underwear no decent woman would wear. She was hysterical and cursing. F-words everywhere. I never heard her say Luther was still inside until more people were around. By that time, it was too late."

"Did you hear Luther scream for help before the fire?"

"No. He couldn't. She murdered him. Poured gasoline on him. She had a can by the door. Belonged to her father. I saw it there before the fire started."

Minnie was shivering and yawning. "It's chilly," Angela said. "Let me walk you home and make you some hot tea."

"No, thanks. It's way past my bedtime. I'll let you get back to work." Angela walked Minnie to Miss Eudora's house, a three-story brick with black-lacquered double doors. She hugged Minnie and waited until the housekeeper waved good night from the living room, then shut the curtains.

Angela saw a big, black Mercedes roar up, the kind most Forest dwellers would sell their souls for. The sleek, arrogant car screeched to a stop next to Virginia, Nick, and Bebe. Angela recognized Eve Delor DeMun. Luther's estranged daughter stuck her head out the window. Eve's normally smooth, pretty face was warped with rage. Emergency lights threw bloody splashes on her blonde hair. "Where is the son of a bitch?" she screamed.

"Your father?" Virginia was unsteady and a little frightened.

"Who else, you ninny?"

"Uh," Virginia said.

Nick stepped protectively in front of his wife. "Eve, I'm very sorry, but you should prepare yourself for the worst."

"What's that?" she shrieked.

"Luther is deceased."

Eve erupted into harsh laughter. Angela shivered at the ugly sound. "You mean he's dead?" Eve wiped tears from her eyes. "That's your idea of the worst? Where is she?" Eve's head swiveled through the crowd. "Is she dead, too?"

"No, she's at the hospital," Nick said. "We think she escaped with minor injuries." His reasonable words failed to calm Eve.

"Now she gets to keep my father's two million dollars? She couldn't even wait to marry him before she murdered him. Well, he's burning in hell now. If there's any justice, she'll die, too."

CHAPTER 6

Day one

Angela headed straight for the shower when she got home. She kept scrubbing her skin, trying to wash away the stench of smoke, scorched flesh, and burned hair. She soaped and rinsed her hair—once, twice, three times—until it squeaked when she touched it under the hot water. She loofahed her limbs until they were red and raw, but she could still smell the smoke and burned human flesh. She pushed away the thought that the horrible odor came from molecules of Luther trapped in her nose.

When her fingers were pruney from the water, she turned off the shower, wrapped her hair in a towel, and slid into her comforting terry bathrobe. Then she carefully walked down the stairs, gripping the handrail and using her cane for balance. When she was this tired, Angela was unsteady.

In the kitchen, she boiled a pot of water laced with cinnamon—her mother's trick for freshening the air. Then she got out the eggs and a loaf of whole wheat and put on the kettle for a cup of chamomile tea. At four in the morning, Angela wasn't sure if this was a late dinner or an early breakfast, but she knew she needed food to sleep. She had to meet Greiman and fire investigator Doug Hachette at nine to finish the death investigation at Luther's death scene. She was dreading the gruesome visit.

Luther's autopsy would be conducted sometime that day, probably by her boss, Evarts Evans. Angela would have to turn in her report as soon as she finished Luther's death scene.

Evarts autopsied all the high-profile cases, unless they were politically sensitive. At the slightest sign that a case could damage his career, he tossed that hot potato to his assistant, Angela's friend, Dr. Katie Kelly Stern.

Angela's kettle screamed, and the wheat bread popped up in the toaster while she scraped her scrambled egg onto a plate. Perfect timing. She plunked a tea bag in a mug and poured the water. Once she sat at the table, Angela realized how tired she was. She quickly forked in her food, afraid she might fall asleep at the table. It happened, now that she lived alone.

No chance Katie will get Luther's autopsy, she thought. His dramatic death promised maximum local—maybe even national—publicity. The cast of characters was a made-for-TV movie script: Old Luther was sleazy, famous, filthy rich, and besotted with a beautiful, young, scheming Mexican American who'd lured him to a fiery death. Priscilla was the victim's virtuous, wronged wife, and Eve was his outspoken daughter, loyal to her abandoned mother. Reporters would break down the morgue doors for this story, and Evarts would be waiting for them with good sound bites. He kept a camera-ready white lab coat and blue shirt in his office. He knew this case would make him a national name, a celebrity medical examiner.

Angela spread strawberry jam on her toast and crunched a bit. From what she'd heard at the fire, the locals had already condemned Kendra as the killer. Greiman and the firefighters thought she was guilty, too.

By the time she'd eaten her eggs, rinsed the dirty dishes, and turned on the dishwasher, Angela's kitchen smelled like her mother had been baking pies. She could pick up only the tiniest hint of roasted human.

Angela dragged herself upstairs to her bedroom. The steps seemed longer and steeper at four in the morning. She spent another half hour blow-drying her shoulder-length brown hair to keep it from turning into a frizzy mess. Her hair had grown back thick after it had been shaved for brain surgery.

While the dryer roared and the warm air dried her hair, she carried on her internal debate. How do I know Kendra is innocent? Angela asked herself. I only talk to her once every two weeks, when she manicures my nails. She showed me her ring once, then never wore it to the salon or discussed Luther. Kendra doesn't seem like a greedy gold digger. But everyone thought so. Except Ann Burris, who believed Kendra was innocent. She and Bryan dared to say that the Forest arsonists were bored rich kids. I wonder what she knows?

You're a death investigator, she reminded herself. It's not your job to prove Kendra is innocent or guilty. That's for Detective Greiman. Who's already made up his mind, whispered an unruly thought. Your job is to collect the facts of Luther's death—and you'll start the rest of that chore in about four hours. She finger-combed her hair. It was dry at last.

Angela couldn't bear to look at her empty bed. She and Donegan had made love on it so many times. Now it was a vast ice floe adrift in a cold, lonely sea. She stumped back downstairs with her cane to the living room and pulled her white wedding album from the living-room bookcase. She carried the heavy, leather-bound album to the couch, wrapped herself in her mother's hand-knitted throw, and looked at the photos of her wedding more than twenty years ago.

She and Donegan had been wildly in love. Their joy in each other radiated from the pages. She saw the photo of her mother, Elise, escorting Angela down the church aisle, the pews decorated with flowers and white ribbons. Elise had been fighting breast cancer. Angela was sure she'd survive, even though her mother had had chemo and a double mastectomy. Elise bravely wore a new dress and a gray Eva Gabor wig on her chemo-bald head to give her daughter away at the altar. Katie was Angela's maid of honor. Angela had threatened to make her best friend wear ruffled pink chiffon. Katie chose her own dress—a long navy gown with white trim—and carried white roses.

Angela wore traditional white and carried a bouquet of red roses, the special flowers for her and Donegan. Donegan gave her red roses throughout their courtship and marriage, until he died too young from a heart attack last February.

At their wedding, Donegan wore a black tux with a red rose in his buttonhole. They were both terrible dancers—so bad they joked it was good they'd married each other instead of inflicting themselves on innocent people who knew how to dance. But their wedding dance was perfect. She and Donegan had floated around the ballroom, laughing and talking, oblivious to the other guests. She was holding her red-rose bouquet, the white ribbons tickling his neck, and she never wanted to stop dancing. She danced and danced until he vanished and the rose bouquet crumbled and turned into the single red rose she'd tossed on Donegan's coffin at his burial service.

The soft sound when the rose landed on his coffin lid shattered her sleep.

Angela woke up crying at eight that morning. She'd been dancing in a dream, and Donegan was dead. She couldn't go back to sleep. She dragged herself off the couch and made coffee, too heartsick and sad to eat. Her sadness was a weight that never left her, but this morning it felt especially heavy. How could she go on? She looked again at the photo of her mother, who'd fought so bravely to live. That photo always inspired Angela. Staying alive was still a struggle. She took comfort in her work as a death investigator and its exacting precision.

A little over a year ago, while still grieving, she'd had six strokes, brain surgery, and been in a coma. She'd made a miraculous recovery, but she still had to fight her sadness and grief. Shape up, she told herself. You have to be at the fire scene by nine o'clock. Upstairs, she washed her face, pulled her brown hair into a high ponytail, and put on dark jeans, a long-sleeved T-shirt, and sturdy boots to inspect the fire scene.

At Olympia Forest Estates, she showed the guard at the gate her ID. The air still smelled like smoke, but now the odor was more tolerable. Either that, or she was growing used to it. The warm spring sun gilded the trees and brick homes, and not a weed dared to show its head in the landscaped yards. The curious crowds who'd gathered on Luther's street were gone, and the development had a slightly hungover, embarrassed feel.

The showcase view stopped at the end of the street, where Luther's blackened house stood out, a rotted tooth in the white perfection of the subdivision. Police cars and other official vehicles were parked amid the ashy puddles. Yellow tape fluttered in the spring breeze, and police, fire department, and other personnel picked through the blackened rubble, occasionally bagging items.

Greiman was at the end of Luther's walkway with fire investigator Doug Hachette, talking and laughing. Hachette was a fit thirtysomething with a lean runner's body, wearing a hard hat and dressed in jeans and work boots. Angela parked her car, grabbed her cane, and carefully rolled her DI kit across the debris-strewn street, avoiding smoky glass shards, twisted bits of metal, and charred wood.

"Finally," Greiman said, though Angela was five minutes early. She ignored him and introduced herself to the fire investigator.

"Captain Douglas Hobart Hachette. But I'm Doug."

And dropping a powerful family's name, she thought. The Hobarts helped run the Forest.

He handed Greiman and Angela each a hard hat and said, "A path has been cleared to the front door. The victim died upstairs, and the stairs are safe. Stick close to me and don't enter a room unless I give the all clear. Miss Richman, I'll take your suitcase. You'll need both hands to negotiate. I've already videoed the scene and flagged, bagged, and tagged most of the evidence."

The front door and jamb were gone. Angela choked on the strong smoke smell as they entered Luther's home. The walls were gray with smoke and streaked with water damage. The sodden furniture was smoke-blackened. "When she ran out of the house, she left the front door open, and it did quite a bit of damage on the first floor."

The gold-framed mirror in the hallway was broken, and a small gold table was smashed and kicked over in the living room. Luther had let Kendra decorate the house, and from what Angela could tell, the furniture was comfortable but not stylish. The house looked like someone had set a garage sale on fire, with meaningless lumps and clumps of blackened debris and broken knickknacks everywhere. Sometimes she could pick out identifiable shapes. They passed a blackened dining room with a table that was supposed to seat twelve people, though Angela doubted that Luther could have assembled that many members of the Forest upper crust after he left his wife. Angela counted eleven chairs near the table, many overturned.

"Where's the twelfth chair, Doug?"

"The seat was burned four days before this fire, and Kendra said she was going to have it reupholstered. Luther was a careless smoker. We answered at least two calls for fires before this one. When I was here before, I saw cigarette burns on the arms of a recliner and the edges of the coffee table. He had ashtrays the size of dinner plates everywhere."

"Bet Priscilla didn't allow those in her house," Greiman said.

"No Forest woman would," Doug said. "Mexican trash."

Angela wasn't sure if he was talking about Kendra or the ashtrays.

A pile of burned rubble had been pushed away from the bottom of the stairs.

"Let's go up," Doug said. "Luther was murdered in the room at the top."

Angela braced herself for Luther's death scene.

CHAPTER 7

Day one

Spring sunlight lit Luther's bedroom, casting bright, garish light on the destruction. Angela could see blue sky through the blackened roof beams, and burned tree branches with shriveled leaves. The damp, gray-smeared walls were bulging and peeling. Angela had no idea what color the walls used to be. Some kind of electrical cord hung down from the ceiling like a noose, swaying in the light spring breeze.

The room's colors were charred black and ash gray: total destruction. She saw the burned mattress of a king-size bed. Across from the bed was a scorched dresser with a melted flat-screen TV. Most of the rest was meaningless debris.

"Go ahead, it's safe to enter," Doug said. Greiman went straight in. The fire investigator rolled Angela's suitcase inside and asked, "Where should I leave this?"

"Near the foot of the bed." Angela took her first steps into Luther's bedroom.

"Floor's carpet on concrete," Doug said, "and the walls are brick over cinder block. That contained most of the actual structural damage to this room."

The bedroom floor was treacherous, with broken, burned debris. Angela's eyes watered from the smoke, and she stepped carefully around shards of blackened window glass. Burned drywall and broken slabs of ceiling were piled on the floor like black ice floes. Next to the bed was a charred nightstand. On the floor beside the burned bed was an overturned lamp with a glass base that was shattered but still intact. "That's heat-crazed glass," Doug said, pointing to the lamp. "It's near the fire's point of origin. I'll be taking this section of the wood bed frame. See these large, shiny char blisters? That's what's known as alligator char. That means an ignitable liquid has been used."

He kneeled down on the burned carpet at an area marked with a small yellow plastic evidence tent. "Look at this. I saved it to show you. These are trailer marks."

"What's that mean?" Angela asked.

"Means we've got her. Looks like she dripped some gasoline when she poured it on Luther."

He pointed at what looked like drip marks on the blackened carpet. "See them? If you move a pot of water from the stove to the sink and spill some on the floor, you'll see trailer marks like these."

The fire investigator photographed them, then cut out sections of the carpet and put them in new tin cans that looked like paint cans. As he stepped backward, Angela heard a crunching sound.

"There's what's left of one of those shitty pottery ashtrays she liked so much," Greiman said.

Why wouldn't Doug or Greiman say Kendra's name? she wondered. Would she become a real person if they used it?

The king-size bed dominated the room, just as it had the last part of Luther's life. Most of the bedstead had burned away. The damage was heaviest on the side closest to the door. "That's where Luther slept," the investigator said. "The sheets were black silk, one of the most flammable fabrics around. She had more of that silky stuff hanging behind the bed. None of it was treated with fire retardant. The mattress was polyurethane, which is equally dangerous."

The mattress was burned down to the blackened springs, except for a soot-streaked section that had been protected by a curled body.

Luther.

She'd already seen his roasted remains, but her stomach lurched. Her nose picked up the choking odors of wet ash and melted plastic— an acrid, synthetic odor—then shorted out like an overloaded circuit. But when Angela looked at the outline of his body, she imagined she could smell that unforgettable charred-meat and burned-hair odor. It lingered like a ghost.

This was where Luther died. Now quit with the drama. You need facts, not vague feelings. She unzipped her DI suitcase, its sides and wheels already smeared with damp, black mulch. She was determined to finish this bizarre, two-part death investigation. Six hours ago, she'd examined and documented Luther's body on the paramedics' backboard.

She photographed the death scene. First, a long shot from the door, followed by a medium shot and several close-ups. Angela didn't see any blood on the blackened mattress surface. When she'd done Luther's body actualization earlier this morning, he'd been lying on his back.

Now, the outline on the mattress showed he'd died curled in the fetal position, his head facing southwest. The body's position on the mattress, from what she could tell, appeared to be natural. She measured the outline: thirty-eight inches from head to the end. She couldn't see any feet. The body's outline was twenty-three inches at the widest part, which appeared to be from the pelvis to the drawn-up knees.

"Did you find any restraints on or around the bed?" Greiman asked the fire investigator.

"You mean like handcuffs or some kinda bondage?"

"Yeah. Did she tie him up or cuff him to the bed?"

"Haven't found anything. Doesn't mean it didn't happen." They exchanged locker-room grins. "The way I see it," Doug said, "she doused

Luther with gasoline when he was passed out, and set the old man on fire."

Greiman shook his head. "Awful way to die."

"He may have been too drunk to feel anything," Doug said. "From what I heard, the old boy really tied one on at Gringo Daze. Drank lots of anesthetic and made a real scene."

"She's a heartless bitch," Greiman said, "setting a helpless old man on fire."

Doug pointed to charring on the carpet by the mattress. "See these burn patterns on the floor? Those can only be caused by gasoline. The gasoline causes a fireball that rises up to the top of the ceiling—whoosh! It hits the ceiling, slams back down, and that's all, folks. All she got was some singed hair, a couple of cuts on her hands and feet, and a little soot on her face and arms. Did you ask her if she tried to save him?"

"Talked to her at the hospital about five this morning. The doctor said she was still in shock, but she sounded fine to me. Had a couple of coughing fits, but she could have faked those. She said she and Luther fell asleep shortly after she got him upstairs."

"Did they screw?"

"She says he was too drunk to 'make love.'" Greiman minced those last words, and both men laughed.

"Next thing she knew, she woke up choking on the smoke and saw the bed was on fire. She said the flames weren't very big and there wasn't much smoke. She tried to wake up Luther but couldn't. She tried to lift him, but she said he was too heavy."

"She sure didn't try too hard. In fact, I don't think she tried at all. I think she set the fire and then ran out of the house screaming her head off."

"She says the flames got bigger, and the smoke and heat were so extreme she had to run out," Greiman said. "By the time she was down the stairs, there was a bright orange glow coming from their room and she heard a roar. She ran outside, wearing practically nothing. Gave the whole neighborhood an eyeful. Perfect way to distract the firefighters. She's still in the hospital for smoke inhalation, but I have a uniform outside her room. I haven't arrested her yet. We're still waiting on test results. Her clothes—if that's what you call those scraps of lace—are being tested for gasoline. Evarts is cutting open Luther today. I told him what happened. I'm sure he'll find gasoline on Luther."

Greiman's already tainted the ME's investigation, Angela thought, before he sees my report. "You going to the autopsy?"

"No need," Greiman said. He wouldn't admit autopsies made him queasy.

"No question she's guilty," Doug said. "Besides these trailer marks, a firefighter found a partially melted gasoline container by the door."

"If she poured gas on him up in the bedroom, why would she carry it downstairs and leave it by the door? Why not leave it in the room where it would burn up?" Angela asked.

"Because she couldn't be sure the gasoline can would burn up," Doug said. "You'd be surprised what survives a fire."

He's determined to make sure Kendra is guilty, she thought. "Any gas in it?"

He glared at Angela. "No, sweetie. She poured it all over Luther. I just showed you the burn patterns."

"My title is death investigator, Captain Hachette." She caught him rolling his eyes at Greiman and suspected the detective had already complained about her.

"There was no gasoline in the container, Ms. Death Investigator." Doug made her title sound like a joke. "But we didn't expect to find any."

"Because it was empty to begin with."

"Because she emptied it on Luther." Doug's voice was a sharp reprimand. "Then she escaped out the front door, screaming hysterically, and paraded around in a sexy outfit to distract the firefighters and hinder the investigation. Her clothes are being analyzed for accelerant. And we've got witnesses who say her father fought with Luther on his doorstep shortly before the fire. Luther had already given her two million dollars, so she didn't need him anymore. I heard he'd embarrassed her at Gringo Daze last night, where he was drunk and grabbing her ass."

"You just told me Luther had a history of careless smoking," Angela said. "The fire department was here at least twice, and four days ago, the dining room chair caught on fire."

"Based on what I've seen today," Doug said, "I believe those were test fires set by her to see how long it would take the fire department to respond. She knew she could escape before we got here, but it would be too late for Luther."

Angela wasn't going to let him go so easily. "If Kendra set this fire the way you say, were any art or valuables removed before the fire?"

"You seem to be quite the arson expert, Ms. Richman, for someone who hasn't worked many fires. No, nothing appeared to be removed from this house before the fire. But when I was here before, the art was mostly cheap crap, the kind of shit people buy because it's pretty or matches the couch."

"So nothing of value was taken out before the fire started," she repeated. Greiman was glaring at her, but she didn't care.

"Not that we're able to tell at this time. But our investigation isn't complete."

"What's on the other side of that door?" she asked.

"The master bath. That door was closed at the time of the fire, and none of the plastics melted, so the heat in the bathroom wasn't too high."

"What about Kendra's engagement ring? Did you find it? A neighbor said she had it on when she came home last night, but I don't remember her wearing it after she escaped the burning house."

"I guess women notice things like that," Greiman answered. Angela ignored the jab. "We recovered her ring on top of the toilet tank in the master bath."

"So she wasn't planning the fire," Angela said. "She didn't wear her ring."

"Diamonds don't burn in most house fires, Ms. Death Investigator. She shut the bathroom door to keep out the intense heat. She knew her ring would be safe. And with two million dollars, she has enough money to buy another one."

CHAPTER 8

Day one

"You've got a problem here, Greiman," said fire investigator Doug Hachette. "I get along with Mexicans. You have to in this job. But the bleeding hearts are gonna say you've railroaded a poor little Mexican slut. I mean, facts are facts, right? She's hooked up with some famous old geezer fifty years older than her. The media's gonna be on this case like flies on shit."

"That's why I'm waiting for the evidence to come back," Greiman said. "As soon as I get Luther's autopsy and the lab report on her whore suit, I'm throwing her ass in jail. We about finished here?"

Her. She. Mexican slut. Neither investigator would say Kendra's name, Angela thought. The two men had been poking through the blackened rubble in Luther's bedroom while Angela worked on her investigation, taking notes on her iPad.

"Did you swab her hands for gasoline?" Doug asked.

"Tried to," Greiman said. "But the ER had cleaned her up. Any results could be messed up by the alcohol cleaning swabs."

"You're sure she's guilty," Doug said. It was a statement, not a question.

There he goes again, she thought. He refuses to use Kendra's name. But that's a smart question.

"Aren't you?" Greiman laughed, and so did Doug.

"What about Priscilla and Eve?" Angela knew that was a risky question: it could damage the small bit of working relationship she had with Greiman. But she couldn't let him railroad Kendra when there were other possible suspects.

The two men looked at her as if she were a talking chair. "What about Luther's wife and daughter?" Greiman asked. Angela heard his belligerence but didn't back off.

"Both women had good reasons to want Luther dead," she said. "He'd given a big chunk of the family fortune to Kendra, and he was going to give her more. Priscilla and Eve were both in the neighborhood last night about the time the fire started. Ann Burris said Priscilla was at a Friends of the Library cocktail party until someone told her Luther had been 'misbehaving' with Kendra at Gringo Daze. Around nine o'clock, Priscilla said she didn't feel well and was going home. Meanwhile, Eve was hanging out with her friends at a poolside barbecue. She left about nine—again, about the time the fire started. She came back later, after the firefighters had removed Luther's body, and Eve said she was glad her father was dead."

"Can't blame Eve for that," Greiman said. "I'm sure his wife is relieved he's dead, too. Why wouldn't she be?"

"But Eve was laughing about it. She was glad her father was dead."

"So? That tells me she's not guilty. I'd be suspicious if she'd made a big scene, weeping for dear old daddy."

"So you didn't interview either one." Angela fought to keep her voice neutral.

"No, and I'm not going to. I'm not bothering two prominent citizens because they didn't cry for a man who turned on his family and took up with a nasty little greedhead."

Doug nodded agreement.

"Last I checked, you're not in charge of this investigation," Greiman said. "It will be run with respect for the suffering family. Luther's wife and daughter have been through enough without the police badgering them."

Well, I tried, Angela thought. My job is to gather the facts and deliver them to the ME, and that's what I did. She turned off her iPad and stashed it in her DI kit, then used her cane to stand up. Angela dusted damp ashes off her pantsuit legs. Her work here was done.

"Ready to roll?" Doug asked. "I'll take your suitcase down to your car."

"We're going to the Burger Den for lunch," Greiman said. "Want to join us?" Angela wished she could take this olive branch, but she couldn't stomach the smell of frying meat in the Den's smoky atmosphere. She wasn't sure she could keep any food down right now.

"Thanks." She smiled at them both. "I'll have to take a rain check. I'm a wuss and feeling kinda queasy right now. I have to write my report at the office."

Greiman seemed pleased with her admission of weakness. They made their way carefully down the stairs. Doug stashed her DI suitcase in the Charger's trunk. Angela said good-bye and then called Katie from her car.

"I'm finished at the fire scene and coming into the office," Angela said. "Wanna do lunch?"

"Can't. I'm getting ready to post the Rhinehart case, the one you caught yesterday. How about an early dinner?"

"Deal, but no meat."

"I'll bring some salads. And hurry up with your report. Evarts can't wait to post Luther and get the glory. I'll stop by about six with the food."

Most death investigators reported to an office at the medical examiner's and stayed for their shift. Thanks to Evarts, Angela's arrangement was a little different. Evarts had heaps of Chouteau County money to spend on his office, but it still wasn't enough for his grand plans. He wanted an executive suite with a Swedish shower, and he needed more space. Angela's cubicle became a lavish marble-tiled shower with a zillion showerheads. She got a desk barely big enough for a preschooler, a chair, and an ancient beige computer she never used. She also got her freedom. Angela didn't clock in. She usually worked from home and showed up for meetings and to write the occasional report. This was fine with her, and, like many Forest deals, it was unspoken. Today seemed like a good time to show up at the office.

Angela opened the iPad and wrote her report—she was an amazingly fast two-finger typist—then sent it to Evarts and knocked on his office door.

"Come in," he called.

Angela's feet sank into the soft, dark-green broadloom. Evarts's office looked like a corner of the Chouteau Forest Country Club, right down to the hobnailed leather chairs and comic golf prints on the plaid-papered walls. A tall bookcase hid a small kidney-shaped putting green, and a putter was propped against the wall.

Evarts, dressed in a polo shirt and khakis, looked like he wished he was on the links. His white hair was perfectly barbered, his pink face smooth and clean shaven, his small blue eyes shrewd.

"Angela! Did you finish your report?"

"You took the words out of my mouth."

"Good, good. I won't ask you to sit down. I'm in a hurry to read your report and post poor Luther. Such a shame. He was one of our finest citizens. Such a horrible death."

"I'm afraid it was," Angela said.

"Well, you can still enjoy this beautiful day. If we need you, we'll call you, but I hope we don't. Our community has had enough sorrow."

"It has indeed," Angela said.

She headed for home, knowing exactly how she'd kill the time until she saw Katie. She parked in her driveway and admired the last yellow daffodils lining the drive, a legacy from her gardening mother. Soon she'd see her mother's trees in bloom—white-and-pink dogwoods and delicate purple clouds of redbud.

She unlocked the door to her two-story white-stone home. She stripped in the laundry room, threw her smoke-saturated clothes into the washer, and left her work boots by the dryer. She'd clean them later. In the kitchen, Angela slapped down place mats, silverware, and napkins, setting the table for dinner with Katie, then fixed herself a quick peanut-butter sandwich. She had to eat something.

Upstairs, she showered away the smoke smell and changed into a blue chambray shirt, skinny jeans, and knee-high boots. She grabbed a bag of peppermints and headed over the hill to the stables at the Du Pres's horse farm.

Angela could see the stables and the horses from her upstairs bedroom window. During her recovery from the strokes and brain surgery, she'd taken long walks on the Du Pres's protected property, trying to tire herself out enough to sleep. She began spending more time at the stables, comforted by the horses' company. She liked talking to old Bud, who'd known her parents. Somewhere in his sixties, Bud was a thin, tanned strip of rawhide, straightforward and comfortable as an old boot. He wasn't much of a talker, unless the subject was horses, and that was fine with Angela: he didn't offer advice or sympathy or ask how she was. She didn't like his tobacco-chewing habit, but she knew smoking was forbidden in the stables. Bud carried around a soda can as a spittoon.

Old Reggie's horse barn was a showcase built in 1902 for the Du Pres carriage horses, and those animals lived in style: Their polished mahogany stalls were bigger and grander than the average Toonerville apartment. Each stall had a brass plate for the horse's name, and the barn had stained-glass windows. Old Reggie was tight with a buck, but he spared no expense on his stables, and a small army kept the stalls painted, polished, and mucked out. Bud lived behind the tack room, near the stables' back exit.

The Forest dwellers no longer kept carriage horses. Instead, they adopted retired racehorses—OTTBs, or Off the Track Thoroughbreds. "Retired racehorses make great pets and riding horses," Bud had told

Angela. "Plus, Reggie enjoys the prestige: He knows all their triumphs and makes sure everyone else does, too. He'll spout the stats for his OTTBs—how many races, how much money they won, and who owned them. Owning a retired racehorse is sort of like dating Elizabeth Taylor in her later years: still beautiful, still a Thoroughbred, with a great past."

"The Forest dwellers are obsessed with pedigrees and the past," Angela had said.

Bud spit into the soda can. "Rich people are like potatoes. The best part is underground. All they care about are their ancestors. At least they treat the horses well. They live in more style than they ever did at the track. And the old man caters to them like they're babies. He gets them pets, if he thinks they're lonely: a cat, a goat, even a pony if they want one. Hell, he loved getting that pony, Snickers, for American Hero. Told everyone Seabiscuit had a pet pony. They never lived like this on the track, where the stalls are falling apart and their pets are mice. Lots of cats at barns for that reason."

Last August, when she first started walking past the stables, Angela had admired the horses from a distance, fascinated by their powerful beauty. She loved their shiny coats, rippling muscles, and slender legs. Their liquid-brown eyes were bright with intelligence. She'd leaned against the white-painted paddock fence, and the horses would come up to greet her. Angela was afraid to touch them, but Bud had encouraged her. He taught her that the horses had unique personalities. He introduced her to a racehorse that was almost black with an unusual white blaze.

"Meet American Hero," Bud had said. "He loves to have his blaze rubbed. Just touch the long white part on his face. He won't hurt you. Now, scratch him under the chin."

"That's a lot of chin," Angela said as she scratched.

"You've got it," Bud said. "Aw, he wants a hug."

Angela wrapped her arms around the horse's powerful neck and head. Hero felt warm and muscular, his dark hair slightly stiff. The horse nuzzled her and very gently blew air out his nose at her.

"You've made a conquest," Bud said. "You're supposed to breathe back into his nose. Some folks say those are horse kisses. He's asking if you can be trusted. He likes you."

"If he likes me so much, why's he sticking his tongue out?" Angela said.

"You're supposed to shake it, like you're shaking hands. Go ahead. He'll never hurt you."

Angela reluctantly grabbed the thick, wet tongue surrounded by those huge yellow teeth and gingerly touched it, then shook it. American Hero tossed his long, black mane.

"You oughta ride him," Bud had said, patting Hero's shoulder. "He's gentle as a lamb."

Angela held up her cane. "I need to walk before I can ride."

American Hero was now one of Angela's favorite racehorses, along with the other OTTB, East Coast Express, a dark bay (brown) horse with a tiny star on her forehead. Angela called her Eecie. She had a pet, too. A pygmy goat named Little Bit liked to hang out in Eecie's stall. The retired racehorse had a sly sense of humor. If Angela wore a hat on a chilly morning, she'd try to pull it off.

Angela came by as often as she could to feed the horses candy, carrots, and other treats, especially after bad DI investigations. Both horses liked peppermint candy.

This afternoon, Eecie was asleep in her stall, lying on her side and snoring gently. "It's hard to believe any creature that big could sound like a tiny kitten, Bud."

"She's a party animal. She was partying with Hero last night, and now she's tired."

Eecie's ears twitched, and her legs moved slightly. "She's dreaming," Angela said. "Do you think racehorses dream about winning?"

"I think people dream about winning. Horses like to run, but many don't like that metal starting gate at the track. It's noisy and frightening.

If Eecie's dreaming about running, she's out on the prairie like her ancestors, running wild and free."

Angela heard a snort from the next stall and went over to see American Hero. She hugged and kissed the dark giant, shook his tongue, and began feeding him peppermints.

"You're here in the middle of the day," Bud said. "You catch old Luther's case?"

"It was horrible."

"Fire always is," Bud said. "You think Kendra killed Luther, or was it the Forest arsonist?"

"That's arsonists, plural," Angela said. "The Forest thinks Kendra's running some kind of Mexican gang. Ann Burris says bored kids are setting the fires. Forest kids—not Toonerville teens."

"Ann marches to her own drummer. I bet that idea got a few folks hot under the collar. From what I hear, most people think Kendra did it. Say she's greedy."

"I guess you'd have to be greedy to hang around with a geezer like Luther, but she already had two million dollars from the old man. I can't see her setting him on fire."

"Me, either. I know her parents, and they brought her up right. I heard she got hurt bad by one of the snotty rich boys, but never knew the whole story. Girl has spirit. She might set one of those boys on fire. But she could walk away from Luther anytime, and that's what she'd do. I want those arsonists caught. I've put extra precautions in the barn—video cameras, so I can watch the grounds and stalls from my room, and smoke detectors. Security watches all that, too, but horses go crazy in a fire. Even if you get them out in time, they'll run right back to the place where they feel safe—their burning stall. I'll keep them safe if it's the last thing I do."

"I know you will, Bud." She thanked him, gave Hero a last pat, and went home to have dinner with Katie, hoping to learn more about Luther's fiery death.

CHAPTER 9

Day two

Dark-green spinach leaves dotted with fresh red strawberries and smooth, creamy goat cheese. Warm, crusty French bread slathered with butter. Katie's salad banished the blackened, ashy horror of Luther's investigation. Angela couldn't wait to dig in.

Katie had left her lab coat at the office and wore her usual subdued outfit: a light-gray shell and a darker pantsuit, sensible shoes, and no makeup. With her short, practical brown hair and freckled face, she should have been plain. But Katie's quick intelligence gave her a brisk, competent beauty.

She demolished her salad while she discussed Luther. But first, she checked Angela, eyeballing her friend until she was uncomfortable.

"It's hard to eat when you're staring at me."

"You're looking pale, but not as bad as I expected." Katie looked at her carefully. "You don't have a migraine, do you?"

"I'm fine," Angela said. "I'm not going to have any more strokes. I know the signs now. I'm almost fully recovered. I hardly need this." She held up her cane.

Angela could see her friend studying her face for signs of a relapse and hoped she didn't look too pale. Long bangs hid the scars from her emergency brain surgery, and her dark hair was long enough now for a high ponytail. She'd gained back most of the weight she'd lost during her three months in the hospital.

"You're still recovering," Katie said. "You scared the crap out of us. You're not as strong as you think."

"I'm okay. I know how to take care of myself."

"Did you go hang with the horses when you got home?"

"Yep. Horse therapy works every time. Eecie was asleep, but I spent time with old Bud and Hero."

"Ever think about riding Hero?" Katie asked.

"I just like being with the horses."

"You'd like riding them even more. Gives you a whole new perspective on life. Think about it."

Angela thought she'd be too scared to get on those huge animals and changed the subject. "What did Evarts say about Luther?"

"You really want to talk about this at dinner?" Katie chomped a healthy bite of spinach.

"I've already seen—and smelled—the worst. Might as well tell me the facts."

She was sorry as soon as Katie started talking. "There wasn't much of Luther left to autopsy. I felt sorry for the poor bastard. Last night, he was slapping ass and raising hell. This morning . . . well, what happened to him shouldn't happen to anyone. Damn, he died bad: hair burned off, eyeballs cooked so bad Evarts couldn't tell his eye color. Evarts said he had trouble getting a blood sample because the body was so roasted. Fortunately, he found a part where Luther wasn't totally cooked."

"So the tests said Luther was drunk?" Angela said.

"Like a sophomore on spring break. I'm surprised the alcohol didn't kill him before the fire got him. Evarts checked with his internist. Doc Bartlett confirmed he had a bad heart and he'd been taking Viagra. She'd refused to prescribe it and put the notes in his chart. Guess she knew he'd sneak around her and get it from India or someplace."

"Do you think the Viagra killed him?"

"I don't know what killed him," Katie said. "I think Evarts did a half-assed job so he could go play golf."

"I think I caught him practice putting at the office. He looked eager to get out on the course."

"Too eager. Greiman came in early this morning and told Evarts that Kendra did it. That's all Evarts needed to hear. He whipped through that post so fast he broke the fuckin' slice-and-dice record. Evarts hates working on burn victims anyway." She stopped for another bite of salad.

"The Forest has already convicted her, Katie. I was there last night and heard them condemn her. It was ugly."

"Do you think she did it?"

"No, but the facts look bad," Angela said. "Doug Hachette, the fire investigator, found a gasoline trail on the bedroom carpet, and a firefighter found a half-melted gas can at the scene. There were significant areas of large, shiny char blisters—alligator char—on parts of the wood bed frame, which means an ignitable liquid had been used. The question is: did Kendra pour the gasoline on Luther?"

"You know Kendra better than I do."

"I know her as well as anyone who holds my hands every couple of weeks. She's pretty and hardworking. She seems ambitious. She never mentioned Luther or wore her giant engagement ring to the salon."

"She's not stupid," Katie said. "The Forest ladies would boycott Killer Cuts. They thought she was a money-grubber and a home wrecker. No point in waving the proof in their faces. Not that Luther had much of a marriage to break up."

"Really?" Angela leaned in and forked a plump strawberry. "You have gossip?"

"Juicy gossip." Katie lowered her voice even though it was just the two of them. "Priscilla's ex-housekeeper works at SOS now.

Connie—Consuelo—had the nerve to ask for a ten-cent raise after working three years, and Luther's wife let her go. Connie said Luther and Priscilla used to argue in front of her like she was wallpaper, and her club-women friends treated the housekeeper the same way. None of them knew Spanish, so if they wanted anything from Connie, they'd say it louder. They'd point to their cups and shout, 'More coffee-ah. Coffee-ah.' Connie would make her English sound worse than it really was, so the gringos talked freely around her. Connie says Priscilla was a real beauty when she was young."

"You're joking. That sour old lady?"

"Connie personally dusted Priscilla's portrait that was painted when she came out as a Daughter of Versailles. It was hanging in the main living room, or whatever rich people call it."

"Portrait painters are kind to rich clients," Angela said.

"Photos don't lie. Well, not too much. Priscilla also kept photos of herself as a deb in silver frames on her dressing table. Connie says your sour old lady was a sweet little honey with big brown eyes, a gorgeous figure, and a dress that showed every asset and then some."

"What freeze-dried her?" Angela asked.

"Clawing her way up to the presidency of the Chouteau Forest Women's Club, the power place for old-school wives. To get elected, Priscilla let her waist thicken, her lips thin, and her hair go gray. The hottie turned into an ice queen and became the most powerful woman in the Forest."

"Who told you that?"

"Nobody. I figured it out. My spies at the Women's Club say that during the ladies' lunches, the old guard make it clear that some of the newer, sexier members are 'too good-looking' and 'need to mature.' That means get old. Priscilla's whole life became the Women's Club and debates about whether the chef should serve cucumber bisque or chicken consommé for lunch."

"You're making that up."

"I shit you not. Laugh all you want, Angela, but the ladies who decree that the chef should serve chicken consommé only on Wednesdays run the Forest, when they're not running their husbands. They're the reason the Forest never changes. Their grandmothers sipped consommé on Wednesdays, and so did their mothers—who donated Grandma's Sevres vases to the club for a fat tax write-off. They want their daughters to have the same life and the same menu. They've kept time standing still.

"Don't get me wrong. The ladies do good works. They even sponsor an annual scholarship for a Toonerville kid. But their lives revolve around the club, and Priscilla dragged Luther along to its silly events. The last straw was when she insisted Luther go to the annual Halloween ball. He wanted to dress as a cowboy."

"He wouldn't even need to buy a costume," Angela said.

"Luther might have had fun, but Priscilla nagged him into wearing her daddy's 1920s Sitting Bull costume, with a real Native American war bonnet that reached the floor."

"I saw the photo in the *Chouteau Forest Chronicle*," Angela said. "He looked so miserable I couldn't stop laughing."

"You and everyone else. His Forest pals started calling him Big Chief Thunder Cloud. Shortly after that, he took up with Kendra."

"Why?" Angela said. "Why would that beautiful young woman go out with Luther?"

"Revenge."

"On who—herself?"

"On Bunny Hobart and Luther's daughter, Eve."

"They're an item?"

"Of course not, Angela." Katie was losing patience. Angela concentrated on her salad while Katie talked. "Kendra's mother, Gracie, has a housecleaning business with a crew of ten. Like her husband, Jose, Gracie is good at business, and her cleaning service is a real success.

She cleaned Eve's house, even though she'd heard Eve joke she'd 'always wanted a BMW.'"

"What's wrong with that?" Angela asked.

"BMW is short for Big Mexican Woman in the wrong circles, and Gracie is on the chunky side. Eve insisted that Gracie herself clean her home, rather than the crew, and she did—until Eve's diamond pendant went missing. She accused Gracie of stealing it."

"When in doubt, blame the help," Angela said.

"Exactly. Eve fired her. Made a big deal out of saying she wouldn't press charges."

"Never mind that she didn't have any proof," Angela said.

"Proof is beside the point in the Forest. Turned out that dear Aunt Eudora Hobart had swiped the necklace when she came to lunch with her caregiver. The caregiver brought it back, along with a note from the Hobarts asking Eve to forgive Eudora, who's become attracted to sparkly objects now that she's ninety. Of course, Eve did. Then she tried to get Gracie back. But Gracie refused. She said someone else had Eve's cleaning day. She had her pride."

"Kendra never worked for her mother."

"Of course not." Katie stabbed a strawberry. "Her parents didn't want their daughter doing hard labor. They tried to send her to college, but she insisted on beauty school. They were disappointed, but thought she'd meet a respectable class of people when she worked at Killer Cuts. Too bad she met Bunny. Kendra liked that she was dating a doctor."

"Huh," Angela said. "If she was going out with Bunny, she still wasn't dating a doctor."

"I forgot," Katie said. "You had an encounter with that jerk-off when you were sick. Your pal Dr. Tritt got so mad he threw the incompetent asshole out of your room."

"I remember," Angela said, and laughed. "I remember the look on Bunny's face, too. No one had ever talked to him that way."

"Bunny dated Kendra. She was beautiful and far too smart for him. I think he was Kendra's first real lover. She thought he would marry her."

"No way he'd walk down the aisle with a Mexican American, no matter how good-looking she was."

"I know. But fairy tales have a powerful pull, and Kendra saw herself as Cinderella. Bunny fobbed her off, saying he still had to complete his residency. But when that ended, Kendra wanted her prince. She popped the question again: when were they going to marry? Something happened. I'm not sure what—it was hushed up. But Bunny hurt Kendra so badly she didn't date for months. That's when Luther came sniffing around. The old geezer knew how to treat her—at least at first. He was kind and respectful. He said he was divorcing his wife. He took Kendra to fancy dinners in Saint Louis and then expensive weekends in Chicago and even New York. He bought her pretty clothes. Kendra was dazzled. She started sleeping with him, and when her parents objected, she said she was nineteen and could do as she pleased. He gave her an engagement ring and two million dollars and promised her another two mil when they got married. Meanwhile, he wanted her to move in with him. He got used to lots of sex and wanted it night and day. At his age, chemical boners wouldn't wait.

"Kendra wanted to be married. I don't think she loved Luther, but she still had that Cinderella fantasy. She rented an apartment in Toonerville and said she'd move into his house after they walked down the aisle. By then, Luther was drinking heavily and pressuring his wife to divorce him. He tried to bribe Eve, but his daughter hated the old goat. Then, after his drunken scene at Gringo Daze, it all blew up."

"Or caught fire," Angela said. "I still can't see Kendra pouring gasoline on Luther. But I think Eve or Priscilla could. And they were both at Olympia that night."

"How would they get in Luther's house?" Katie asked. "Do they have keys?"

"Don't need them. It's a gated community. Nobody locks their doors."

"How did they get in his room? Kendra was right there in bed next to him. If they poured gasoline on Luther, wouldn't some of it get on Kendra? Wouldn't she smell it and wake up?"

"Not if she had a couple of drinks before bed," Angela said. "She may have needed some booze to put up with getting groped by Luther. Maybe she was exhausted after dealing with the old coot. Greiman's refusing to even question them. Instead, he got Evarts to lie and delivered the verdict the Forest wanted."

"Hey, I don't like our boss any better than you do, but I don't think Evarts lied. He just didn't look for anything that didn't fit Greiman's conclusions. His report said Luther had a high blood alcohol level and he'd been doused with gasoline before he burned to death, just the way Greiman explained it to him. He said there were traces of gasoline on Luther's body and concluded he'd been set on fire by 'person or persons unknown.'"

"Meaning Kendra."

Katie nodded. "It gets worse. Greiman convinced Evarts that Kendra's the Forest arsonist."

CHAPTER 10

Day two

Angela had planned to sleep in the next morning, but Katie called at 7:00 a.m. "Wake up! I have news! Someone videoed Luther the other night."

"You mean the fire?" Angela was too groggy to figure out what Katie was saying.

"No, someone caught him on a cell phone when he 'misbehaved' at Gringo Daze. The old boy was on a tear, and the video has gone viral on YouTube. I'll be right over, bringing breakfast. It's the shitstorm of the year."

Angela still wasn't sure what Katie was talking about, but she dressed quickly and used her cane as she made her way downstairs to put on the coffee and set the table for breakfast. By the time the coffee was ready, Katie's red pickup screeched into Angela's drive, and the assistant medical examiner rushed in with a bag of quiche and fresh fruit.

Angela quickly plated their ham quiche and divided the container of cut strawberries into two bowls. "Who recorded it? When?"

"I don't know, but the video hit the Internet last night. I've got it on my iPad."

The video had a slightly yellowish cast, but Angela could clearly see the interior of the bar in the crowded Mexican restaurant. The sound was slightly tinny, but she could hear the splashing Spanish-tile fountain and the soft guitar music. There was scrawny-legged Luther in his black Stetson with the diamond hatband and his handmade Lucchese boots. He swung his arms in the exaggerated moves of a drunk and slurred his words when he yelled, *"Kendra is the best piece of ass in Chouteau Forest."* A polo-shirted pack of patricians egged on the drunken Luther, applauding his crude comment.

"Oh my god," Angela said. She dropped her fork.

"Someone sold this video of his drunken rampage to cable news," Katie said. "Priscilla's fucking head is gonna explode. Her randy old goat is all over the Net. Damn! The Gringo Daze scene is on the website of every news station I can find." Katie flipped from site to site while she gave Angela a play-by-play.

"Ha! Here he is grabbing Kendra's ass on CNN! You can see his schnockered pals laughing and slapping his back. Bet those dumb fucks are living in shit city now—all their wives belong to the Women's Club. Hey, here he is on Fox News!"

"What a pig," Angela said. "Luther called his fiancée a piece of ass."

"With big tits," Katie said. "Listen up." A loaded Luther shouted, *"Look at those massive mammaries, boys. How'd you like to wake up to that mountain view?"*

Angela had abandoned her breakfast to watch the Internet sensation. Katie said, "Here's HLN."

"Is Luther *that* famous? I know he's rich, but this is a Mexican restaurant in Nowhere, Missouri."

"Ever hear of Warren Buffet in—where is it—Nebraska? Don't sell Missouri short. We have our share of major money—the Pulitzers, the Busch beer barons, a Walmart heiress. Everyone knows Luther's payday loan slogan 'You get more with Delor.' They're really getting an eyeful now. Kendra's a natural for TV. Even in this amateur video she looks like a million bucks."

"Two million. To be exact."

"Luther looks older than God," Katie said. "You'd think he was ninety instead of seventy."

"His rhinestones and diamonds sure sparkle," Angela said. "Almost as much as her engagement ring. Look at that rock. It's bigger than a doorknob. Who took the video? One of Luther's pals?"

"You kidding? No matter how drunk those old boys were, they knew they looked like assholes. Spilling Forest secrets is a death sentence. I'm guessing some waiter or dishwasher took the video and cashed in. I hope they got paid a mint. This is real fuckin' reality TV. Look! Here's a close-up of Kendra's backside as she tries to drag Luther out."

Kendra was haloed in the bar light, her form-fitting white dress a beacon. Angela heard Luther's fiancée say, *"You're tired, sweetie. Let's go home."*

"This early?" howled a hanger-on. *"You're losing it, Luther."*

"Losing it? I can go all night long." Luther's leer showed obviously false teeth.

"Kendra's frantic to get him out of there," Katie said. "Watch this. He's grabbing her ass on CBS and air-fucking."

"God, I love this heart-shaped ass. I'm up for anything. And I do mean up." Luther bucked his hips suggestively, and his dog pack sniggered. *"It's magnificent. Any of you fucking anything this good? Kendra has the hottest ass in Chouteau County. In Saint Louis. No . . ."*—Luther flung his arms wide—*"the whole state of Missouri. Hell, the United States and Mexico."*

"She should have punched him and walked out," Angela said.

"Sh! Here's where he insults Priscilla. I hope she had a stiff drink at the club before she saw Luther say this."

"Let me tell you, this little greaser gal is one hot tamale. Not like my dead-ass wife."

"I almost feel sorry for Priscilla," Angela said.

"Me, too, except I know she's a major shit disturber. Just when she thought it was safe to shovel Luther six feet under, Luther insults her from beyond the grave. Look at Kendra, still trying to get him to leave, pulling his arm."

On the video, Luther slapped Kendra's round rump. *"She knows how to dress to please a man."* He extended his pinkie and minced his words. *"No lady would dare wear anything that tight. Kendra's so deliciously low-class. That's why I'm getting the best sex of my life."*

"Please, Luther, let's go home," Kendra said. But his friends howled like demons, and their bawdy comments encouraged him. Luther bragged, *"She even lets me smoke in my house. She furnished it herself, too. Stuff you can enjoy. No pansy-ass decorators. No antiques."*

"Except for you, Luther," someone yelled over the hoots.

"Our great room really is a great room, where I kick back in a big, fat recliner, watch my sixty-inch flat screen, and smoke cigars. In the house. Any of you do that? She doesn't mind a few cigar burns, not even after I accidentally set a chair on fire. And it wasn't the first fire in that house. Won't be the last, either."

"Why didn't she dump him and walk out?" Angela asked.

"Who knows? Here's the last part."

Kendra said, *"Please, sweetie, let's go home."*

This time, he looked at her face instead of grabbing her body. *"You're right, love bug. Boys, I'm going home for a sweet piece of Mexican ass. This,"*—he gulped down what Angela guessed was Viagra with the rest of his Dos Equis beer—*"and this"*—he grabbed Kendra's backside again—*"guarantee hot sex. Expect to hear about another fire tonight. The flames will be in my bedroom."*

The manicurist's face was scarlet, though Angela couldn't tell if Kendra's deep-red color was caused by shame or anger. Eduardo, the restaurant owner, arrived and guided Luther toward the door. The video followed Luther's black shirt. Then it was over.

Angela sat in stunned silence and then said, "What a pig."

"That video will poison the jury pool," Katie said. "They'll say he predicted his own death. Anyone who sees this will assume Kendra had a good reason to kill him."

"So did Priscilla. And his daughter, Eve."

"And Jose, Kendra's father." Katie returned to her quiche.

"Did Luther ever do anything but make sleazy money?" Angela took a sip of strong coffee. She needed it.

"He gave money to underprivileged children's programs. He seemed to feel sorry for them—at least sorry enough to write an occasional check."

"You're telling me that perv was a good guy," Angela said.

"No, I'm not. But he's got a few redeeming qualities, which is more than I can say for the brainless boobs in the bar. Luther even read, which made the others suspicious, but it was mostly military history. They forgave him because he was so rich."

"I can see he had money," Angela said. "And he wasn't afraid to wear it."

"Those cowboy boots are handmade American alligator tail. I saw a pair online for thirteen thousand dollars."

"Why did he dress like that?" Angela finally managed a forkful of quiche.

"That's how Luther rebelled. Cowboy clothes may not seem like much of a rebellion, but they're radical for the tight-asses who run the Forest. I kinda felt sorry for the old boy. His life was mapped out at birth. There was only one place for him to go to school, one way to dress, and one career—running his family's payday-loan scam. He didn't want to do it but didn't have the guts to tell his rich family to go to hell."

"How do you know so much about Luther?"

"He's friends with our boss. You're hardly ever in the office, but Luther was there all the time. He'd kick back in Evarts's office and leave the door open. Once those two started shooting the shit, I was the invisible woman."

"With big ears."

"Not my fault they couldn't keep their mouths shut. In the '70s, Luther knuckled under and married Priscilla Du Pres, from the finest Forest old money, and settled into the family business. I'm surprised Luther's dick wasn't too frostbitten to screw Kendra." Angela choked on a bite of her quiche. Katie was forthright and foulmouthed. "Last year, Luther's father died and left him in charge of the company. Luther had money to burn."

"Katie!"

"Okay, Luther had no one to rein him in. He went off the rails and took up with his manicurist—and yours."

"Kendra delivers the best gossip."

"Now *she's* the best gossip," Katie said. "Kendra refused to shack up with him, and Luther liked that. Gave him a chance to fuck with his well-bred wife. Didn't matter how important she was—Priscilla was a joke when her soon-to-be ex was nailing a nail technician, and a Mexican one at that. When Luther married Kendra, he'd be barred from Forest society. He couldn't wait."

"No more stupid fancy dress parties at the Women's Club," Angela said.

"Yep. Luther moved out of their mansion and exiled himself in Olympia Forest Estates. Too bad he didn't get to live happily ever after. Thanks to this video, he's still screwing with Priscilla from beyond the grave."

There was a moment of silence while they pondered the enormity of Luther's social sins. Angela finished her strawberries. "Have you found any interviews with the Forest creatures?"

"They wouldn't dare. They're all running for cover and bolting their doors. The Toonerville folks are another matter. They can't wait to talk to the national media. They hit town two hours after this hit YouTube.

Here's part of an interview with Luther's former driver." She called it up on her iPhone.

A thin, gray-haired man somewhere in his seventies was shaking his head and telling a reporter, *"I can't believe the old boy's dead. He was a force of nature. Generous, too. When I retired, he gave me a nice chunk of change and said, 'Go have some fun while you still can.' The old boy lived life the way he wanted and went out with a bang. What more could a man want?"*

Katie glanced up from her phone. "That's all I can find. You know no one in the Forest will say a word to the press. They've got their drawbridges up and the boiling oil ready if any reporters land on their doorsteps."

"What about *The Scoop*?" Angela asked.

"Damn, I must be brain dead. How could I forget that scandal rag? Let me call it up."

"Any idea who writes that blog?"

"Not a clue," Katie said. "But if you want to make a quick ten thou, Old Man Du Pres is offering ten large for that information. No takers, so far. We're all having too much fun reading it. Ah, here it is. Read it carefully, Angela, and then keep your ears open. *The Scoop* has poured more gasoline on this fire, and we're going to have to work hard if we want to save Kendra."

There was the website's distinctive header: *The Chouteau Forest Scoop* in curly script above a row of horses' rear ends. Under the horses was this slogan: THE SCOOP ON THE HORSES' ASSES WHO RUN THE FOREST—AND WE MEAN NO DISRESPECT TO OUR EQUINE FRIENDS.

It was a sad day when pedigreed horndog and no-table barfly Luther Ridley Delor burned to death in his Olympia Forest Estates mansion. Flames twenty feet high shot out of the roof. Did the devil come to fetch his soul? We at The Scoop have good sources, but they're not that good. Before he went for the final roundup, Luther gave us some infernally good entertainment his last night at Forest hangout Gringo Daze.

"*The Scoop* was at Gringo Daze?" Angela said. "The blogger has to be one of the local bigwigs."

"What? Nobody in Toonerville knows how to write? Go back to reading."

The Scoop happened to be on the scene to witness Luther's last performance, and we give it five stars. Never in Forest history has there been so much public ass slapping (and what a firm, young ass it is) and spouse dissing. Luther basically called his wife, Priscilla, a lousy lay. Don't look so shocked. Priscilla is a new widow, but we don't think she's crying in her beer over Luther's loss. Excuse us, in her manhattan. Our friends at the Chouteau Forest Women's Club say Pris likes a stiff one in the afternoon, but not from Luther.

"Now that's a low blow," Angela said.
"Shut up and read."

Luther died in a blaze of glory. (Hey, we couldn't resist.) So who killed Luther? We're seeing more horseshit than a stable hand. The Forest is divided on whether "the Mexicans"—the Salvatos, father and daughter—had help. Some witnesses say they actually saw another dastardly evildoer. The dastard was a mysterious black man. You know, the dude who commits all the crimes against white folks. We find ourselves agreeing—maybe for the first time—with two local grandees: Ann Burris and Dr. Bryan Berry. Yes, they're rich and connected, but those two refuse to follow the crowd. The Forest's glamour couple believe all the fires were started by the Forest arsonist. And, they say there's more than one arsonist. But wait, there's more! Ann and Bryan say the arsonist is a local Thoroughbred. Hard to believe, right? The whole Forest knows Toonerville kids are setting the fires because Our Kind would never do that.

CHAPTER 11

Day two

Later that same morning, a tentative knock at Angela's door dragged her away from her housecleaning.

"Ms. Richman?" A man's voice.

More knocking. Angela peeked out her kitchen window and saw a sparkling white truck and trailer emblazoned with crossed flags and **Proud American Lawn Service** in red, white, and blue.

Jose Salvato's lawn service. Kendra's father was at the front door.

Angela set down her dust rag and grabbed her cane. She'd seen Jose around the Forest but had never formally met him. Up close, she could see where Kendra got her beauty: Jose was a lean, tanned man with a chiseled face and black hair lightly silvered with gray. He was neatly dressed in a clean, dark-blue work uniform with his company's logo.

He spoke formal English with a slight Spanish accent. "Forgive me, Ms. Richman. You don't know me, but my daughter says you are always nice to her at Killer Cuts. I am here to see you. She needs help."

"Come in. Let's sit in the living room and talk. I'm sorry Kendra's having problems. Would you like something to drink? Coffee? Ice water? Beer or wine?"

"Nothing, thank you. I'm not going to stay long." Jose glanced around the book-lined living room, then perched on the leather couch as if he were about to bolt for the door. "I understand you're investigating the death of Luther Delor, my daughter's fiancé."

"I did investigate Luther's death, Mr. Salvato, but—"

"Jose, please."

"And I'm Angela. My investigation was at the death scene. I did the body actualization—I photographed and noted the damage to his body, and then I investigated the room where he died. I've turned in my report to the medical examiner. Dr. Evans will release his autopsy findings today, but the actual investigation is being done by the fire department's Doug Hachette and police detective Ray Greiman."

"I know, Ms. Richman, but they've already made up their minds that my daughter is guilty. She's living with us now. She was afraid to go to her apartment because of the press. She cannot work. Everyone canceled their manicures, except you. You must believe she's innocent."

"I have a hard time believing Kendra could set a man on fire. But—"

Jose rushed in with "See, I knew it. Everyone else says she killed Luther."

"Unfortunately, there's evidence against her, Jose. Physical evidence. And what happened at Gringo Daze the night Luther died didn't help. The whole Forest was there, and someone recorded his drunken rampage."

Jose winced and studied his calloused hands. "That's another reason why Kendra is living with us. She can hardly bear to leave home after that terrible video. My beautiful daughter has been shamed all over the country. The world! The names people call her! The e-mail! It's disgusting. I admit I never liked Luther, but he was her fiancé. Not the best choice, maybe, but she wanted to marry him."

"Why?" Angela knew it was rude, but she had to ask.

Jose sighed and settled back into the couch. "She'd been badly hurt by another man. The people here in the Forest, they seem nice and polite, but they can be mean to outsiders. Her mother and I weren't born in the United States, but we became citizens. We are proud to be Americans. You can succeed here if you work hard. We did everything to help Kendra fit in. I wanted to name my daughter Graciela after her mother, but Gracie insisted her daughter have a modern, American name. We sent her to the high school where the best families go. It was a sacrifice, but she's a smart girl and we wanted to give her every opportunity."

Jose and Gracie must be doing well, Angela thought. The Chouteau Forest Academy was thirty grand a year.

"Her mother and I wanted Kendra to go to college. She made good grades, and we wanted her to work with her brain. But Kendra refused. She wanted to go to beauty college, which is not the same. Still, it was an honorable living. She was hired at Killer Cuts right after graduation. Her mother and I thought she would meet good people. She started dating Bunny Hobart. He's a doctor."

"I met him at the hospital." Angela's voice was flat.

Jose picked up her guarded tone. "Bunny! What kind of name is that for a man? Gracie said we should be glad our daughter was going out with a young man who had a good job and a future. Kendra was sure he would marry her, but he didn't propose. She never told me what happened, but she was very upset. Her mother said I should leave her alone—losing your first love was painful. I followed her advice. Kendra started dating Luther.

"Now my beautiful daughter is shamed all over the country and branded a killer. If she was going to kill anyone, it would have been Bunny. She didn't care enough about Luther to murder him. She's going to be arrested any day now. Her mother and I will give all we have to save her. Kendra is rich and can pay you more."

He handed Angela a check. Her eyes bulged when she saw the zeros—$20,000. She handed him back the check.

"That's very generous, Jose, but I can't investigate on Kendra's behalf. It's not my job. You need a good lawyer. You should call Montgomery Bryant. Monty's a respected attorney who dates Dr. Katie Kelly Stern. Do you know him?"

"Yes, I cut his grass."

Angela had one chance to clear up a mystery about Luther's death. "The fire department found one of your gasoline containers at Luther's house. Did you leave one behind?"

"I don't know. Renaldo, the new man, is careless. He could have lost it. Who cares?"

"It could make you a suspect. There are witnesses who said they saw you at Luther's house."

"I was there. Like I said, I didn't kill Luther, but I would sacrifice my life to save my daughter."

Jose shook her hand and left. She watched him back his rig out of her driveway. Would Jose be railroaded for Luther's murder? Worse, would he confess to a crime he didn't commit to save his daughter?

CHAPTER 12

Day two

As soon as Jose left, Angela called Katie and was grateful her friend picked up her phone on the third ring. "Jose just tried to hire me to investigate Luther's death. He told me a little bit about why Kendra took up with Luther. He says she was in love with Bunny Hobart, and he broke her heart."

"Could be. I heard fuckface was dating one of the Du Pres girls—what was her name? Emmy? No, Esme. That's it. He was using Kendra as a fuck buddy while Esme was away at school."

"Poor Kendra thought he was serious."

"So the dickhead sweet-talked her into bed. He's the lowest of the low."

"Snake's-basement low. I don't think Jose knows the whole story about what happened between Kendra and Bunny. She's living at home now, and the media have the house under siege. Know anyone I can talk to?"

"Yeah, Mario at Killer Cuts. Women tell their hairdressers everything—they hear more confessions than priests. He was her boss. Talk to him. And Connie. Consuelo. She's working here at SOS now. Used to work for Luther and Priscilla. Connie's good friends with the family, and Kendra calls her Aunt Connie. I usually see her outside about noon. I'll ask her. If you don't hear from me, that means the meeting is on. Stop by the picnic area at noon and I'll introduce you."

At noon, Angela was outside at the SOS employee picnic area behind the medical examiner's office, waiting for Katie. The small concrete pad was used mostly by low-level hospital staff. Angela rarely went there. The place gave her the creeps. The only view was of the mortuary and funeral-home vans loading and unloading bodies. Two women wearing the maroon scrubs of the hospital laundry department munched sandwiches at one table. At another, two cleaners in dark-blue scrubs picked at salads. Angela took an open table and watched a black body bag being wheeled into a funeral home's black van. Katie came out the ME's door and waved. "Connie will be right out. She's nuking her lunch. I have to work."

Angela watched another funeral-home van park by the door. "How can you stand this place?"

"View's not much," Katie said. "But you can't beat the company. The place is boss-free: no doctors, administrators—even the nurses don't come here. Just the people who do the work. Great information and good company. Ah, here's Connie."

Connie was a slim, round-faced Latina with short, shiny dark hair. Mascara made her shrewd brown eyes look bigger, and she had laugh lines around her generous red-lipsticked mouth. Angela could smell her sweet, flowery perfume. She guessed Connie's age at fortysomething. She had a can of Coke and a burger on a tray. "You mind if I eat while we talk?" Her English was only slightly accented.

"Please. I'm taking your lunchtime."

"For Kendra, I'm glad to do it. Katie said you need to know about that . . ." She stopped, and Angela could see the anger in her eyes. "I can hardly say his ridiculous name. Bunny." Her contempt should have incinerated her sandwich. She carefully cut the burger in half.

"Jose told me a little about her romance with him," Angela said, "but I get the feeling he doesn't know the whole story."

"If he did, he'd kill the creep. I don't know enough bad English words to describe what he did. Katie says you will promise not to tell Jose the whole story."

"Never!"

"You called it a romance, but it was only a romance for Kendra. He's a predator. I'm old enough to recognize these men—they think sex with a Latina will be exotic. When Kendra told me she was in love with him, I tried to warn her. But she was only nineteen then, and I was an old lady of forty-two. She thought Aunt Connie was too old to understand love. What do I know, a married lady with three children?"

Connie bit into her burger, then said, "Kendra was very romantic then."

Then, Angela thought. But no longer.

"He gave her cheap flowers and took her for long walks. She told me they would talk and talk for hours. She was sure they would marry. I tried to tell her that rich men like him don't marry poor Latinas, but she thought America was the land where dreams come true. The girls at her high school had been mean to her—really mean. Now she had a handsome young doctor courting her, and she was sure she would march down the aisle and become Mrs. Hobart. I finally gave up warning her that would never happen. I was afraid I'd drive her away. I love that girl, and she was so innocent."

Was. Connie took a swig of Coke and another bite of burger.

"Was he her first lover?" Angela asked.

"Yes. That meant a lot to Kendra but nothing to him. She wanted to get married, and he kept making excuses. He said he had to finish his residency, and she promised to wait. Then he did, and he invited her to a party at his apartment. She was sure she'd get a ring. I went shopping with her for a dress. She chose pink lace—she thought white would look too bridal."

Angela thought Connie had tears in her eyes. "I hoped she was right. I even bought her high heels to wear with the dress. She stopped by before she went to his apartment, and she looked so young and beautiful and hopeful. I thought he'd have to have a heart of stone to hurt her. Well, he did." Connie poured ketchup on the rest of her burger as if she were squeezing blood out of the packet, then savagely bit into the sandwich. After she washed it down with more Coke, she continued.

"Kendra showed up at his apartment, all dressed up, expecting a ring, champagne, flowers, maybe even candles."

"She was a romantic," Angela said.

"And he was disgusting. She was puzzled by what she saw. Only Bunny's two best friends were there—no other women. There was no engagement champagne, flowers, or candles. Just beer and pizza."

"Kendra asked where was the party and that . . . that *pig* introduced her to his two friends and told her to relax and get to know his 'bros.' He said he had some coke and weed. They were grinning at her. Kendra realized she was the party. He was bored with her and wanted to pass her around to his friends."

"Cruel."

"She was embarrassed. Humiliated. She had no idea he thought she was a slut. She slapped his face and ran out of there. She went home and cut her new dress into pieces and threw out her shoes. She locked herself in her room and wouldn't talk to her parents. Gracie stayed home the next day, and Kendra finally confessed what had happened. Gracie called me, and I went to see them. We cried together and agreed her father must never know the truth.

"But Kendra was a different girl. She was quiet. She no longer laughed. And that crafty old Luther must have seen she was wounded. She was ripe for the picking. He treated her with respect, took her to the finest restaurants and on glamorous trips. He wanted her to move in with him, but Kendra said no. She no longer wanted love. She told me she was finished with that. But she wanted to be a Forest wife. She thought all the other wives would bow down to her if she married an important man like Luther."

"No chance of that," Angela said.

"I know that, and so do you. Like I said, Kendra was young. Luther gave her an engagement ring and two million dollars. He said it would make her independent. He wanted her to move in with him because they were engaged, but she refused unless he married her. Luther became the talk of the Forest, and he loved the attention. He loved showing off his beautiful, young fiancée—especially since he knew how much it angered his wife, Priscilla."

"She wouldn't give him a quick divorce," Angela said. "And his daughter hated him."

"Right. And Gracie was worried about her daughter's reputation. She told Kendra she was no better than a prostitute to take that money from Luther. Kendra was heartbroken—and angry at her mother. She moved out of her parents' home and got a flat in Toonerville. After that, Luther's behavior grew wilder and more drunken. Kendra didn't seem to care. I don't think she knew how to go back home. She had her pride. The one good thing that came out of this is that Luther is dead, and Kendra is back with her parents. Gracie has forgiven her. They've forgiven each other."

"What about Bunny?" Angela asked.

Connie's lip curled, and rage flashed in her eyes. "I wish he'd been set on fire. Luther was an old fool, but Bunny was a killer. He killed my sweet Kendra. I don't know this new girl anymore."

CHAPTER 13

Day three

Angela was on call that night from midnight to 8:00 a.m. She fell asleep about two in the morning. Butch Chetkin's call woke her up.

"Angela, sorry to wake you up at four thirty." The Forest detective sounded rushed and apologetic on the phone. "We've got a bad one. A headless motorcycle rider."

Angela's sleep-fogged brain flashed on "The Legend of Sleepy Hollow," except she saw a headless motorcyclist holding a pumpkin under one arm. She quickly stomped on that thought. She'd been dragged out of a sound sleep for an early-morning death investigation, but at least she'd be working with her favorite detective.

"The deceased is sixteen, according to his driver's license," Chetkin said. "Tried to pass a car and smacked head-on into a semi. He was going about a hundred miles an hour."

Angela whistled. "Poor kid. Where's the accident?"

"Bodman Road, in southwest Chouteau County. About half a mile from I-55. Kid lived in Bodman in Jefferson County."

Bodman was a huddle of run-down houses just over the county line, and Bodman Road was the main drag. "I'm on my way." Angela splashed cold water on her face, then slipped into a dark pantsuit, tied her shoes, and pulled her hair into a ponytail. She grabbed her cane and was out the door and at the scene twenty minutes after Chetkin called.

She saw the accident half a mile away on the twisting two-lane road. In the harsh glare of the portable lights was a sad carnival of flashing light bars and police cars, ambulances, tow trucks, and other official vehicles. As she got closer, a jackknifed semi blocked the road at the top of a hill. A white delivery van was parked at the east side of the road, with a blue late-model Toyota behind it. Bodman Road was blocked from the south by a patrol car, and a pair of uniforms directed the few cars driving at this hour to an alternate route.

Angela parked her car by the roadblock, pulled her DI case out of the trunk, and carefully caned her way along the potholed asphalt. The police had opened a portable folding nylon screen in front of the truck, and another one was about twenty feet away in the middle of the road. The body and the head. She shivered, and not only because it was a cool morning.

Butch Chetkin waved and hurried over. He was about thirty-five— a big barrel-chested man who looked dangerous. He was, to the wrong people, but Angela found him to be smart and thorough. He wore a dark police windbreaker, dark pants, and a turtleneck.

"What happened?" she asked.

"According to the wit in the Toyota, who was on his way to work at the 7-Eleven, the driver of the motorcycle was going at a high rate of speed and tailgating. The motorcyclist flashed his high beams and proceeded to pass the Toyota and the white Chevy van when the semi crested the hilltop at about fifty miles an hour. The truck driver applied the brakes, but it was too late. The motorcycle collided head-on with the semi, and the truck jackknifed. The kid's body is stuck on the radiator like a bug on a grille, and his head separated from his body. It landed about twenty feet away. Judging by the skid marks, I'd say the motorcycle was going at least a hundred."

Angela hissed in horror. "How's the truck driver?"

"Minor injuries and shock. He blames himself, but there's no way he could have stopped. Both he and the wits say he was driving the posted limit. He's on his way to the hospital, but I don't think the doctors can remove the sights and sounds from his mind."

"What was a sixteen-year-old doing out at this hour?"

"We found heroin in his saddlebag. The ME's going to have to test for it in his system, but we think the deceased may have been out buying drugs."

"More heroin in the Forest?"

"We're seeing lots of it lately," Chetkin said. "We think it's being brought in from Saint Louis."

"Do you have a name for the victim?"

"No formal ID yet, but the motorcycle license is in the name of Shane Mathrews, with an R." He spelled the name for her. "The photo looks like him." They both knew licenses were unreliable, especially for teens, who often used fake IDs.

Angela thanked him, opened the Vehicular-Related Death form on her iPad, then wheeled her suitcase over to the truck. Her stomach slid sideways when she saw the victim's headless body flattened on the truck grille. That cab must have been the trucker's pride and joy: shiny black with custom-painted red-and-yellow flames and gleaming chrome bumpers, radiator, and cab steps. The chrome-winged lady on the radiator must have taken off the victim's head. There was a dark trail of blood where his head had slid across the hood, cracked the windshield, then landed in the road. He was still wearing his helmet.

Shane, she told herself. His name is Shane. Even if she couldn't officially use his name until he'd been identified, she'd think of the lost boy as Shane to humanize his horrible death. Angela's stomach lurched, and her hands shook slightly. The only way to handle this nightmare was to concentrate on the facts. She photographed the body and the head.

She noted the time, the temperature—forty-two degrees—and the number of lanes. The road was two potholed asphalt lanes divided by a faded double-yellow line. Shane had illegally passed those two vehicles. The accident had happened at night in an open area in clear weather. The roadway was dry. There were no visual obstructions and no streetlights.

Butch ran the plates and gave Angela the year, make, and model for the vehicles. The crushed motorcycle was a 1973 Suzuki T500 with a rusted fender. She picked her way around the broken bits of reflectors and twisted metal, using the cane to steady herself, and examined the truck, a 2012 Peterbilt 587. She noted both the motorcycle's and the truck's plate numbers and the trailer's height, length, and weight. Butch told her the cargo was light bulbs. Both vehicles had their headlights on and their wipers off. The CD player had been turned off in the truck cab after the accident. The driver had been listening to Michael Bolton. There were no alcoholic beverages in the cab, a plush affair with red leather seats.

These mundane details calmed and centered her. Now Angela was ready for the body actualization.

She started with Shane's head, lying near the center lines in a modern, artsy arrangement of blood slashes, arcs, and an oval puddle like John the Baptist's platter. The victim's helmet was decorated with flames similar to the ones on the truck he'd smashed into. The ME would remove the helmet. From the crown of the helmet to what was left of the neck measured eleven and three-quarters inches. The head had been detached just below the hyoid bone. Angela photographed the head and mangled neck.

Shane's face had road rash on the unprotected left cheek. His dishwater-blond hair was in a blood-drenched ponytail. His pale blue eyes were open, his two upper front teeth—numbers eight and nine—were chipped, and both upper incisors were broken. His mouth was surrounded by scrapes and contusions, but she could see enough to tell that, before the accident, he must have been handsome.

Angela moved on to the body embedded in the shiny truck grille, painted with blood. She photographed the body and the bloody hood ornament that had sheared off Shane's head, then measured the rest of the body. He appeared to have been of average height for his age: about five foot seven. One red athletic shoe was on his right foot, and the left one was in the road. He wore a dirty white crew sock with a hole in the heel. His body measured four feet eleven and three-quarters inches from his neck to his shoeless toes.

She photographed and noted the lumps of bloody tissue on the truck's hood, then started at what was left of the neck and worked her way down. The yellowish jigsaw puzzle of the fourth cervical vertebra and the top of the spinal column—with its sheared-off veins, arteries, and ligaments—were drenched in blood.

Shane was wearing a black leather motorcycle jacket with reflective skulls on the back. She pushed away the thought that his skull was in the middle of the road. His jeans were worn and oil stained. Both hands were badly broken, with compound fractures of all ten fingers. Jagged bones broke through the skin. She suspected nearly every bone in Shane's body was broken, but the ME would determine that when the body was X-rayed before the autopsy. She did not see any open fractures through his clothes. She photographed and measured the significant areas of blood on his clothes and at the base of the truck's radiator.

The sun was nearly up when she finished her body actualization. She found Chetkin talking to a uniform near a patrol car and asked, "Can we take the body off the radiator?"

"No way. He's embedded in that grille. We'll have to remove the grille and take the whole shebang to the ME's. I don't envy the transport service having to lift that."

An hour later, the grille with Shane's body had been detached from the truck cab, and the tissue and remains on the rest of the truck had been collected. When the transport van arrived, Angela signed the paperwork, and Shane was taken to the ME's office. By nine o'clock, the trailer had been righted and the truck towed, along with the wrecked motorcycle.

Chetkin brought Angela hot coffee and a glazed doughnut. They sat side by side on his car bumper while she ate. The coffee revived her. "We should notify the next of kin," Butch said. He looked weary in the bright morning sun, and Angela knew she must look equally tired.

"This is going to be a hard one," she said. "If that's his right address, we'll have to take whoever's at home to ID the body at the ME's."

"The face isn't too damaged. If the ME puts sheets over the rest of him, the kid won't look too bad. But the undertaker's going to have a hell of a job putting him back together. Follow me to the house on Bodman Road to inform the next of kin?"

"Might as well. The day can't get worse."

As soon as she said those words, Angela knew she'd regret them.

CHAPTER 14

Day three

The house on Bodman Road looked like a junkyard. The tiny, white shoe box had faded to a dirty gray, and its weed-choked yard was piled high with rusting cars, a commode, a child's stroller, sun-faded plastic toys, and broken, unidentifiable objects. Angela felt another stab of pity for Shane Mathrews. If this was his home, his life must have been as miserable as his death.

Butch Chetkin offered to break the news, and Angela gratefully accepted. Telling people they'd lost a loved one was always difficult, and at times it could turn violent. She'd seen newly bereaved fathers punch their fists through walls. One mother of a murdered girl had lunged at Angela and tried to claw her face. Luckily, Chetkin was with her that afternoon and grabbed the woman before Angela was hurt. Later, the grief-stricken mother had apologized. But "kill the messenger" is a common impulse when parents lose their children.

The front porch of the Bodman Road house was a concrete slab with a yellow aluminum lawn chair and a dead plant in a clay pot. A tired, scrawny woman with colorless hair, raging acne, and a sagging dark-blue T-shirt answered the door. Bruce Chetkin introduced himself and Angela, and they both showed their identification.

"I'm Tiffany Mathrews." The woman talked as fast as a tobacco auctioneer. She was missing at least four teeth, and Angela wondered if she was a meth head. She sure looked like one. Angela couldn't guess her age, except that she seemed somewhere between forty and sixty. But if she was a drug user, she could be in her thirties.

"Do you know a Shane Mathrews, age sixteen?" Butch asked.

"What's he done now?" Tiffany flared into anger. "He in jail? He didn't come home last night." She didn't invite them inside. She padded outside in her bare feet and closed the door. Angela wondered if she was hiding her own drugs.

"Mrs. Mathrews, is Shane Mathrews your son?" Butch is tactful, Angela thought. Tiffany looked old enough to be Shane's grandmother.

"Yes, he's my son. Since his father took off, he's been nothing but trouble: skipping school, lying to me, and staying out late. I told social services I can't control him, but they don't do nothing. Now he's taken up with some Forest kids, and he doesn't even bother coming home, like last night. Third time this week."

"He drives a motorcycle?" Butch asked.

"Blue one. Rusty old thing ain't worth two shits. Did he hit someone?" There was a challenge in her voice.

"Ma'am, do you want to sit down?" Butch said.

"Why?" Now she looked frightened. "What did he do? Shoot somebody? Hold up a gas station? It's not my fault. I told—"

Butch interrupted her. "Ma'am, I'm sorry, but we have reason to believe that your son was killed in an accident."

Tiffany kept talking as if she didn't hear him. "I told him, 'Next time you're in trouble with the law, you're on your—'" Suddenly, she stopped and blinked. "Shane's dead?" She seemed to realize there would be no "next time."

"We think so, ma'am," Chetkin said. "We need you to come with us to identify him."

"Where's he at?" She was picking at a scab on her arm, and her hands were twitchy.

"At the medical examiner's office at Sisters of Sorrow Hospital. Ms. Richman and I will take you there."

"Are you sure he's dead if he's at the hospital?"

"Yes, ma'am. The body is in the county morgue, which is at the hospital. Now we need to make sure the deceased is your son."

"Let me get my flip-flops. Can I ride with her?"

"Of course," Angela said.

While Tiffany went back inside, Angela said, "If you want to go back to work, Butch, I can handle this."

"Look, Angela, I don't like her riding in your car. She's probably using. Meth would be my guess, and meth heads are erratic and paranoid."

"You know she won't ride with you. And you don't have any reason to arrest her. You'll never get a search warrant for that house."

"At least turn on your cell phone now so I can hear what's going on in your car. I'll lead the way. Flash your lights if she gets hinky, and I'll pull over and help you. And stow your cane in the trunk so she doesn't use it on you. Once we're at the ME's office, I'll try to talk to her. I want to find out more about those Forest kids that Shane's started hanging around. She may give us some leads on who's selling heroin in the Forest."

"Think she'll be in any shape to talk?"

"She's not exactly broken up over his death, is she? The ME's office is my one chance to talk to her. She looks like she's been around the block a few times. She's smart enough not to ride with me. If she lawyers up, I won't find out anything."

"I'll see what I can find out when I drive her to the ME's." Angela turned on her cell and dialed Chetkin's number. He answered and left his phone on in his shirt pocket. Angela stashed hers in the pocket of her pantsuit jacket.

The door slammed, and Tiffany was outside, dressed in jeans and flip-flops. Sandals slapping, she followed Angela to her car. Chetkin took off first in his black, unmarked Dodge Charger. The Forest had money for the latest equipment and vehicles.

For the first few miles, they drove in uneasy silence. Tiffany shifted restlessly in her seat. She was in constant motion: nodding her head, drumming her fingers on the armrest, and picking at scabs on her arms until Angela felt itchy.

Tiffany didn't talk about Shane. She never mentioned his boyhood or baby years. No fond memories at all. She didn't ask any of the questions that usually tormented grieving relatives: Did he suffer? Was he alive when you got there? Did he say anything? Did he die alone? Where did the accident happen? Angela had seen people who were more upset when their dogs were run over.

Finally, Tiffany asked, "Who'd he hit?"

"The motorcycle collided with a truck heading for I-55. It happened on Bodman Road, about half a mile from the highway."

"Bet the trucker was high."

"No, he wasn't," Angela said.

"Then he was going too fast. Damn truckers tear along that road when they're carrying a load."

"According to two witnesses, the truck was going the speed limit."

"Ha! He probably bribed them to say that," Tiffany said. "Those long-distance haulers are worried about lawsuits. Might give me a few bucks to shut up and go away if I get me a good-enough lawyer."

Angela was shocked into silence. Tiffany was trying to make money off her son's death. Twitch. Shrug. Pick. The grieving mother acted as if she had bugs crawling under her skin.

Angela saw Chetkin's Charger turn right at the sign for SOS Hospital. She'd have to ask her about Shane's drug use soon. "You mentioned that your son was running with some kids in the Forest. Do you know their names?"

"Never mentioned any names. He said they were rich, and he did some favors for them. That's how he got that black leather jacket with the skulls on it. Can I get it back?"

"If the deceased is your son, you're entitled to his personal effects. But I think it's been damaged."

Like your son, she wanted to shout. Your boy was decapitated, and you don't care two hoots about him.

"Too bad." Shrug. Twitch. Pick. "He paid two hundred eighty bucks for that."

Angela wanted to smack the heartless bitch, but she had to ask her about the Forest drug dealers. "So you don't know anything about who Shane was hanging around with or what he was buying?"

"Buying? What do you mean, buying? Why you asking these questions?" Tiffany's flat eyes grew meaner. "Do I smell bacon?"

"Huh?"

"You a cop? That why you're asking these questions? You keep talking that way and you can let me out now, bitch."

"We're here." Angela was relieved the ME's office at the back of SOS was in sight. She parked behind Butch Chetkin's unmarked car and fished her cane out of the trunk. The three of them headed toward the building, Tiffany walking a little in front of them, scratching and twitching.

"I didn't get much," Angela said, her voice low.

"More than I'll probably get from her," Chetkin said. "I heard it. I'll handle it from here. Why don't you see if Katie's free? It's almost noon."

"Already?"

"Time flies, whether you want it to or not." Butch punched in the code for the door and held it open. Angela got behind Tiffany, in the unlikely event that Tiffany was overcome when she entered the medical examiner's office. More than one person had fainted on the doorstep when they caught the distinctive odor of disinfectant.

"Stinks in here," Tiffany said.

"Thanks for your help, Angela," Chetkin said. "I'll stay with Mrs. Mathrews for the identification."

Angela peeled off down the hall to write her report. After she turned it in, she stopped by Katie's office and knocked on the door.

"Come on in. You're just in time to watch Kendra get arrested."

CHAPTER 15

Day three

Angela squeezed into Katie's claustrophobic office and perched on the edge of her cramped desk. The assistant medical examiner was staring at a pint-size TV sitting atop a file cabinet. Katie had papered the wall behind her desk with an autumn forest scene and glued a plastic skull in the foliage.

"You won't want to miss this. Shut the door." Katie turned up the sound. They watched an unruly media mob roiling outside the Chouteau County Sheriff's Office and county lockup. The CCSO, painted a soft green with black accents and expensive landscaping, looked more like a boutique hotel. The Forest liked to pretend crime didn't exist in its privileged precincts.

"I can pick out the newspaper reporters," Angela said. "They're the worst-dressed, and they're all waiting to take notes. Where did those guys get those baggy pants? From a clown costume? The TV reporters are blow-dried and burnished."

"Cut the freakin' fashion report." Katie waved Angela into silence. "This one's talking."

A stylish brunette with short hair and a serious suit told the TV audience, "Kendra Salvato, a suspect in the murder of her fiancé, Luther Ridley Delor, has agreed to surrender at the Chouteau County Sheriff's Office in approximately five minutes, according to detective Ray Foster Greiman . . ."

"Your friend Detective Greiman set up this clusterfuck," Katie said. "The great detective was all set to clap the cuffs on Kendra and make her do the perp walk. But Monty did some negotiating and . . ."

"Really?" Angela said. "I know your boyfriend can work miracles, but he actually negotiated with Greiman?"

"Okay, he did some ball twisting. And threw in a few subtle reminders about Greiman's last screwup. Monty heard through the grapevine that Greiman's got orders from on high to cut the hard-nosed crap—he made the Forest look bad—but the Forest first families are pressuring the police to close this embarrassing episode and arrest Kendra. Greiman finally said Monty could escort Kendra to the sheriff's office and hand her over in private. Then he called every reporter from here to California."

"Does Monty do murder cases?"

"He's doing this one. For now. Kendra needed someone fast. She'd barely sat down in Monty's office this morning when her cell phone rang. Her mother said Greiman was at their home with an arrest warrant for Kendra. Poor woman was crying her eyes out. Monty talked to Greiman and . . . Sh! Here they come!"

Kendra, makeup-free and demurely dressed in a navy suit and high-necked white blouse, her long, glossy hair pinned in a tight chignon, looked like a lawyer. Angela saw no sign of her injuries from the fire, except for her bandaged hands. Monty, with his blue eyes and chiseled cheekbones, looked like an actor playing an attorney.

Pointed questions flew like flaming arrows: "Did you kill Luther Delor, Kendra?" "Did your father help you?" "Can a Mexican girl get a fair trial in Chouteau Forest?" "Did you have sex before you set him on fire?"

Kendra and Monty ignored them and pushed toward the steps.

"Good grief," Angela said. "Did you hear that?"

"I'm not deaf. Hush! Monty's going to talk."

Monty stood at the top of the stairs, Kendra at his side, and held up his hands. The crowd quieted. "My client, Kendra Salvato, is voluntarily surrendering. She is innocent of any and all charges, and that's how she'll plead at her arraignment. We are confident the jury will find my client innocent. One of you asked if a Mexican *woman*"—he emphasized that word to counter the demeaning description of Kendra as a girl—"could get a fair trial. I want to remind you that Ms. Salvato is an American citizen. She was born at Sisters of Sorrow Hospital, graduated from the Chouteau Forest Academy, and also from beauty school. She is gainfully employed at the Killer Cuts Salon. That's all I have to say. There will be no further questions."

The media pelted the pair with questions anyway: "What are you going to do with the two million dollars, Kendra?" "How could Luther Delor be your fiancé if he was still married?" "Mr. Delor's widow says you killed her husband, and so does her child."

"Child?" Angela said. "Eve is forty-two."

"You can see which way the wind is blowing. Kendra's in for a real shitstorm."

Monty and Kendra fought their way through the bristling sound booms and mics and disappeared inside the sheriff's office, and a uniform shut the door. Katie clicked off the television and leaned back in her chair, her head nearly touching the plastic skull she'd glued onto the wall.

"Won't Greiman be making a statement?" Angela asked.

"Probably, but I'll watch it on tonight's news. I already know what he's gonna say, and he'll wear his mediagenic suit and blue shirt. The judge will read the charges and then set a preliminary hearing and send her to the county lockup. Monty expects Kendra's bail will be denied."

"When did you two discuss this?" Angela said.

"Last night. Kendra called for an appointment right after her father left your place, and it's a good thing she did. Monty knows I have my doubts about Evarts's autopsy, and Priscilla can't wait to cremate Luther."

"What! Her husband burned to death, and she's going to cremate him?"

"She'd watch him burn in hell if she could get a seat. Besides, if Kendra really is innocent, any evidence that frees her goes up in flames along with Luther. Monty's going to have to work fast. As soon as a trial judge is assigned, Monty will have to ask for a writ of mandamus, which will seriously piss off the judge."

"Why?"

"It clutters up his docket. Also, it's rude to question an ME's opinion. Many Missouri counties don't even have medical examiners. Chouteau County is supposed to be grateful we have one and keep our mouths shut."

"We're a death-penalty state. Giving Kendra the needle is pretty rude, too. Any idea who the trial judge will be?"

"Best guess is Monty will get Chauncey Boareman."

"Fat old cigar chomper with white hair and a red face?"

"That's the one. And if he doesn't do something about his high blood pressure, he's heading for my slab real soon."

"Chauncey's part of the Forest old guard," Angela said. "Kendra doesn't stand a chance."

"There are worse choices. Sometimes Judge Boareman is pro-prosecution, but he has occasional outbursts of objectivity. Monty's hoping the trial can be delayed until Kendra is no longer a hot issue."

"Good luck with that. The Forest has a long memory, and Luther's last video will keep it alive." Angela shifted on the edge of the uncomfortable desk and sent a pile of papers over the edge. While she scooped them up, she asked, "Didn't you used to have a guest chair?"

"I traded it for that file cabinet. There's not room for both, and I wanted a place for my TV. What brings you to the ME today?"

"I worked the decapitation death out on Bodman Road."

"The motorcyclist? I'll probably post him. I helped prep what's left of him for the ID. Poor kid. We fixed him so he doesn't look too bad, then took photos. Who's the next of kin?"

"His mother, and I've seen rattlesnakes with more maternal feeling. I think she's a meth head. Didn't seem to care about her son at all, once she discovered she couldn't make any money off his death."

"Poor little bastard. You wonder why some of these women even bother to have the kid," Katie said. "It's almost noon. Wanna do lunch?"

"No meat. But I could eat a salad."

They heard a brisk knock on Katie's door, and Butch Chetkin stuck his head in. "Hi, Katie. The accident victim has been identified, Angela. His mother says that's definitely Shane Mathrews."

"Are you taking the Mother of the Year home?" Angela asked.

"Nope, she won't get into a cop car. Says her boyfriend will pick her up. I think she needs a fix. I asked her if Shane was using, and she said she didn't know. Didn't know any of his Forest friends, either, and she was probably telling the truth that time."

"What about the boy's father?" Angela asked. "Maybe you can talk to him when he shows up for the funeral."

"Shane's father is no prize, either. He's been in and out of the pen since before Shane was born, and there's an active warrant on him for armed robbery. There may not even be a funeral. Mommy Dearest complained she didn't have any money. She may let the county bury him." Chetkin looked sad.

"Why don't you join us for lunch?"

"Something light. No meat."

"Both of you? That scene must have been a slaughterhouse."

"It was," Chetkin said. "But the boy's mother really made me sick. When she saw her dead son, she said, 'Now I'll never get any child support out of his fucking father.'"

"Touching," Katie said. "Lunch is on me. Both of you."

"Thanks," Angela said. "That's generous."

"Not really. Neither one of you has any appetite, and you can take me out when I'm hungry."

CHAPTER 16

Day three

The three were at lunch, tucked in a quiet booth at the Forest Salade Shoppe. Despite the cutesy spelling, the restaurant's vegetarian food was always fresh. The tiny place smelled of warm cookies. Angela found the light-green walls and flower photographs cool and restful, especially after that brutal, red, raw morning.

Like most cops, Chetkin preferred to sit with his back to the wall so he could watch the entrance. Angela doubted they'd be attacked by rabid salad eaters, but if Chetkin felt comfortable, he'd talk more freely. She nibbled on a caprese salad—buffalo mozzarella, olive oil, and tomatoes. That's all her queasy stomach could manage, and she wasn't too sure about the tomatoes. In deference to their delicate appetites, Katie ate an avocado-and-sprout sandwich on whole wheat.

Butch Chetkin speared a fat crouton in his Caesar salad. "Greiman and Hachette, the fire investigator, believe Kendra is the Forest arsonist."

Katie and Angela knew that, but Butch's pronouncement was disturbing.

"What's their proof Kendra set the fires?" Katie asked.

"Didn't say. But Greiman and Hachette found out that either Kendra's mother or father worked at the places where the arson fires were set. They think that's how she got the inside knowledge of the owners' schedules and got into the properties."

"So what?" Katie said. "Gracie and Jose work for every rich family in the Forest."

"Greiman and Hachette are lazy," Angela said. "If they blame everything on Kendra, they can close all the arson cases. Ann Burris says the arson fires are inside jobs, set by Forest kids. They'd know how to get into those properties without being seen, too."

"Ann is the only one saying that," Chetkin said.

"Bryan Berry agrees with her," Angela said.

"Of course he does. She's one hot lady. I'd agree the earth was flat if Ann said so. Look, I'm telling you what I heard. You can believe it or not. Greiman and the fire investigator are holding a joint press conference this afternoon. You can hear what they have to say yourself."

"Do you think Kendra killed Luther?" Angela asked Butch.

"Luther? Not my case." Butch munched his Caesar salad.

"Off the record, what do you think?" Angela took a bite of dripping tomato.

"On *and* off the record, I'm glad Ray Greiman caught the case. And I can tell you this, because it's no secret—he believes Kendra poured gasoline on Luther and set him on fire. That's premeditated. Murder in the first degree."

"Do you believe that?" Angela said.

"Doesn't make any difference." Chetkin shrugged. "Greiman and the fire investigator have a solid case against Kendra. Along with Greiman's usual half-ass—" He stuffed a big hunk of romaine in his mouth, as if to stop his criticism. After Butch swallowed, his tone was more measured. "Although Greiman sometimes makes hasty assumptions, there seems to be solid physical evidence that Kendra set the fire that killed Luther. Hachette, the fire investigator, found pour patterns and things like that. I know you don't like Greiman, Angela, but this time he may be right."

Butch had finished his lunch. He sounded fed up. "Want a cookie and coffee?" Katie asked, and broke the tension.

Butch and Angela both said yes. Katie came back to the booth with hot coffee and three hubcap-size chocolate cookies, and they spent the rest of the lunch discussing Butch's wife and two boys, who were both in grade school.

By two o'clock, Angela was home. Exhausted after the early-morning death investigation, she napped. At ten after six, she flipped on the TV news in time to see the report about Kendra. The announcer, a heavily hair-sprayed brunette, looked like a high-priced dominatrix with her tight black sheath and the face of a disapproving schoolteacher.

The video showed Monty escorting Kendra into the Chouteau County Sheriff's Office, while the announcer said, "Bail was denied to Kendra Salvato, the Mexican American manicurist charged with murder in the first degree and multiple counts of first-degree arson. Miss Salvato was employed at this popular Chouteau Forest salon."

Now Killer Cuts' elegant black awnings and chic, gray storefront were on-screen. Poor Mario, she thought. His salon had been dragged into Luther's murder. He didn't deserve that.

The announcer continued: "Miss Salvato, age twenty, is accused of deliberately setting fire to her fiancé, the distinguished Forest business-man, Luther Ridley Delor, age seventy." Was that a disapproving grimace? Hard to tell. The announcer looked like she'd disapprove of everything, even Mom's apple pie (fattening) and fuzzy kittens (they shed).

"Miss Salvato's last evening with Mr. Delor was the subject of a viral video at Gringo Daze, a local Mexican restaurant."

Angela groaned. Lourdes and Eduardo, the restaurant owners, were also part of Luther's murder.

"In this excerpt," the announcer said, "Luther Delor appears intoxi-cated as Miss Salvato attempts to persuade him to leave the restaurant."

The infamous scene was replayed again, with Luther roaring, *"Kendra is the best piece of ass in Chouteau Forest."* And that was no excerpt. The station played three full minutes of the scandalous video while Luther's octopus hands roamed Kendra's curves. Angela meanly enjoyed the prospect of Priscilla's outrage. She was sure the furious phone calls to the station had already started.

The announcer was back, looking like a hanging judge. "Witnesses said Miss Salvato, Mr. Delor, and Miss Salvato's father, Jose Salvato, had a loud altercation outside the late Mr. Delor's home before the fire. No one was injured, and the police were not called. Mr. Delor's home caught fire about three hours after the disagreement."

The fire video was dramatic: columns of flame devouring Luther's roof, dark smoke rolling into the night.

"Miss Salvato escaped the blaze, but Mr. Delor was pronounced dead at the scene. Viewers are warned that the rescue scene may be disturbing, and discretion is advised."

A firefighter in a turnout coat and SCBA gear carried Luther's badly burned body down the aluminum ladder. Angela winced when she saw Luther's blistered hide and charred, hairless head. At least there was no video of Kendra running around in that skimpy lace bodysuit.

The announcer solemnly said, "Miss Salvato's attorney, Montgomery Bryant, told the court that the defendant was not a flight risk, but Chouteau County prosecutor Mick Freveletti argued that she could flee across the border to Mexico."

The Forest was already distancing itself from Kendra, Angela thought, playing up her Mexican heritage. There was no mention that Kendra had gone to the Chouteau Forest Academy. That tony school was probably scrubbing her name from their files and records. What would they do with those giant framed photos of each class lining the halls? Block out Kendra's face? Or hope memories would fade and no one would recognize the dark-haired killer? At least neither business owned by Kendra's parents was mentioned. Were the Salvatos losing customers now that their daughter had been arrested for murder?

The announcer continued: "When her bail was denied, Miss Salvato was remanded to the Chouteau County Jail to await trial." More video of the exterior of the hotel-like lockup. The county jail wasn't the Ritz, but at least it was fairly new.

"After the arraignment, Chouteau Forest detective Ray Foster Greiman and fire investigator Douglas Hachette held a joint press conference," the announcer said.

As Katie predicted, Greiman was wearing his tailored TV suit. Doug Hachette did most of the talking. He looked professional in a dark outfit and jacket. Hachette didn't sound as polished as Greiman, but he was charmingly awkward, his deep voice strong and sincere. "We want to thank the prosecuting attorney for making sure that this dangerous woman no longer walks the streets of Chouteau Forest."

Hachette hesitated. Midway through, he must have realized he'd made a double entendre, and stumbled over the next sentence. He blushed and said, "I mean, she's no longer at large in our community. Mr. Delor's death was terrible, and we'll prove beyond a reasonable doubt that she's the perpetrator. We have airtight evidence. This heartless criminal is locked up, and the jury will soon put her away for good. Chouteau County can sleep at night, thanks to the good work of the fire department and my colleague, Detective Ray Greiman."

Angela switched off the TV, disgusted by the biased broadcast. Yes, the fire investigator had found pour patterns. But how did he know that Kendra poured the gasoline? The residents of Olympia Forest Estates didn't lock their doors. They felt safe in their gated community. Anyone could have sneaked inside while Kendra and Luther slept: Priscilla, his not-quite-ex-wife. Eve, his irate daughter. Or Jose, Kendra's father. Angela didn't want to think about that last—and more likely—suspect, but she knew the investigators would.

How long would it be before Jose was locked up, too?

CHAPTER 17

Day six

Today was the day. Angela would deal with Donegan's MINI Cooper. Since her husband had died last March, Angela hadn't even started the sporty little car, much less driven it.

The MINI needed the freedom of the road.

But first, she would deal with Donegan's clothes. She'd clean out his closet and donate them to Goodwill. It was the right thing to do. He'd been a generous man.

She finished the last of her breakfast coffee, then climbed the stairs to her bedroom. The stairs seemed steeper than usual. I'm just tired, she thought. This was her third day off work since the Shane Mathrews death investigation. She'd spent a whole day cleaning house and doing laundry. Yesterday, she had three doctors' appointments, each one an eternity on an uncomfortable chair with stacks of old magazines. That would wear anyone out.

But today, she thought, I'm stronger. I can handle this. It's time.

Angela opened Donegan's closet and caught the faint scent of his sandalwood soap. Could she let that go? Yes, it was just soap. She'd read that mourners kept the dead earthbound by refusing to let go of them.

She couldn't let that happen to Donegan. She loved him. She would always love him. But shirts, sports coats, and shoes had nothing to do with love.

She reached in for his navy Ralph Lauren sports coat. She could feel the quality of the fabric. There was dust on the shoulders. The coat had been in there too long. The jacket even looked good on the hanger. She remembered how the students—no, how she'd—admired him in that coat. She saw him again, his shoulders straight and strong, his brown hair thick and slightly too long. The well-tailored jacket looked elegant, especially when he wore it with his blue shirt. This blue shirt, still in the cleaner's bag. She put both of them on the cedar chest at the foot of their bed. Her bed, now. Her empty bed.

She sighed and reached for his brown suede jacket. That buttery-soft suede was her favorite. She held it in her arms, and for a moment—just a millisecond—she felt like she was holding Donegan. She hugged the jacket to her and carried it to the cedar chest, but she couldn't let go. Instead, Angela collapsed on the bed, weeping.

I can't let you go, she thought. I know I should, but I can't. I'm keeping you earthbound. I had a chance to go with you when I had the strokes. I could have joined you and been happy forever. Instead I lived, and each day is so hard. I'm so lost without you. Her tears spotted the soft suede, but she couldn't stop crying. She wanted Donegan so badly. She was tired of struggling to live without him. It wasn't worth it.

Angela woke up as the late-afternoon sun slanted across the bed. She was still holding the crumpled suede jacket. She hung Donegan's clothes back in the closet. Another day, perhaps. Right now she needed comfort. Through the lace-curtained bedroom window, she could see the Du Pres horse farm. She'd visit Eecie and American Hero. She changed into boots and jeans. Downstairs in the kitchen, she forced herself to eat a peanut-butter sandwich, then found the bag of carrots and package of peppermints she kept for her favorites. Time for horse therapy.

She picked up her cane and stepped out into the sweet spring afternoon. Eecie was out in the pasture today, her pet pygmy goat, Little Bit, at her side. The big bay racehorse with the tiny white forehead star hurried to greet Angela, moving delicately to avoid stepping on her little white pal. Angela hugged the horse's long, warm neck, and Eecie covered Angela with kisses, then nudged her gently.

"You want something?" Angela asked.

The horse's ears twitched, and she nickered. Angela fed her carrots while petting the Thoroughbred's warm, dark-brown nose. The pasture had the green smell of growing grass. The soft, spring air was scented with flowers and a slight undercurrent of horse manure. The white goat's shrill demand sounded like a rusty door, and Angela gave her a carrot. Eecie nudged Angela's hand with her nose. "Hey, you can spare a carrot for your friend. You're supposed to treat your pets."

After Eecie had chomped half the carrots in the bag, Angela said, "That's enough. How about some peppermints for dessert?"

The powerful racehorse crunched the sweet treats greedily, then licked the last of the candy off Angela's hands.

Bud came out of the mahogany horse palace to the pasture, carrying his portable soda-can spittoon. "Her ladyship making demands?"

"She didn't want to share a carrot with her goat. One lousy carrot."

"She's the boss of the barn." Bud rubbed Eecie's nose. "She lays down the law to American Hero. He may be a bigger, stronger male, but when they're roaming the pasture during the day, she lets him know if she doesn't want him to come back into his stall—just by pinning back her ears or giving him a glare. And he knows she means business."

Angela's cell phone rang. "Sorry, Bud, I have to take this. It could be work."

It was Katie. "Where are you?"

"At the Du Pres stables."

"See you in ten. I've been dealing with horses' asses all day. I'd like to see the whole animal."

Angela clicked off her phone and went back into the Du Pres's showcase stable. "Katie's on her way."

"Fine with me. American Hero can use some attention. I'm too busy to deal with him. You give him his treats, and I'll send her back when she arrives."

American Hero looked stunning in his luxurious mahogany stall. Red-and-blue stained-glass shadows dappled his shiny, dark hide, and his white blaze glowed in the late-afternoon light. Angela hugged his neck, and Hero stuck out his huge tongue. She gravely shook it, and he blew kisses through his nose.

"If I can interrupt you two for a minute." Katie clomped up to them in her riding boots.

"You're dressed for the barn. Did you wear boots and jeans to the office?"

"Nope, I keep them in the truck for when I visit Monty's horses. You okay? You don't look so good, Angela."

"Thanks."

"Your eyes are red. You were crying."

"It's allergies."

"Bullshit. Something upset you. Don't lie to me."

"This is a hard time of year. I miss Donegan. We went on our first date on a spring day like this one and had lunch at an outdoor restaurant in South County. Now the restaurant's gone, and so is Donegan."

"And? What's the rest of it? What set you off today?"

"I tried to pack Donegan's clothes for Goodwill, but I couldn't. I started crying and had to put everything back in the closet."

"I'm sorry." Katie looked sad and sympathetic. "That has to be hard to do on your own. If you want, call me next time, and I'll help. The clothes can wait. Goodwill isn't going to close down because it didn't get Donegan's old shirts."

"I know that." Angela started sniffling again. She wiped her eyes, but she couldn't stop the tears. American Hero moved closer and blew her a kiss. Angela wrapped her arms about the Thoroughbred's neck and cried.

"Angela, honey, what's the problem?" Katie's voice was soft. She patted Angela's back as if she were a skittish horse.

"I'm afraid I'm keeping him earthbound." Angela cried harder.

"Who? Donegan? What do you mean?"

"I read somewhere that if we don't let the dead go, they can't ascend to a higher plane and enjoy the afterlife."

"Where the hell did you get that horseshit?"

"I don't know. I just read it."

"Well, it's wrong. God doesn't work that way. If she did, I wouldn't have room to work in the autopsy suite, it would be so crowded with earthbound souls. Angela, when you're dead, you aren't tethered to the earth like a freaking weather balloon until you're set free. Donegan is wherever good people go—in heaven, or absorbed into the universal consciousness—I don't pretend to know exactly what happens after we die. But I do know this: you miss him and love him, and he loves you and always will."

Angela was sobbing hard now, clinging to Hero's neck. He nuzzled her and tried to lighten her mood by blowing kisses. She rubbed his muscular neck until she was cried out. "I'm sorry."

"Don't be. I wish I could help."

Angela smoothed Hero's coarse, dark mane. "It's like he knows how I feel."

"He does. Horses fall in love with us. He'll be your rock through this. He already is."

Angela blew her nose on a tissue she found in her pocket. "What's going on? Why do you need to meet with me away from your office?"

"Kendra's in big trouble, and I didn't want anyone to know we met."

Angela handed Katie half the carrots. "Help me feed Hero. Bud's working outside and wouldn't talk if he did overhear anything."

"We've got problems. Shitloads." Katie held out a carrot for Hero. The horse delicately took it with his big yellow teeth and crunched it. Angela patted Hero on his velvety nose and fed him another carrot.

"I should have a freaking blackboard and pointer to explain," Katie said. "It's that complicated. As expected, Monty got the old cigar chomper, Chauncey Boareman, as trial judge.

"Monty wants to bring in his own expert to autopsy Luther. He knows I think Evarts did a half-assed job. Monty asked Judge Boareman for a second autopsy. Luther's wife and daughter fought it. The fight was short, hard, and expensive. The family hired their own lawyer to stop the second autopsy. Priscilla and Eve said the dearly departed should rest in peace without a stranger carving on him again. Besides, his cremation date was set, and the invitations had been sent. The family would have to delay the service.

"Monty argued that once the cremation took place, any additional evidence would go up in smoke, and the rights of the living trumped the rights of the dead. The prosecution said there was no additional evidence—Evarts is a respected medical examiner, and the county can't afford to pay for a second autopsy. They went back and forth. Finally, Judge Boareman granted the order."

"I bet Evarts was thrilled," Angela said.

"He was so mad, I thought he'd burst into fucking flames. Judge Boareman said Kendra would have to pay for the second autopsy because she has money. Monty says it looks bad, but Kendra agreed to pay for it anyway."

"So Luther paid for his own autopsy?"

"It gets better. Judge Chauncey said Evarts did the first autopsy, so he could attend the second one. As a courtesy."

Angela whistled. "Evarts's head must have exploded."

"It nearly did. Evarts claimed he was too busy, but I could go as his representative."

"Evarts doesn't know you think he screwed up Luther's autopsy?"

"If he did, I'd be out on my ass. That's why I'm meeting you here."

"Is Monty holding the second autopsy at the ME's office?"

"No, what's left of Luther will be hauled to the East Missouri State Medical Center in Franklin County."

"That doesn't sound too bad."

"There's more. Monty's having trouble getting experts for Kendra. The court gave him money, but when the experts found out they'd be testifying for Kendra, they tripled and quadrupled their fees. A fuck ton flat-out said no."

"Somebody got to them," Angela said.

"That's my guess. Monty filed an appeal saying the experts' fee increases were way beyond a reasonable amount."

"What did Judge Boareman say?"

"Whatever the legal term is for 'tough shit.' Now Monty has to do a nationwide search for new experts."

"Poor Kendra."

"It gets worse." Katie gave Hero another carrot. "Monty's bringing in another lawyer. Kendra's been charged with murder in the first degree, and it's technically a death-penalty case. Missouri loves giving felons the needle. Monty's not playing games with Kendra's life. This is his first trial for a first-degree murder case."

"But he represented that doctor accused of first-degree murder last year."

"And he's damn lucky that case was dropped. It looks like Kendra's case is going to trial. Even if she doesn't get the death penalty, she could spend the rest of her life in prison—and she's only twenty. Monty will be committing gross malpractice if he represents her. He needs a top-flight defense attorney who's won an assload of first-degree murder cases in appeal."

"Uh, is an assload more or less than a shitload?"

Katie frowned at the interruption and gave Hero the last carrot. "Less than a shitload but not as much as a fuck ton. You wanna hear this or not? We're lucky we've got a good lawyer nearby in Saint Louis—Lin Kalomeris. She's smart and tough. We want to meet at her office tomorrow for a summit—a secret meeting outside the Forest. This is risky for both of us. I could lose my job if Evarts finds out I'm helping the defense. So could you."

"I can get a job in another city," Angela said. "I'm not going to stand around and suck my thumb while Kendra is railroaded for murder."

"Good. We're meeting at Lin's office on Fourth Street, near the Arch. It's a big glass skyscraper. Here's the address. Park in the garage across the street. The building is crawling with lawyers, and there's an Italian restaurant on the first floor, so if anyone sees Monty and me there, it's no big deal. Monty and I will go out to dinner afterward, maybe stay in the city overnight. Everyone knows we're dating. We'll drive up to Saint Louis together. You come by yourself. We'll meet you at four o'clock Saturday afternoon, okay?"

"Sure."

"Keep quiet," Katie said. "This really is life and death."

Angela patted American Hero's nose one last time. "He has too much horse sense to talk."

CHAPTER 18

Day seven

The law offices of Brandt, Bosman, and Kalomeris had a spectacular view of the Arch and the Mississippi River flowing past, muddy brown and muscular. The huge law firm sprawled over four floors in the twenty-story Bosman Building in downtown Saint Louis.

The law firm was two blocks from Saint Louis's Old Courthouse, scene of the Dred Scott decision decreeing that Scott, an enslaved man, could not be a citizen or sue in a federal court. He was property. Arguably the Supreme Court's worst decision, the Dred Scott case haunts Saint Louis—and the nation—to this day.

Kendra's arrest was a more modern form of racism, and the secret Saint Louis summit was held at BB&K to stop this injustice. Angela met Katie and Monty in the lobby of the building a little before four o'clock Saturday afternoon. Both were dressed for a date night in the city. Monty wore a pin-striped suit, and Katie had on a rare black sleeveless dress and high heels.

"What's Lin Kalomeris like?" Angela asked.

"Smart. Tough. Hates the death penalty on moral and religious grounds," Monty said.

"You keep saying that. How religious is she?" Katie asked. "Will I have to watch my fucking language?"

"Would it do any good if I said yes? She's a little uptight. But I've seen her enjoy a glass of wine. She'll fight hard to save Kendra, and that's what we need."

The three signed in at the gray marble security desk, and the guard opened the elevator for them. Lin herself met them at the fourth floor. She was almost as tall as Angela and wore her blonde hair in a twist. Even on Saturday she had on a somber, dark suit. Angela wondered if she wore the severe dark-framed glasses because she needed them, or to tone down her striking looks.

After the introductions, Lin said, "We can meet in the conference room next to my office." The trio followed her down endless halls painted in vibrant colors: orange, maroon, and lime green. The walls were lined with art that looked abstract and expensive. Angela wondered how many billable hours it represented.

The conference room was as impressive as the view. They sat at a round table overlooking the Arch and the river: Monty was across from Lin, with Katie and Angela on either side of the lawyer. They helped themselves to coffee from an urn and got down to business. Monty explained Kendra's case and said, "I can't tell you how risky this meeting is for Angela and Katie. They can both lose their jobs for defying their supervisor and the local powers that be."

"Point taken," Lin said. "We're all here to help Miss Salvato."

Katie added cream and sugar to her coffee until it was the same color as the Mississippi.

"We believe Kendra isn't guilty of murder," Monty said. "But the prosecution, the police, and the fire investigator say the evidence is against her. They say the pour patterns on Luther's bedroom carpet were caused by gasoline. They claim she doused the old man with gasoline and then set him on fire, creating a fireball that rose to the ceiling, then hit the floor, singeing Kendra's hair when the scary thing exploded."

"And what does Miss Salvato say?" Lin sipped her coffee. "What was she doing when the fire started?"

Monty checked his notes. "She was asleep in bed next to her fiancé when she was awakened by the smell of smoke. She saw small flames on the sheets on Luther's side of the bed."

"What material were the sheets?" Lin asked.

"The sheets and spread were both silk. There was no blanket. She said the flames were only a couple of inches tall. She jumped out of bed and tried to wake Luther, but she couldn't get him to move. She tried to lift him, but he was too heavy.

"She said the flames were getting bigger and the smoke was thicker. She couldn't breathe and ran out of the room. By the time she was down the stairs, there was a bright orange glow and black smoke pouring out of their room—the fire was everywhere. She heard the fire roaring and ran out the front door. She was choking and having trouble breathing. The firefighters arrived maybe five or six minutes later, she's not sure. When she tried to get help for Luther, it was too late."

"Did she call 911?" Lin asked.

"No," Monty said.

"Had her fiancé been drinking?"

"Yes. We have video evidence to prove he was drunk. He'd had a raucous scene at a local restaurant, where he was videoed drinking. We have a copy of the video."

"I believe I've seen it on TV, but I'd like to study it."

"Here's a flash drive with the video." Monty handed it to Lin.

"It's like *Animal House* for geezers," Katie said. Angela was relieved her friend didn't say something more outrageous.

"Had Mr. Delor been smoking before the fire started?" Lin asked.

"Yes. Kendra said he was smoking a cigar in bed when she fell asleep. She said he usually smoked a cigar before he fell asleep, and she tried to get him to stop because it was dangerous. She says that's what started the fire—careless smoking. Luther had a history of it. The fire department had been called to his house at least twice before this fire."

"How serious were the previous fires?"

"The first was minor. The second time, Luther burned a dining-room chair, but there were no injuries."

"When was the chair fire?"

"Four days before the fatal fire."

"Did Mr. Delor's house have smoke alarms or a fire-suppression system?" Lin asked.

"You mean like a sprinkler system?" Monty said. "No. But the house did have smoke alarms."

"Why didn't they work?"

"Kendra said Luther had disconnected them. He kept setting them off with his careless smoking, and he got tired of the noise."

"The night of the fire, did Miss Salvato have sex with her fiancé before he fell asleep?" Lin asked.

"Luther tried, but he couldn't . . . uh, perform. He'd taken Viagra earlier—that's on the video, too. He took it in the bar at Gringo Daze and washed it down with beer. When they got home, Luther asked Miss Salvato to put on a sexy outfit, a sort of white-lace bodysuit, and she did. It was, uh . . ." Monty looked embarrassed. "It didn't have any . . . uh . . ."

"It was crotchless for easy access," Katie finished, and Monty turned bright red. Katie looked pleased with herself, and Angela guessed she'd had to struggle to describe Kendra's outfit without using the F-word.

"Was Kendra wearing the bodysuit at the time the fire started?" Lin asked.

"Yes, she went running out into the yard dressed only in the lace bodysuit. The prosecution says she deliberately donned it to distract the firefighters from their job." Angela drank the last of her coffee.

"Did she do that?" Lin asked.

"She was definitely a distraction. But it wasn't on purpose. She didn't have time to grab a robe or change clothes—the heat was too intense."

"What does Miss Salvato say happened after she tried to save the deceased?" Lin asked. Katie watched a barge power down the river.

Monty looked at his notes again. "Kendra said she was dizzy and confused by the smoke. She had trouble breathing and thinking after she escaped the house. It took her a while to realize that Luther was still inside and in danger. She tried to tell the firefighters, but they didn't seem to understand. The paramedics tried to force her into an ambulance to go to the hospital, but she broke free and ran back in to save Luther. She got as far as the living room on the first floor when the smoke got her and she had to turn back. She was coughing and choking. That's when she was taken to the hospital and treated for minor cuts and burns on her hands and smoke inhalation. She did not resist treatment that time. The firefighters and paramedics described her behavior as hysterical and said she fought with and injured at least two paramedics trying to get away from them."

"She fought the paramedics to run *into* the burning house?" Lin asked.

"Yes. Kendra said they were forcing her into an ambulance, and she was trying to get away to save Luther."

"And she escaped and made an unsuccessful attempt to save her fiancé."

"Correct," Monty said.

"Did the hospital find any traces of gasoline or other accelerant on her body or clothes?"

"The ER nurse said she didn't smell any gasoline when she cut away Kendra's bodysuit or cleaned up her hands, arms, and face so they could treat her injuries."

"What were her injuries?" Lin asked. "How serious were they?"

"They were fairly minor. According to the discharge papers, her hair was singed slightly, and she had first-degree burns with small blisters on her hands and a few small cuts on her hands and feet. She was given a topical cream. She was given oxygen for the smoke inhalation, and they put a clip on her finger to check her oxygen levels. She had a cough, itchy eyes, and was a little confused, but the confusion cleared up when her oxygen levels began to rise. She was kept in the hospital overnight for observation. Chouteau Forest detective Ray Greiman got a warrant and took scrapings from under her fingernails while she was at the hospital. He also confiscated the bodysuit she'd been wearing. She was released the next day."

"What's the other evidence against her?"

"Kendra's father, Jose Salvato, received a call from the restaurant owners about Luther's shocking behavior. About three hours before the fire started, Salvato went to Luther's home and got in a shouting match with his daughter and her fiancé. She refused to come home with her father. She said she would stay with her fiancé for a while and then spend the night at her rented apartment. Witnesses heard Luther say he would ruin Salvato, who has a lawn-care business in the Forest."

"Could the deceased have ruined Mr. Salvato?"

"I don't know," Monty said. "Jose is a respected businessman and takes care of most of the local lawns. Luther was rich but not well liked."

"What else?" Lin asked. "The prosecution must have more."

"A firefighter found a partially melted gasoline container near the door of Luther's home with the logo of Salvato's landscaping company on it. Salvato admitted it was his. He said a careless employee may have left it behind when the crew cut the grass there. Salvato cuts most of the grass in Olympia Forest Estates, the gated community where Luther lived."

"Are Miss Salvato and her father the only people with motives to kill Luther?"

"No, Lin," Angela said. "Not according to the people I interviewed during the death investigation after the fire. Both Luther's estranged wife, Priscilla, and his daughter, who refused to speak to him, were in Olympia Forest Estates that night. Priscilla was at a cocktail party. The witness said Priscilla left about nine o'clock, citing illness. Luther's daughter, Eve, was at a barbecue in the same community and went home about the same time. Witnesses told me that Luther offered Priscilla major money to give him a quick divorce, but she was fighting him every step of the way. Luther offered Eve a million dollars to persuade her mother to divorce him. Eve sided with Priscilla."

"So Mr. Delor's estranged wife and daughter both had good reasons to want him dead."

"Yes," Monty said. "Luther's behavior was a continual source of embarrassment. That viral video I gave you was just one example."

"It's got more fossils than the science museum," Katie said.

"One more question. Why didn't Kendra leave for her own apartment that night?"

"She told me she was exhausted after calming down Luther and attempting to have sex with him," Monty said. "She often woke up about midnight and went to her own apartment. She never stayed the night at his place. We have witnesses to confirm that was her habit."

"Why would she refuse to stay overnight if they were engaged?" Lin asked.

"Luther gave her two million dollars when they got engaged, but he wanted her there all the time." Monty hesitated, and Angela could see his ears turn pink with embarrassment. Katie shifted restlessly. She seemed tired of this verbal fencing.

"Luther was hooked on Viagra-fueled sex," Monty said. "Kendra refused to spend the night until they were married. He promised her another two million when they officially tied the knot. Kendra had a two-million-dollar incentive not to murder her fiancé."

"That's one way to look at it," Lin said. "But she was what—a manicurist? Two million dollars may have seemed like enough money."

"Hell," Katie said, "I wouldn't fuck him once for two million, much less give the old geezer a license to do it every day."

CHAPTER 19

Day seven

"So, who wants more coffee?" Lin Kalomeris said, in the deafening silence after Katie's F-bomb.

"Me." Angela was grateful for the distraction.

"I think we can all use some." Monty didn't glare at Katie. He knew it wouldn't do any good. "Look at that barge going by."

It looked like every other barge churning down the mighty river, but the three admired it effusively. "Then why don't we get some," Lin said.

After everyone had refilled their mugs, Lin checked the notes on her yellow legal pad. "Now, to summarize our discussion so far, you believe that Miss Salvato is innocent. Angela and Katie are in a dicey situation—if they're caught helping her, they could be summarily fired. Is that correct?" Lin's voice was a little too bright.

"Exactly." Monty resumed the role of group spokesman. "Chouteau County has been hit with two other arson fires in two weeks, all in Chouteau Forest, the main city. The first fire was at a historic nineteenth-century barn that belonged to the Du Pres family."

"They're a big-deal name in Chouteau County," Angela added.

"They're a big-deal name everywhere," Lin said.

"The barn wasn't on the Du Pres estate," Monty said. "It was on Old Gravois Road, and it was going to be converted into a restaurant. Old Reggie Du Pres hadn't closed the sale yet, and the potential buyers backed out after the fire. He's livid at the loss."

"Was it insured?" Lin asked.

"Barely," Monty said. "Old Man Du Pres won't get much, certainly not as much as if he'd sold it. He's been hounding the police and fire investigators to make an arrest. The second fire was the Hobarts' pool house."

"Hobart . . . Hobart . . . why is that name familiar?" Lin said.

"Their sixteen-year-old daughter was killed in a car crash last spring," Monty said.

"That's it." Lin shook her head. "Tragic, just tragic."

Angela winced at the memory. She'd been the death investigator on that case, and her dreams were still haunted by the gruesome scene and senseless death of a promising young woman.

"Any loss of life in that fire?" Lin asked.

"No," Monty said. "But it's doubled the pressure for an arrest. The victims are powerful, influential families, and they want action. They want someone to blame. And they're not the only ones. The whole county is on edge with these firebugs. Now Luther Delor is dead, and that's made it a hundred times worse. The police and fire investigators took the easy way out and charged my client with setting the arson fires, as well as murdering her fiancé and burning his home."

"What's the evidence for these additional charges?"

"Circumstantial," Monty said. "There's no DNA or witnesses placing Kendra at these other fires. There are no security videos or fingerprints. The investigators claim that because Kendra is Mexican American, she has a grudge against the rich people in the Forest."

"Does she?"

"As I understand it, she was badly hurt by a love affair with a rich young man in the Forest," Angela said. "She thought he was going to marry her. He thought she was a casual fling."

"Was his family's property targeted by the arsonist?" Lin asked.

"He's Dr. Bunny Hobart, a distant cousin of the Hobarts who had the burned pool house," Angela said. "But I was told that if Kendra wanted revenge, she'd have gone after Bunny. The investigators say that Kendra had direct access to the three arson sites because of her parents' businesses—her mother owns a cleaning service, and her father has a lawn-care company."

"Circumstantial evidence isn't necessarily bad for Miss Salvato in the arson cases," Lin said. "Juries expect forensics now, and the prosecution can't deliver them."

"Don't underestimate the fact that Kendra is an outsider," Angela said. "She's a brown-skinned woman in a lily-white world. And she's a home wrecker. She stole the husband of Priscilla Delor, a much-admired Forest matron who's president of the Chouteau Forest Women's Club. A jury of Forest wives would give her the needle for that alone."

"You think the Forest has that kind of lynch-mob mentality?" Lin asked.

"Yes," Angela said. "I did the death investigation interviews at the scene after the fire where Luther Delor died. That's when the transformation started. Before the fire, Luther was a dirty old man having an affair with a woman half a century younger than he was. The local good ol' boys admired him for doing what they didn't have the nerve to do—break out of their rigid lives and have some fun. The women were disgusted. They refused to invite Luther and Kendra to any of their parties. Luther didn't care. The women were deeply sympathetic to Luther's wife, Priscilla.

"When I was interviewing the Forest insiders the night of the fire, people began talking about him differently. They started calling him 'our Luther' and dismissing his sexual escapades as endearing foibles.

Kendra, fifty years younger than Luther, was a scheming black widow who'd trapped the poor, foolish old man and bled him dry.

"We can't forget this fact," Angela said, "because it's crucial to the Forest: Kendra made off with two million dollars of the old man's money, and he promised her another two mil—money she wasn't entitled to by birth or a properly sanctioned marriage. In the Forest, money *is* blood. She is a poacher, an interloper, and she tried to rise above her place. They want to punish her."

"They're already punishing her," Monty said. "I'm having trouble finding experts to testify, once they know I'm representing Kendra. Suddenly, their calendars are full."

"Our boss, the Chouteau County medical examiner, blew a gasket when Monty asked the court for a second autopsy," Katie said.

"Why do you need one?" Lin asked.

"Because Evarts Evans did a half-assed job," Katie said. "He hates slicing and dicing fire victims. Before he even saw the body, Ray Greiman, the Chouteau Forest detective, said Kendra did it, and that's all Evarts needed to hear. He rushed through the autopsy so he could get out on the golf course in time for his tee off."

"Do you think he fudged the evidence?" Lin said.

"No, Evarts, for all his faults, isn't a liar," Katie said. "But he did his best to interpret the facts to give the Forest the verdict it wanted. He's a political animal. I'm convinced a second, more careful autopsy would give us different results. The problem is compounded because the usual experts refuse to question the opinion of their respected colleague. Evarts hates having his opinions questioned—which is why he'll roast my sweet, rosy—"

Angela tapped her coffee mug with a spoon, and the china rang like a bell. Katie stopped and recalculated her words. "He'll be absolutely furious if he finds out I'm helping the defense."

"To be fair, you are conspiring against him," Lin said.

"*Fair* is a four-letter word in the Forest," Katie said.

"You're having trouble getting a pathologist for a second autopsy," Lin said.

"Exactly," Katie said.

"Have you called Carol Berman?"

"*The* Carol Berman, from Florida?" Katie sounded impressed. "The one who worked on the Howe murder-for-hire arson? You know her?"

"She's a friend." Lin tried to look modest. "Carol lives in Delray Beach. If she's free, she'll do the autopsy. I'll make the call for you." She made a note on her legal pad.

"That would be a real help." Monty didn't bother hiding his relief.

"What about expert testimonies from fire investigators?" Lin said. "Do we need them?"

Angela heard that "we." Lin was ready to come on board.

"At least two," Monty said.

"Have you contacted Laurie Hartig and Mo Heedles?"

"I know of Laurie Hartig but haven't contacted her," Monty said. "Never met this Heedles guy."

"Mo Heedles is a woman," Lin said. "I think Mo is short for Maureen. Again, I can get in touch with them for you."

"Could you? That would make my life much easier," Monty said.

Lin glanced at her watch, a none-too-subtle reminder that her time was money. "What else? If you think your client is innocent, who set the arson fires? And who killed Luther Delor? Juries want answers. We have to give them the killer."

"The most likely suspect for Luther's murder is his wife," Monty said. "Priscilla is a leader of Forest society, and her husband's drunken skirt chasing made her a laughingstock. If he was dead, she could play the grieving widow."

"So you think this Priscilla slipped inside Luther's house and set fire to her husband?"

"Yes," Monty said. "People don't lock their doors in Luther's gated community. She's definitely angry enough to kill him. So is his daughter, Eve, for that matter."

"Then why didn't Priscilla or Eve pour gasoline on Ms. Salvato?" Lin said. "I can see why Priscilla would want her husband dead, but it would be just as easy to kill Ms. Salvato."

"Because she wanted to frame Kendra for his murder?" Monty said.

"I hear a question in your voice. Do you have a good investigator?"

"Yes," Monty said. "I can get him on the case."

"Did Priscilla set the other arson fires?" Lin asked.

"Of course not," Monty said. "It could also be that whoever is setting the arson fires killed Luther by accident—the house fire got out of control. I certainly don't believe Kendra is the arsonist. Some locals blame Toonerville kids—that's the nickname for the area where the blue-collar families live in the Forest."

"Any names?"

"No," Monty said. "The Toonerville kids are the usual suspects. Kendra's father has also been mentioned."

"As well as the inevitable black man," Angela said.

"Two people in the Forest believe that the fires have been set by bored rich kids. They'd have easy access to all the estates."

"But you have no proof and no suspects," Lin said.

"If we can find the real Forest arsonists, we can save Kendra," Angela said.

"And have all the fires tied up in a neat package? I don't think so," Lin said. "Monty, I'll be your lead on this case, but your investigator needs to start looking for the arsonists."

She stood up, indicating the meeting was over. Monty shook her hand, then said, "May we use this room to discuss a few things? It's not a good idea for the three of us to be seen together."

"Of course. I'll start drafting up an agreement."

After Lin left, Katie said, "Who's your investigator? KJ Lakker?"

"He's the only one I trust to poke around in the Forest," Monty said. "I'll contact him when we're back home."

"Call him now," Katie said. "He can get started today."

They waited while Monty dialed the number. "Hi, Angie. Monty Bryant. Is KJ available?" A pause. "Montana!" The lawyer sounded as if the investigator had gone to Mars. "Could you tell me when he'll return?" Another pause, then a shocked "Three more days! Is there any way I can reach him now? Okay, I understand. Please have him call when he returns."

When he hung up, Katie said, "That didn't sound good."

"He's off on some white-water rafting adventure with no cell phone. I didn't realize he was like that."

Monty sounded as if he'd discovered the investigator had a shameful secret.

"Hey, it's not like he's running around the woods after Bambi," Katie said. "We've got time. He'll get rolling as soon as he's back. What can we do in the meantime?"

"Angela, I need you to go to Killer Cuts and ask Mario what he knows about Kendra and how she really felt about Luther. Right now, she sounds like a heartless gold digger. We need to know more about her."

"What about me?" Katie said.

"You can stay out of trouble," he said. "You've got the hard job. Angela, while we're all together, Katie and I wanted to ask you something. There's a new associate at the Forest law firm of Du Pres, Hanley, and Hampton. Kinkade Rushman. He's forty-two, sing—"

"No," Angela said.

"No what?"

"No, I'm not dating this Kinkade."

"We call him Ken," Monty said.

"I don't care if you call him sweetheart."

"I met him on a case, and we've become friends. I told him all about you. He'd really like to meet you, Angela."

"I really don't want to meet him. It's too soon."

"It's just lunch," Katie said. "We're not asking you to do anything but sit down at a restaurant—anyplace you choose—and have a meal. Think about it, Angela. That's all we ask."

"All right. I'll think about it. But I'm not making any promises."

"We're off to dinner," Monty said. "Thanks for driving here."

"No problem." Angela watched them walk hand in hand toward the brightly lit restaurant.

She turned toward the vast, nearly empty parking garage, her footsteps echoing on the cold concrete. On the long drive back to the Forest, Angela wondered how she would face her empty house.

CHAPTER 20

Day seven

Sirens.

Lead-footed Angela heard their haunting wail and checked the Charger's speedometer. The police are after me, she thought. I can't get a ticket. The Forest cop let me off with a warning last time, but tonight I'm toast.

Wait! I'm going forty-five, the speed limit. Maybe I slid through a stop sign. As the patrol car's flashing lights approached, she pulled over. And watched it zoom past.

Angela breathed a sigh of relief as a gust of cold wind slammed her car. She flipped on the heater. The temperature must have dropped thirty degrees since she'd left the Forest this afternoon. In the unpredictable Missouri spring, she could expect anything from cyclones to snowstorms. The streetlights glowed against the preternaturally dark sky.

Up ahead, the cop car turned into Du Barry Circle, a pricey outpost of privilege. Thick, oily black smoke billowed over the treetops.

Fire?

Angela followed the patrol car's dancing red-and-blue lights to the looping, carefully landscaped road. She passed two mansions guarded by black wrought iron gates. Fire engines and emergency vehicles blocked the drive to Dr. Porter Gravois's estate. The late Dr. Gravois—the neurologist who'd misdiagnosed her.

The patrol car stopped at the roadblock, and Angela pulled off onto the side. She grabbed an old sweater from the back seat and leaned against her car's fender to watch the fire. Despite the freezing wind, she couldn't take her eyes off the scene.

Hell had erupted in this sleek, extravagant neighborhood. Sirens howled like demons in the choking smoke. Yellow-and-orange flames roared through Gravois's elegant French chateau, shooting through the mansard roof and cracking its fine bones. Angela counted three fire engines, two ladder trucks, the battalion chief's van, and a hopeless tangle of cop cars and emergency vehicles among the hoses.

As she watched the fire devour her old enemy's estate, a hot, fierce triumph burned through her. Gravois's body was rotting in the cemetery overlooking his home. She hoped he was frying in hell as he watched his family home burn.

As if she'd conjured him out of the swirling smoke, the man who'd nearly killed her stood before her in his sleek Savile Row suit. He'd died without dignity. She'd seen his nearly naked body wearing blue boxers and black socks, like a porn-movie reject. Right up until his death, he'd been a respected member of Forest society. Thanks to Gravois's blue blood and deep pockets, most of his mistakes were either overlooked or cured with a cold cash compress. But he'd misdiagnosed Angela when she'd showed up at SOS with migraines so severe she could barely see. Gravois had sent her home and told her to come back for a PET scan in a couple of days.

Instead, she'd had six strokes—including a hemorrhagic stroke—brain surgery, and a coma. During her three-month recovery in the hospital, Gravois never saw her, much less admitted his near-fatal blunder. When he was murdered last summer, Angela didn't feel triumphant—she didn't feel anything at all. She was too sick and numb. She was one of the few who didn't mourn his death. But she did share the local shock when she learned Gravois was flat broke.

His widow was forced to sell his horses, her jewelry, their summer home in Michigan, their art collection, even their family antiques. Their Forest estate, a fake French chateau with topiary, two pools, and twenty acres of land, was still for sale. The price had been dropped twice in the last year, but there were still no buyers.

Now the fire was taking it.

An icy breeze blew away the swirling, red-tinted smoke, revealing fire investigator Doug Hachette with a camcorder perched on his broad shoulder. He wore a firefighter's turnout coat, protective clothes and boots, and a hard hat.

"Angela! What are you doing here?"

"Is anyone in that inferno, Doug? I saw the smoke and followed a cop car here, in case I had to start a death investigation."

"As far as we can tell, the place was empty. Thank God for that."

"Is this another arson?"

"Incendiary fire," he corrected her. "Arson is the crime, and this looks like it was deliberately set. I'll know more when the fire's out and I can flag, tag, and bag in daylight."

He means investigate, Angela translated.

"Right now, I'm documenting the conditions, suppression, and progression, and interviewing individual witnesses. I'm looking for two juvenile witnesses. Males, estimated age fifteen to eighteen. Did you see them go by?"

"No, but I just got here. I didn't see anyone walking along the road when I was driving up Du Barry Circle, and there were no cars in the other direction. Why do you think the fire was set by teen arsonists? Kendra's in jail—she couldn't have started this fire."

"I didn't say they set the fire. I just saw them when I was taping the observers, but I didn't recognize them. One was wearing a T-shirt that said . . ." He stopped and looked embarrassed. "It had the F-word. I don't like four-letter words."

"I've heard them before. I work with Katie."

"Okay, it said, 'I Just Came Here to Drink and Fuck.'"

"Sweet." Doug shifted uncomfortably, and Angela changed the subject. "The Gravois place looks like a total loss. I thought these old homes were solid."

"They look solid. But like most of the big houses here, the Gravois home was built at the turn of the last century—it's old-school balloon-frame construction."

"What's that?"

"The worst kind for a fire. In balloon construction, the exterior wooden wall studs extend from the foundation to the roofline. This creates wall cavities from the foundation to the roof. Unless there are fire stops between the studs, these cavities can be an open path for the fire to spread quickly, like smoke up a chimney. Whoever built these houses cut corners and didn't put in the fire-stops. With balloon construction, the fire travels from the first floor to the attic and spreads through the HVAC system and across the attic."

Heating, ventilation and air-conditioning, she thought. Typical Forest—a good front hides massive problems.

"The building style, along with many remodels over the years, created interstitial spaces with no fire-stops between the interior and exterior walls and the ceiling and the floor above it. That helps the vertical spread of the fire."

The way the house was built, along with the Gravois family's nearly constant home improvement projects, created gaps that fed the fire, she translated, proud that she could keep up with Doug's professional jargon.

He shook his head in disgust. "Fires in balloon-frame walls destroy the structural integrity, and collapse is a serious threat."

On cue, there was a doomsday crack and cries of "Get back, get back," and the roof of the Gravois mansion fell in. Sparks exploded in the night sky as geysers of flame shot up through the ruins.

"Holy shit!" Doug forgot he disliked four-letter words. "Now the whole structure will collapse. We'll have to bring in heavy equipment to move the debris so we can investigate this fire. I just hope it doesn't spread to the woods behind the house."

"Mrs. Gravois will be lucky if she can sell the land. Is Celine here?"

"You mean at the scene? No. She's not even living in the Forest right now. She's staying at her mother's house in Michigan. At least she's spared the sight of her home going up in flames. That poor woman has had enough sorrow."

"Did the house have a fire alarm?"

"It's no secret that Celine Gravois is broke," Doug said. "She couldn't afford to pay the security company to monitor the property. She may have had battery-operated smoke detectors, but the house was unoccupied, and no one lived near enough to hear an alarm. A neighbor called it in when she saw the smoke, but by that time the fire was well advanced. The weather conditions don't help. The high winds are spreading it. Mrs. Gravois stopped using a lawn service, and the dead topiary and trees are feeding the fire."

"Do you think she set the house on fire for the insurance?"

"She's in Michigan, Angela." He came down hard on her name. "I'm not even sure she has insurance anymore. Besides, Celine's a good woman."

And her husband was a good doctor. At least on the surface. Angela knew she'd get nowhere asking anything else about Celine. "Are you going to search for the boys?" An icy drop of rain hit Angela in the face.

"I'm sure they're long gone," Doug said.

Another drop slammed into Angela's neck.

"I have to finish my preliminary fire-scene documentation. I still need to record the address number on the gate and street sign to establish the scene." He patted his camcorder like a faithful pet.

She said, "Nice camcorder." The two drops had turned into twenty as Angela edged toward the driver's door to make her escape.

"It's a professional model. A Sony PXW-X70 XDCAM compact camcorder, with a one-inch type sensor, which is larger than a super-16-size sensor . . ."

He rattled off a dizzying list of features that Angela didn't bother to figure out. The Forest grandees gave those who served them the best equipment—for their own protection, not to keep the workers happy.

The cold drops had turned into stinging, slashing sleet. "Feel that?" he said. "The sleet may help put out the fire, but it ices up the ladders."

"I feel it, all right," Angela said. "It's like being hit in the face with a bucket of ice water. I'm heading for my warm home. Good luck, Doug."

CHAPTER 21

Days seven, eight

Angela drove carefully home through the sleet storm. Once inside her house, she kept her cell phone on the coffee table and prayed everyone stayed safe tonight in the Forest.

Her prayers were answered—sort of.

Her cell phone rang the next morning at 3:00. She fumbled for the phone and gave a groggy hello to Butch Chetkin.

"Bad night to call you out, Angela, but we've got a possible fatal overdose out on Du Pont Close."

"It was bound to happen," she said. "Last Saturday night, there were two near-fatal ODs: high school seniors who'd scored heroin so pure it was nearly white. They weren't used to the good stuff. It sent both of them to the hospital."

"I heard about that," Butch said. "The girl's an A student, and he's just been accepted into Yale. Heroin is no longer a junkie drug. Nice white suburbanites switched to it when the street price of prescription painkillers shot up—heroin was cheaper. There's something off about this one. I'll show you when you get here. Meanwhile, I got a warrant to search the car, just to be safe."

"That's why I like working with you, Butch. You play by the rules."

"This one's bad, Angela—another kid. Seventeen, if we can believe his driver's license."

She sat up on the living-room couch, nearly knocking over her mug of cold coffee. "Who is it?"

"Alexander Soran. License says he lives on Harris Avenue in Toonerville, but he hasn't been formally ID'd. We found his wallet on the passenger seat with more than six hundred dollars, most of it in twenties, a Chouteau Forest Library card, and a Chouteau Forest High School ID, all in the name of Zander Soran. The photos on his school ID and license look like him, but we'll still need formal identification."

"Give me the address and I'll be there."

Chetkin did, then said, "He's driving a new black Beemer. You'll see the patrol car first—its emergency lights are on. The officer saw the BMW on the side of the road and stopped to see if the driver needed assistance. This poor boy was beyond help. Bundle up. The sleet has stopped, but it's still slippery and cold as a stepmother's kiss. Hurry! I'm freezing my tail off."

Angela was fully awake now. After she came home from the Gravois fire, she'd been too tired to bother fixing dinner. She'd scrambled two eggs—her default meal—and fell asleep listening to the sleet patter against the windows, grateful no one had died in that fire. She'd slept on the living-room couch again, wrapped in a yellow throw her mother had knitted. The old stone house was cold and drafty, even with the thermostat pushed up to eighty. She would have been more comfortable in her own room, but she couldn't face that vast, lonely bed and the memories of how Donegan had warmed her on nights like these. Then, she'd loved the cold. They both had.

She shook off her sad thoughts, caned her way to the kitchen to flip on the coffee maker, then hurried upstairs to dress. She couldn't believe this gorgeous spring had relapsed into winter. She rooted in her closet for sweaters, long johns, and her heaviest winter coat.

By the time Angela was ready, she wore so many layers she could hardly move. She carefully made her way down the stairs in her sock feet, cane in one hand and railing in the other. In the kitchen, she poured steaming coffee into an insulated cup, found her winter boots in the mudroom, and put on the antislip ice-and-snow grips. She'd hoped she wouldn't have to wear them again until next winter.

She was sweating by the time she made it outside, grateful for the cold wind that slapped her face. In the satiny moonlight, her yard was an ice garden with diamond-dusted grass. Her colorful spring flowers were encased in glittering ice. They'd be brown and dead by morning, but at this moment their fatal beauty was arresting.

She carefully made her way down the drive to her icy car, once more cursing her cowardice. If she could find the nerve to move Donegan's car, her Charger would be sheltered in a warm garage and she'd be at the scene quicker. She ripped the magnetic cover off the front windshield. Holding on to the car and using her cane, she walked carefully back and pulled off the other windshield cover, then dumped both in her trunk. She sprayed de-icer on the mirrors and the passenger windows, then pressed the key fob. The driver's door opened.

She tossed her cane on the passenger side and rewarded herself with a sip of hot coffee. The roads were a lethal combo of ice and slush. Whenever she pushed past twenty miles an hour, the Charger slid sideways.

After twenty minutes, she spotted the patrol car's lights first, then saw the crime-scene van. Zander Soran's black BMW coupe was parked on a deserted stretch of Du Pont Close, another cluster of century-old mansions about a mile from Du Barry Circle. She parked her car and saw Butch Chetkin, red-nosed and miserable in his hooded sheepskin coat.

Angela popped the trunk latch on her Charger, and Butch pulled out her death investigator kit. The crime-scene techs were working on the BMW's trunk. One was Sarah "Nitpicker" Byrne. That nickname was a compliment—Sarah was famous for finding trace evidence in hopeless cases.

"Looks like the kid was a dealer." Butch stamped his feet to warm them. "We found four cartons of thirty-six preloaded 'love roses' in the trunk."

"Every time I see love roses at a convenience store, I wonder if anyone actually buys them for romance," Angela said. "They're so chintzy. A teeny silk rose in a little glass tube. I know they're drug paraphernalia, but how do you preload them?"

"Stick in a bit of copper scouring pad—Chore Boy is a favorite brand—for a filter, add some heroin, and you've got yourself a preloaded pipe. Also works for crack cocaine. The local convenience stores live up to their names—they carry Chore Boys and love roses for one-stop shopping."

"Kid must have been a super salesman," Angela said. "Not many seventeen-year-olds in Toonerville drive fifty-thousand-dollar Beemers."

"You don't have to be good to sell heroin. Anyone willing to risk Missouri's tough drug laws will make a fortune. Zander had an advantage. A nice preppie-looking kid like him fit in with the white suburbanites. Too bad he started using his product."

"Let's go see him."

He started to take her death investigator suitcase, but she refused. "I can handle it, Butch." She rolled it carefully along the slushy blacktop road. A uniform greeted Angela and moved the crime-scene tape so they could pass through. Butch hovered beside Angela. She wished he wasn't so protective, but it beat working with Greiman—even the so-called improved edition.

She unzipped her case and opened the Death Scene Investigation Form on her iPad. She stuck her warm wool gloves in her coat pocket and put on four pairs of latex gloves. As she examined the dead boy, she would strip off the gloves so the evidence wasn't contaminated.

She was ready to begin her body actualization—the investigation. Photos came first. Zander Soran was in the driver's seat. She took wide shots of the BMW from the front, back, and both sides, then medium shots, then close-ups of the exterior and the license plate.

"Finished with your photos?"

Angela nodded, and Butch opened the door with latex-gloved hands. "No prints on this door. This was a carsicle when the uniform opened the door."

Seventeen-year-old Zander's slumped body was held in place by his seat belt. The boy must have been a chick magnet, with his thick, dark hair, long lashes, and straight nose. His lips were blue, and he'd vomited on his expensive plaid shirt.

"Did you see a froth cone coming from his nose or mouth?" The froth cone was a sign of pulmonary edema—the lungs weren't working. Often found in drug overdoses, a froth cone was the most fragile evidence. It had to be photographed quickly before it disappeared.

"No. I looked for one," Butch said. "He's sure not dressed like a Toonerville kid in old jeans. He looks like he was going to a country club, right down to the khaki shorts and boat shoes."

"He must have died before the weather changed," Angela said. "He's wearing shorts and didn't have a winter jacket."

Butch laughed. "You don't know anything about preppie boys. They'll freeze their legs off before they'll admit they're cold. They only wear jeans when they have to."

The brisk wind didn't blow away the powerful smell of feces and another odor filling the car's interior.

"Do you smell gasoline on him?" Angela asked.

"Definitely. See the spike in his left arm?" The needle was still stuck in Zander's arm. Angela's stomach heaved. She hated needles. "Why did he use a needle when he had a car full of pipes?"

"Exactly. What else?"

"I don't see any track marks. Is that needle in a vein?"

"I don't think so. That's what's off about this," he said. "It could be suicide or murder, but I'm guessing murder. I'm hoping we can get DNA from the needle and maybe a print on the syringe."

"Poor kid." Angela shook her head. A fatal heroin overdose was an ugly way to die. He'd be shaking and fighting to breathe. She could see where he'd thrown up.

She photographed the needle site, then shot more photos of Zander in the car seat. Next, she wrote down the body's location on her iPad. Zander left this world in style, in the elegant ebony leather seat of a jet-black BMW 440i Coupe, with both feet on the floorboards. His car was facing north on Du Pont Close.

She noted the fingerprint powder on his seat-belt buckle. "Can we move him for a full examination?"

Butch nodded. "His seat belt and harness have been printed. The techs will work the rest of the interior after we move the body. I've got a body bag."

Angela and Butch spread the black body bag on a soggy patch of grass near the car, then covered it with a sterilized white sheet. They carried Zander to the sheet, careful not to dislodge the needle. She photographed the needle again and noted her and Butch's suspicions about the setup. She'd also warn the contractors who transported the body to handle that spiked arm like fine china.

"He's only seven years older than my boy, Butch Junior." Angela heard his sorrow—and his fear. He knew, better than most parents, that bad things happened to good kids.

She was relieved when Nitpicker Byrne interrupted them. "Hey, Butch, we found something you should see in the trunk." Butch left Angela to work on her investigation. She used her cane to carefully lower herself to the cold ground.

She'd have to get Zander's demographic data, including his name, age, and birth date, when his identity was confirmed. She took the ambient temperature—thirty-two degrees at 3:57 a.m. Then she made a slit in Zander's shirt under his rib cage to get the body core temperature. She used a refrigeration thermometer that cost fifty bucks at a food-supply outlet. The overpriced forensic models didn't have as good a temperature range.

After she removed the thermometer and circled the slit on the body in indelible ink, she initialed the mark so the ME would know that was her work. It was her job to note every cut, known as a cutlike defect, every scrape, and every bruise (contusion) on Zander's body, from his head to his feet.

She started with his head, carefully examining it and probing around the hairline with her gloved fingers, but she found no scrapes, cuts, or contusions. She checked for "burns," or irritated areas around his mouth, in case he'd drunk some corrosive liquid like Drano. Some suicides checked out that way.

The boy's clothing had no rips or tears on the front, except the one she'd made to take his temperature. She noted a yellow-brown, eight-inch-by-four-inch irregular stain on his shirt front that "appeared to be vomit." She did not see any blood. He was wearing brown Sperry boat shoes.

He wore no jewelry and had no visible tattoos or piercings. Many drug users who injected used tattoos—including spiderwebs—to hide their track marks.

His muscular arms were bruised. She noted a twelve-inch contusion on the inside of his left arm and a one-inch contusion on his left elbow. He had a three-quarter-inch cutlike defect on his left index finger and a three-inch contusion on his left palm. His right arm had a two-inch contusion on the elbow, a six-inch contusion on the inside of his right arm, and a two-inch contusion on his right palm. Angela didn't think the cuts, scrapes, and bruises were defensive wounds, but the medical examiner would make that judgment.

His hands had other, puzzling injuries: big blisters, ranging from half an inch to three-quarters of an inch, above the first knuckle on the thumb and on the first two fingers of his left hand. He had a three-and-a-half-inch red mark on his right palm that appeared to be a first-degree burn.

Angela did not find any drugs, pill bottles, or paraphernalia in his shirt pocket or shorts pockets. She had to turn the body, and the black van for the contractor who removed the bodies had arrived. Angela had worked with Jim and Terrell before. She waved at them.

"Would you please help me turn him?" she said.

"Jim and I will do it," said Terrell, a burly linebacker with a deep voice. "You stay there." Together, the two men rolled Zander onto his stomach. As they did, his shirt rode up, and Angela saw a huge purple spot on the dead boy's right side. Livor mortis. After the heart stopped beating, the blood had pooled in the areas where the body rested. The pair went back to wait in their van while Angela measured the livor mortis on his side.

She quickly finished the back of Zander's body: he had a four-inch contusion on his left calf and an irregular brown stain on the back of his khaki shorts.

Butch ambled over, and she asked, "Did you find his cell phone?"

"No, I was hoping you would. Who would take a cell phone and leave behind six hundred dollars in cash?"

"Look what I did find. Livor mortis on his right side. He didn't die sitting up in the front seat of his car. His body was moved. And his hands are burned and blistered."

"Interesting. There were two twelve-packs of toilet paper, a bag of potato chips, and a can of vegetable shortening in the trunk—all Cheap and Easy house brands."

"Weird. Why would he have that?"

"They're all fire starters. Arsonists love chips. They make a trail to the ignition source, and the fire consumes it. Toilet paper works well, too. Smear the walls with vegetable shortening, and that adds more fuel. Nitpicker found a receipt from Cheap and Easy for thirty packages of potato chips, six cans of shortening, and thirty twelve-packs of TP. Looks like he paid cash and bought the stuff last night at eight nineteen p.m."

Why were Zander's hands burned and blistered? Why did he smell of gasoline? Was he the Forest arsonist?

And who killed him?

CHAPTER 22

Day eight

Jackie Soran, a small, worn woman, opened her front door at six in the morning and saw Angela and Butch Chetkin on her doorstep. The blood drained from her face before they presented their credentials.

"He's dead! My baby's dead," Zander's mother shrieked. "I knew it. I knew it!" She rocked back and forth in the doorway, weeping and tearing her short, dry brown hair.

Angela and Butch had yet to a say a word. A chill morning wind whipped across the concrete slab rustling the corpses of the spring flowers.

"Mrs. Soran," Angela said, "may we come in? Please?"

She put her arm around Jackie Soran's thin shoulders and guided her inside. She could feel the woman's nearly fleshless bones and smell her rose perfume. The living room was barely big enough for the bulky brown couch and recliner, a pair of end tables topped with brass lamps, and a boxy old TV. Styleless and scrupulously clean, the room's only decorations were framed photos of Zander, from a smiling baby to a sullen, sultry teen. The dead boy looked like a doomed movie star.

Angela helped Jackie to the recliner and handed her a fistful of tissues from a box on the nearest end table. Butch sat on the brown corduroy couch.

"May I fix you some coffee?" Angela asked.

"There's coffee in the thermos," Jackie said between sobs. "In the shopping bag on the kitchen table. I was on my way to work." She wore a blue housekeeper's smock with a logo for the Forest Executive Suites, a well-run motel for business travelers near the highway.

"Do you clean at the Executive Suites?" Butch's voice was soft. In difficult interviews, he often started with easy, obvious questions. Angela found a clean mug in the spotless kitchen cabinet and filled it with steaming black coffee.

"Yes." Jackie wiped her eyes. She did not cry prettily. Her face was red and blotchy, and her nose dripped. She dabbed at it with a crumpled tissue and sniffled. "I'm head housekeeper. Zander hates my job. He's ashamed of me. We used to be best friends when he was little. It was Zander and me against the world. His father took off when he found out I was pregnant.

"Cleaning hotel rooms is hard work and doesn't pay much. But it's an honest living and puts food on our table. There are perks, too. We never have to buy soap, shampoo, or conditioner. If a hotel guest leaves behind a partly full bottle, I can have what's left. When the toilet-paper rolls are near the end, I get to take those home. I can't make Zander see this. He hates my scrimping and saving. He's sick of using short rolls with only a few sheets. One day he went out and bought a twelve-pack of bathroom tissue and said, 'Here. I want a whole roll for once.' He got Quilted Northern! We can't afford that, but he said, 'I've got my own money, Mom.'"

"He hates," "He's sick of," Angela thought. She still doesn't believe her son is dead.

"Is that when he was selling drugs, Mrs. Soran?" Butch asked.

"I think so." She sniffled and blew her nose. "You can call me Jackie."

Angela handed Jackie the mug of hot coffee and sat next to Butch. They were both wired from countless refills during an hour-long diner breakfast. After they finished Zander's death investigation, they had decided to wait until 6:00 a.m. to contact his mother. Angela dreaded delivering the news that would destroy this woman.

"Was it usual for Zander to stay out all night?" Butch asked.

"Lately, yes. He'd come dragging home about two or three in the morning, and some nights he didn't come home at all, especially on weekends. But tonight felt different. He left about nine o'clock and said he was going to meet some friends. When he wasn't home by midnight, I walked the floors, waiting for him to pull into the driveway. I called him and texted him. I even used our special code, with 911 on the end. He didn't answer. I tried to tell myself this was just another night, but I knew it wasn't. Please tell me what happened. I've been expecting this, but I didn't think it would happen so soon."

"Does your son drive a black BMW 440i Coupe?" Butch asked.

"I know it's some kind of fancy black Beemer," she said with a flash of anger. "But I don't keep track of cars. He's so proud of it, and I can't even look at the thing. I make him park it out back. Was he in an accident? Was it that stupid car?" Now her voice was a plea, almost a keening wail.

"No," Butch said. "A patrol officer found your son parked in his car on a deserted section of Du Pont Close."

Jackie wailed louder. Angela rubbed her back and fought her own tears. Breaking this news to a family member was the worst part of her job. She'd seen grief before, but this poor woman was in agony.

"Was he alone? Please tell me he wasn't alone."

"We're not sure," Angela said. "But we didn't find anyone with him."

"Who did it? What dirty bastard did that to my Zander?"

"We don't know," Butch said. "When did your son start selling drugs?"

She winced, then took a deep breath. "He never admitted he was dealing, but I knew he did. He had to. That car cost five times what I make in a year. There's no way he could afford anything like that. No honest way. Was he shot by another dealer? What happened? Why won't you tell me?"

Because this is the best time to get information, Angela thought. "We're not sure how he died. He was found in his car with a needle in his arm. It appears he may have been the victim of an overdose."

"No! That's not right. Zander sells drugs, but he doesn't use them. I went and got a pamphlet about the signs of heroin abuse, and I know what to look for. Bad grooming is supposed to be a major sign—addicts don't shower or put on clean clothes. But Zander always looks nice. Drug addicts steal to support their habits. Zander never takes money from me. Instead, he tries to give me things. He wanted to buy me a new car, but I wouldn't have it. He gave me a sixty-inch TV, but I gave it to Goodwill. I watch him for the other signs of addiction. He doesn't have a runny nose or sniffle constantly, his speech isn't slurred, and I've never found any pills or needles in his room or in his clothes."

Angela glanced at Butch and thought of those loaded love roses in Zander's car. The trunk was his hiding place. But Butch told her they didn't find any signs of personal use: no pipes or needles. The techs had checked the obvious stash sites in the car—the wheel well, under the center console, the cup-holder molding, the hood insulation—and came up with nothing. They'd found a felony amount inside the fuse box, a moderately clever hiding spot.

"Did you check your house for places where he could hide drugs?" Butch asked.

"I remembered some spots from years ago, when I was dating his father." For a brief moment, Angela saw an impish, attractive woman, until the tired drudge overwhelmed her. "I checked the drop-down ceiling in the basement, the heating vents in his room, and between his mattress and box spring. I looked in the toilet tank—but I knew he was too smart to use that. I took apart his dresser and checked the drawers. I even took them out to see if he'd taped anything underneath or in back of them. Nothing. You can search the house if you want."

Jackie seemed to sense their skepticism. "I started spying on my own son. I knew something was wrong. Teenage boys sleep like they're d—"

The word *dead* nearly slipped out, but she stopped, sipped her coffee, and finished, "sleep like they're darned unconscious. He'd be out cold, and I'd check his arms and legs. I even looked between his toes, 'cause I read that's where some people shoot up. He didn't have any track marks."

"When did he change, Jackie?" Angela asked.

"The summer before his junior year. He was a good boy until he started hanging around with that Forest trash." She made a sour face. "He was a pool boy at the country club, and the rich girls made a big fuss over him. He's handsome, and it went to his head. Those girls are pretty. I could see they weren't serious about him. But he was too young to know they'd go out with him for kicks but go steady with their own kind. Zander started running errands for rich white trash, getting them beer and drugs. Pot at first, then heroin. My son is one of many stupid white boys who go into the city to buy heroin in dangerous neighborhoods because he makes so much money."

"How do you know this, Jackie?" Butch asked. "Did you check his cell phone?"

"I couldn't. It was password protected. I couldn't follow him, either. You can hear my old beater coming a mile away. It needs a new muffler. God forgive me, I put a little digital recorder on his windowsill—he keeps the drapes closed—and I picked up part of a conversation. Zander said he was going into the city—Saint Louis—and he'd meet someone 'at the usual spot on Grand Avenue' and buy 'buttons.' A button is five dollars' worth of powdered heroin. A tenth of a gram. I looked that last part up on the Internet."

"You didn't hear any names or nicknames?"

"No, Zander is careful not to say names on a cell phone." Jackie was still talking about her son as if he were alive. "Rich kids don't have normal names. They go by Muffy, Miffy, Kiki, Chip, Trip. Not one of them has a decent Christian name.

"I only used the little digital recorder once. I tried to talk to Zander about going into the city, but he wouldn't listen. Maybe if he'd had a father, he would have listened to him."

"Do you know where he went last night?"

"I'm sure he went to another party at one of the rich kids' houses. Don't ask me which one. They all look alike—blond hair, good teeth, sneery smiles. Something happened and they made it look like Zander OD'd. Stuck a needle in his arm and left him on the side of the road to die like a dog. A dog!"

She wept and rocked back and forth. "He's gone, he's gone. The only good thing in my life is gone forever."

Jackie had finally realized that her son was dead.

CHAPTER 23

Day eight

"I'm going to show you a photo, Jackie," said Ginevra "Viv" Easter, the medical examiner's grief counselor. She worked in the identification room. Viv was a sweet-faced, motherly fifty with a soothing voice. She was dressed quietly in a soft-pink blouse, modest gray skirt, and low heels.

The shell-shocked Jackie Soran sat across from Viv at a polished oak table, flanked by Angela and Betty, Jackie's supervisor at the hotel. Betty patted Jackie's trembling hand. Jackie gripped Angela's hand so tightly her fingertips were white.

"I don't have to identify my Zander's body?" Jackie's voice was unsteady.

"Identifications are not like you see on TV, Mrs. Soran. We take a photo. Just a photo of the face. In this case, the young man's face is unmarked, and he's lying peacefully on a blue sheet. There are no bruises, cuts, or blood."

And no drama, Angela thought. TV shows love those morgue ID scenes. How many times have we seen this scene: The grim, dark morgue is alive with shifting shadows. The steel drawer opens with the sound of approaching eternity, and the bored morgue attendant whips back the sheet. The bereaved mother screams, "That's him! That's my son!" and faints.

That's death porn in all its gory glory, and as phony as a Halloween haunted house.

The reality? Barbaric visual IDs have all but disappeared. Most dead people are identified by photos after their loved ones are carefully prepared for the process by an experienced counselor. Afterward, the bereaved person is given sympathy and counseling.

The Chouteau County medical examiner's identification room could have been a sitting room in a comfortable home. Its light-blue walls were hung with pleasant, forgettable art. The flowered sofa was piled with pillows, and a teddy bear slouched on the coffee table. The oak table and chairs where the group sat would fit nicely into a suburban dining room. The room was soundproof, the lighting was soft, the coffee strong and served in china cups.

Viv had spent more than half an hour explaining to Jackie what the photo would look like. Alexander Soran's case was easier than some—the dead young man had no facial cuts or bruises, and the paramedics hadn't worked him over. Identifying him would be an emotional ordeal, but it wasn't needlessly cruel.

The worst part was telling a family member a loved one was dead. That's when Angela encountered fury, fear, denial, shock, and pain. These emotions were so raw she needed a police officer with her to keep the bereaved from hurting her—or themselves. Even worse was the case of poor Shane Mathrews, the headless motorcyclist. His heartless mother's greed and indifference took a bigger toll on Angela than Jackie Soran's genuine grief.

Viv was explaining the ID procedure for the third time. "I'm going to show you a photo, Jackie. The photo will be presented face down on a clipboard. You can take as long as you want to turn the photo over and make the identification."

"I'm ready." Jackie's voice was flat. "Let's get it over with before I lose my nerve."

"All right, then." Viv brought out a white clipboard with a photo on it and set it on the table in front of Jackie. "Can you identify this man? Take as much time as you need. I'm willing to wait as long as you need."

Jackie closed her eyes. Betty, her supervisor and friend, rubbed her hand. Jackie opened her eyes and quickly turned over the photo. Once again, Angela was shocked by the surreal beauty of death. Alexander Soran looked like a marble statue. The vomit had been cleaned away, his hair was combed, and his sculpted features were pale blue.

Jackie made a small sound between a whimper and a moan, then said, "That's my . . . that's Zander." Her voice was a January wind, and its hopeless sound tore Angela's heart.

"Thank you," Viv said. "I know that was hard. I'd like to speak to you a little while longer. Do you want Angela to stay?"

Jackie shook her head no. Betty had her arm around her friend. "Let's move to the couch, where it's more comfortable, and we can talk," Viv said. "May I get you more coffee?"

Angela escaped out into the hall, so tired she felt drugged. Jackie's wrenching grief and the long, cold hours at Zander's death scene weighed her down. She saw a broad-shouldered figure leaving the medical examiner's office down the hall. Doug Hachette was heading her way. Doug had showered and changed his clothes since last night at the Gravois fire, but his eyes had dark circles and bags.

"Angela!" he said, and sneezed. "What brings you here? Excuse me."

She waited while Doug blew his red nose. "A heroin overdose. Seventeen years old."

Doug shook his head. "We're seeing way too much of that now. We even found heroin at the Gravois fire in the kitchen, along with empty beer cans, empty snack bags, used heroin pipes, and other drug paraphernalia. The kitchen was vandalized before it was set on fire—unbelievable damage. Broken windows, vomit, excrement smeared on the walls. People defecated on the floor."

"Disgusting. Was it the arsonists? Did it happen the night of the fire?"

"That's my guess," Doug said, "but we don't know, since the estate has no working security system anymore. We found some prints, hairs, and fibers, plus enough vomit and excrement to get DNA." He sneezed again. "Those Mexicans are disgusting."

Angela couldn't imagine Kendra or her father doing any of those activities. It sounded more like kids to her.

Doug sneezed again.

"Sounds like you're getting a cold. Did you work all night in the sleet storm?" Angela asked.

"Yeah. I went home to clean up and get breakfast about six o'clock, but I want to document as much as I can while the evidence is fresh. We'll have to bring in earthmoving equipment for the main house, but we caught a break. The arsonist set fire to the kitchen, but it went out. That kitchen is a later addition to the house and sort of sticks out in back. It was safe for me to enter, and I investigated it this morning. I found toilet paper draped over the appliances, potato-chip trails, vegetable shortening smeared on the walls, and gasoline. There were prints on an unburned TP wrapper and a shortening can."

Angela was instantly alert. A receipt for TP, chips, and shortening had been found in Zander's trunk. "Do you remember the brand names of the groceries?"

"Sure do. They were all from Cheap and Easy."

"You may want to get in touch with Butch Chetkin. He caught the heroin homicide early this morning. I think the crime-scene techs found a receipt for those items in the decedent's car—and it's dated. He also found toilet paper, a bag of potato chips, and a can of vegetable shortening."

"Thanks, Angela. I'll get in touch with him now."

"Was the Gravois fire arson?"

"Looks that way." Doug sneezed again and headed wearily for the exit.

Angela felt energized. This was news, and she hurried to Katie's office. She found her friend working on reports. "Come in, Angela. Did you get the heroin OD?"

"Yes." Angela perched on the edge of Katie's desk. "What a waste. The kid was a dealer, and his mother's devastated. Butch and I had to break the news, and I went with her to make the ID."

"I'm posting him this afternoon. Poor dumb bastard. Was he running with the wrong crowd?"

"Yeah, the Forest rich kids. According to his mother, he was their errand boy. Started buying beer and ended up dealing drugs. Mom is head housekeeper at the Forest Executive Suites. Kid couldn't resist the easy money and the shiny toys it bought and wound up dead. The old story."

"With the same fucking ending." Katie shook her head. "They never learn. Did you see where your pal Gravois's place burned to the ground?"

"I saw it all right. I followed the police there on my way home last night and watched it burn."

"Give you a warm feeling?" Katie grinned.

"Yep," Angela said. "He devoted his life and fortune to that white elephant, and now it's gone up in smoke. Doug Hachette was there, working the scene. I saw him again this morning, coming out of Evarts's office. Why do you think he's seeing our boss?"

"Beats me, but I'll keep my ears open."

"Doug says the Gravois fire is arson. Does this get Kendra off the hook for arson?"

"Nice try, but no. I called Monty this morning after I saw the news. He says it's a crappy defense, but he'll try it anyway. He and the prosecutor, Mick Freveletti, aren't asshole buddies, but he expects Mick to laugh him out of the room. We still have to find the real arsonists to spring Kendra."

"I've got some info that may help Monty. Zander Soran, the dead heroin OD, had potato chips, vegetable shortening, and TP from Cheap and Easy in his car trunk."

"A fucking fire-starter kit," Katie said.

"That's what Butch said. Zander paid cash and bought it at 8:19 the night before the Gravois fire."

"So he's the Chouteau County arsonist?"

"I don't think he set the fires by himself. He was an errand boy for the local rich kids. Hachette says there was a party in the Gravois kitchen before the fire and that the place was trashed. They left behind prints and DNA in the unburned kitchen. Hachette says there's no way to figure out when the party happened, but that purchase could tie it to Zander and his rich friends."

"Who are . . . ?" Katie prompted.

"Haven't a clue. His mother didn't know."

"We've got to find them before their fuckin' parents' lawyers find out and protect the overprivileged little shits. Mommy and Daddy will make sure they get away with murder. Have you made your appointment to see Mario yet and ask him about Kendra?"

"Give me a break. I've been working all morning. I still have to write my report."

"We don't have time to waste. Call him now, before you forget."

Under Katie's watchful eye, Angela made an appointment to have her roots colored at nine tomorrow morning. When she hung up, Katie said, "You should be rehabbed by noon. You can lunch with Ken tomorrow."

"Ken? You mean Kinkade Rushman, the lawyer?"

"He's a hunk, Angela, and Monty says he's a good guy."

"Then Monty can have lunch with him."

"He already has. That's why he thinks Ken would be someone you'd enjoy. Look, I promised I wouldn't lecture you, but it's lunch. You can go anywhere you want. How about Gringo Daze? You like the place. Just sit down and have a freaking tamale with the guy. What's the big deal?"

Angela felt the panic freezing her heart. She hadn't been on a date with another man for almost twenty-five years.

As if she had read Angela's mind, Katie said, "It's not a date. When you have lunch with Butch, is that a date?"

"No, that's business. I can't go out with this Ken. I don't want another man. I won't be able to eat." She could feel herself starting to sweat. She'd throw up. She tried to make Katie understand, but her friend barged ahead.

"Angela, you owe me. You owe me your life. I found you after you had the strokes. I've never asked for anything, but I can't stand to watch you bury yourself alive. Go to lunch with Ken, please? That's all I'm asking."

Angela hesitated, then managed one word. "Okay."

"About fucking time," Katie said.

CHAPTER 24

Day nine

"You wish to cancel your appointment with Mario for this Friday, Mrs. Hobart?" the Killer Cuts receptionist said into the phone. Raquel's artfully made-up face was frowning, and she poked her shiny, wavy, dark hair with a pen.

Angela could hear garbled shouting from Raquel's receiver, then the Cuban receptionist said, "Oh! You want to cancel your appointment for *every* Friday. As you wish." Her voice was freezingly polite.

Angela glanced over the top of the salon's black marble counter and saw the elegant black appointment book, as big as a ledger. Nearly all the appointments were crossed out on both pages. No wonder she'd been able to get an appointment yesterday on such short notice.

"Have a good day." Raquel ended the call and smiled at Angela.

"How's Mario?" The salon was unusually quiet for 8:50 in the morning. Angela heard the lonesome roar of a single hair dryer. She missed the customary cheerful background created by chattering customers and laughing staff.

Raquel lowered her voice so Angela could barely hear. "He's hanging in there, Angela, but customers are canceling left and right.

Ungrateful people! Mario helped so many of them. He flew to New York, to Newport, even to Paris, to do the hair and makeup for their daughters' weddings. He went to their homes and did their hair when they were housebound. If they were in the hospital, he brought them flowers and visited them."

"I know. He brought me orchids and Cuban coffee when I was in SOS."

"See? You remember. You're loyal. But the others? *Pfft!* They forget. After everything he did for them, this is how they repay him!" She opened her arms to the empty salon. The group of client chairs looked like elegant leather-and-steel sculptures. Untouched magazine racks held the latest fashion news. Kendra's abandoned manicure station looked forlorn, the vibrant nail-polish colors lined up in racks. Next to Kendra's station was a second one, where a ponytailed blonde read a gossip magazine.

"Is it because of Kendra?"

"Yes. He refused to denounce her. He hired another manicurist, and he's made it clear that she's temporary until Kendra returns. The old Forest families have been boycotting him, starting with that b—" She stopped, and her caramel-colored skin blushed red. "With that awful woman Priscilla Delor and her witchy daughter, Eve. Then the Du Pres and the Hobarts started canceling—one of them just canceled now."

"I heard." It was Angela's turn to blush for eavesdropping, but Raquel shrugged.

"It's no secret. Eve and Priscilla are leading the campaign. All the blue-blood wives and their hangdog husbands have boycotted Killer Cuts. I don't know how much longer Mario can keep going. This is a one-man shop with beauty services, and he's paying the staff out of his own pocket—the cleaners, the manicurists, the facialist, the massage therapist, and me. Right now, there's no income except for a few faithful customers like you. I'm so grateful you're here, and he is, too. We're learning who our real friends are."

She glanced at the wall clock. "It's almost nine. And I talk too much. Mario will have a fit if he finds out I told you this. Change into a smock, and I'll take you back to his chair, then get you a café Cubano."

"My lips are sealed." Angela headed for the purple dressing room with the lavender curtains. All the cubicles were empty. She unzipped her dress and put on a black robe. She'd dressed so she could go straight to lunch when Mario finished her hair, and wore a pink sheath with beige heels. She couldn't risk getting hair dye on the light-colored fabric—Donegan had loved that dress.

Katie had never asked her for a favor, so despite her reluctance to lunch with Ken, Angela worked hard to look good. She kept her serviceable pantsuit in widow's black and sensible shoes in her closet. She wore a dress with color for the first time since she came home from the hospital. She'd changed her clothes—but she couldn't do anything about her feelings. Every nerve in her body longed for Donegan. Katie was right. She'd buried her feelings along with her husband, and resurrecting them was too painful. But she'd honor her promise.

The dressing room's gold-framed mirror revealed she was past due for a color touch-up. She had a good half inch of gray roots, and her hair was slightly frizzy. Mario's magic would tame it. Angela hung her dress on the dressing-room clothes rack, and the hangers rattled and jangled. On a normal day, she would have had to fight for an empty hanger.

She pasted a smile on her face, and Raquel escorted her to Mario's station, a light-filled alcove at the back of the shop. Peach orchids perched on clear Lucite shelves, and sun spilled through the high, arched window, gilding two feathery palms. Mario was dressed dramatically in his signature black.

"Angela! So glad you came!" He hugged her. Mario's English had only a trace of a Cuban accent. He carefully examined her hair and shook his head. "You waited too long again. But I can fix it. You need a trim, too." He looked down at her shoes. "And what's this? Where's your cane? You're wearing heels."

"Katie talked me into having lunch with a lawyer. I can't handle heels and a cane, and this dress doesn't look right with sensible black shoes."

"Well, I'm glad to see you out of your uniform. What kind of lawyer?"

"No idea. She claims he's handsome and entertaining."

"It's about time. Don't frown at me. You're a young, beautiful woman. You should be with men."

"I don't need a man."

He mixed her touch-up color in a bowl on a small rolling table. "You don't have to fall in love with him, but you need friends, especially people who aren't connected to your work. I know you love your job, but it's hard. What's so difficult about lunch with a handsome man? You eat good food, you listen, you laugh, you think about something besides the sorrow you encounter in your work." He used a small brush to paint her gray roots with a creamy brown solution.

"It's just that—that—I still love Donegan." She stumbled over her words, but she had to let him know why she dreaded this lunch.

"Of course you do." He deftly divided her hair into sections so he could paint the roots. "Are you afraid you'll stop loving Donegan because you have lunch with this man?"

"No, but—"

He leaned across her head to paint a swatch by her ear, then began sectioning and painting the back of her head. "No one can take away your love for Donegan. That's real, and you'll always have that. But make room in your life, if not in your heart, for new people."

Raquel arrived with two tiny shots of Cuban coffee so strong, sweet, and thick Angela could almost eat it with a spoon. She and Mario drank it in respectful silence. The caffeine bomb gave Angela the courage to change the subject. "I heard that some of the Forest old guard are boycotting you."

"They're going to that fraud, Nikolai of New York. Ha! Nick of Newark is more like it. Nicolai claims to be 'just back from New York with the latest styles.' Oldest scam in the stylists' book: he goes to Manhattan for a few days, takes an overpriced class from some celebrity stylist, then opens a salon and announces that he's 'just back from New York.'

"Wait till Nikolai starts working on those ladies. He better know how to keep a straight face. Mrs. Du Pres told me, 'I may be seventy-two, but I have amazing skin, Mario. I've never had a face-lift.' I'm combing her hair as she tells me this. I can feel the face-lift scars! But I am polite and pretend she's telling the truth. And Miss Eudora Hobart—cheapest woman in the Forest. Tips me fifty cents for doing her hair—what's left of it."

"You're joking. Everyone tips you at least fifty bucks. Why do you put up with that?"

"Because her caregiver usually remembers to tip me for Miss Eudora. And if she doesn't, my book is full next time until she gets the point. Priscilla, the ringleader, is a piece of work. Last time, she was eating a banana while I did her hair. She ate half and then handed it to me, asking, 'Would you like the rest?'"

"She tried to give you a banana she'd been eating?"

"Yes! With her teeth marks in it."

"That's revolting."

"They're all revolting." Mario dabbed hard at her gray roots with the brush. "I'm glad to be rid of them." They both knew that wasn't true.

"Do you like Kendra?"

"I love Kendra." Mario's voice was soft. "Such a sweet, innocent girl."

"Why didn't she go to college? She's smart enough, and her parents had the money to send her to the Forest Academy."

"She got good grades there, but she was miserable. The students, especially the girls, called her ugly names."

"I can imagine."

"I'm not sure you can, Angela. I know your parents were servants, but you at least looked like the other students. Kendra is brown-skinned."

"And beautiful."

"That made it worse. Kendra told me she'd come home crying at least once a week."

"Didn't the school have rules about bullying?"

"Gracie would talk to the principal, and it would stop for a while, but then it would start up. Her tormenters had rich parents."

"And the school didn't want to offend major donors."

"Exactly." Mario gave Angela the ghost of a smile. "She said she'd go to beauty college, which was not the same. I hired her right after she graduated. Her parents thought she would meet good people here. Instead, that Bunny Hobart—that doctor—went after her. I never liked that man. He's a snob with a silly name. He seemed to sneer all the time. What's wrong with him?"

"He was born that way," Angela said. "The silver spoon did something to his lip."

Mario's laugh was bitter. "He walked in like he owned the place and we should be grateful he's here. He went straight for Kendra, like all the men did. I tried to warn her, but she was dazzled. She thought he was sophisticated, when he was just another preppie. She thought he was courting her with those long walks and supermarket bouquets, when he was cheap and didn't want his fancy friends to see him with a Mexican girl.

"I knew he was dating Esme Du Pres, who was away at college, and escorting her to the Daughters of Versailles Ball. Kendra was his part-time . . ." Mario stopped, then said, "girlfriend" because he didn't want to insult Kendra. "I warned Kendra that Bunny would never marry her.

But she said they were in love, and to her, love meant marriage. She had visions of being a Forest doctor's wife. A lady."

"She'd be bored silly," Angela said. Kendra didn't have the social skills or connections to advance Bunny's career, but Angela didn't need to say that. Mario knew.

"He used Kendra until the woman he was serious about came home. I tried to get up the nerve to tell Kendra about Esme, but she found out right here at the salon. Esme's mother booked a day of beauty for her daughter before the DV Ball—facial, massage, manicure, and then I did her hair and makeup. Esme showed Kendra the photo of her dress on her iPhone and asked Kendra what color nail polish she should choose. Then she spent the rest of her manicure chattering about Bunny. I knew Kendra would never be engaged to Bunny. It wasn't long after that he tried to pass her around to his disgusting frat friends like a door prize. You know about that?"

"Her Aunt Connie told me. The man's a pig."

"People don't understand why someone as beautiful as Kendra took up with a wrinkled old man like Luther. They think she's a gold digger. But she wasn't like that until Bunny Hobart." He spat the name. "After what he did to Kendra, I wouldn't let him soil my shop. Every time he called, Raquel was instructed to say I was booked. He was one of the first who went to Nikolai.

"After Bunny betrayed her, she was a different girl. Like shattered glass. I was afraid she'd been assaulted. She lost weight; she couldn't eat. People judged her harshly when she took up with Luther. They didn't understand. She was devastated. She didn't care about men anymore. Luther started asking her out. He treated her well—I made sure of that. He said he'd left his wife, and he was waiting for a divorce. Some women won't date a man until the divorce is final, but Luther could be persuasive. He offered her two million to wear his ring and another two when they married. Kendra said no, at first.

"Then Esme came in waving her engagement ring with an outrageous diamond. It was so big it looked fake, but she swanned around, calling it the Hobart Diamond. She wanted a manicure. Kendra did her nails and told her the ring would look best with green polish."

Angela laughed.

"The next day, Kendra came in wearing Luther's diamond. It was even bigger than Esme's rock. She'd accepted his offer. She showed it to me and then put it away. She knew better than to wear that diamond to work here, but the Forest women knew anyway. They called her a gold digger—but not around me."

"What other kind of woman puts up with abuse from a man like Luther?"

Suddenly, Mario's eyes were lit with fire. "You don't understand, Angela. You were born here to American parents. You never had to listen to the cruel words that Kendra did. You don't understand what a hard, harsh life she'd had. She did what she could to survive." Mario's accent was suddenly thicker, and she remembered he was a Cuban refugee. "We all do."

CHAPTER 25

Day nine

Kinkade Rushman was waiting in the nearly empty bar at Gringo Daze with a frosty Dos Equis in front of him. Angela recognized her lunch date—no, the man she was supposed to have lunch with—by Katie's description. "He's tall, about six two," her friend had said, while Angela had silently objected to every attribute. "Nice shoulders. Brown eyes."

But not like Donegan's, Angela thought.

"A jaw so strong he could crack walnuts with it."

Why do I want that, Katie?

"He's got thick, dark hair any woman would want to run her fingers through."

She means me.

"It's frosted with a little gray, so you know he's a freaking grown-up. He's forty-two, and works out, but he's not a frickin' fanatic."

"If anyone needs a shirt model, I'll recommend him," Angela said out loud. Katie sounded like a used-car salesman, and she wasn't buying.

"Hey, there's a good bod in that shirt. Women are dying to go out with him."

Angela started to say, "Don't let me stand in their way," but she sensed Katie was getting seriously ticked. She owed her so many favors, she couldn't pay them back in this lifetime.

Now that Angela saw Ken, he was everything Katie described and well dressed, besides. He wore a tailored charcoal suit, blue shirt, and blue-and-navy striped tie. Predictable, bland, and dull, she decided, as she crossed the bar to meet him. Kinkade was a name destined for some pompous profession like the law.

You're judging the man already, before he even opens his mouth. He can't be all bad if he drinks beer. Still, she wished she'd lingered in her car until noon. She was five minutes early for their lunch.

Her heels clicked on the Spanish tiles, and she walked carefully to keep from stumbling. She wished she had her cane. The heels pinched her toes. She felt like a poodle fresh from the groomer. Mario had tamed her dark hair into a stylish long bob and insisted on doing her makeup for free. "Just a little shadow to make your eyes look bigger." But he'd put on layers of makeup, and even false eyelashes that weighed ten pounds apiece.

"I'll look like a hooker," Angela said, then saw Mario's face. She'd insulted her friend, and he was going through a bad time. His makeup was skilled and subtle. She let him finish. When she saw the results in the mirror, she knew she looked good. Now Angela noticed appreciative males eyeing her long legs and body-skimming sheath, including Ken. She should have been flattered, but she vaguely resented the unwanted attention. He stood up to meet her, an old-fashioned courtesy she rather liked.

"Angela Richman." She smiled and extended her hand.

"Ken Rushman." He had a firm, straightforward handshake. "Glad you suggested this place. It's a hoot."

A hoot? She hated that condescending preppie compliment.

Eduardo showed them to an alcove near the fountain, the most secluded, romantic table in his restaurant. He reminded Angela of the man in the Spanish bullfight poster in the bar: dark-haired, lithe, and neatly made. He presented them with menus and lit the candle on their table with a flourish. "This is nice and quiet, so you can talk, yes?" Angela wished he hadn't done that. Now she was aware that their booth was dark and cozy, and felt even more awkward.

"Would you like a drink?" Eduardo asked.

"Club soda with lime."

Ken held up his beer. "I'm fine for now, thanks."

The waiter quickly arrived with her drink. "Are you ready to order, or would you like more time?"

Angela panicked at the thought of more time. "I know what I want. What about you, Ken?" Anything to hurry this along.

"I'll have the steak fajitas. Would you like guacamole, Angela?"

"Yes." She sounded more grateful than necessary for a bowl of mashed avocados. Guacamole and chips would be another distraction. "And I'll have the chicken fajitas."

After the waiter left, Ken said, "Thanks for taking the time to meet with me. I haven't lived in the Forest for many years. I met your friend Monty when I was deposing his client. We hit it off, and he and Katie asked me to dinner. She's a hoot and a half."

"Uh, yes, she is." Angela wondered if Katie had dropped any F-bombs on Ken. Maybe he thought those were a hoot, too. Or two hoots.

"I asked Monty if he knew any more girls like Katie, and he said she was one of a kind."

"She certainly is."

"But he mentioned Katie had a good friend who was a widow. I didn't expect you to be so . . . uh . . . attractive."

I'll have to have a little talk with Monty the Matchmaker, Angela thought. "I am widowed." That word had a fearsome, final sound. For months after Donegan's death, she couldn't even bring herself to say it. Every admission of her changed status seemed to reinforce her loss.

"I'm a *recent* widow, Ken. My husband's death was unexpected, and it's too painful to discuss."

"I understand."

Angela hoped he understood that was all she was going to say about Donegan. If Ken had any sensitivity, he wouldn't ask her anything else.

Their silence stretched on, until their server arrived with brown pottery bowls of chips and guacamole. "Your fajitas will be out soon."

Not soon enough, Angela thought. She sneaked a glance at her watch: 12:17. The minute hand refused to move faster. Ken dragged a tortilla chip through the guacamole and crunched it.

Angela waited until he finished chewing. "What brings you back to the Forest?" she asked. Her chip held a healthy scoop of guacamole.

"I needed a change of scene. It was time to explore new horizons. I'd lived in Memphis since I graduated from law school. I was a junior partner in a firm there, until my wife divorced me. She had an affair with the senior partner, if you can believe that. While I was racking up billable hours, she was spending time in the sack with Richard the Third—Richard Q. Pershing the Third. All big-time lawyers have at least one initial and a number in their name." He smiled to lighten the bitterness in his tone.

"Richard's wife tumbled to the affair, but by that time, it was too late. Richard the Third wanted to marry my wife. He fixed it so she got everything—the house, the Mercedes, my 401(k). Fortunately, we didn't have any kids. You'd think as a lawyer I'd know how to fight for a good divorce, but I didn't handle divorces at the firm—that was his specialty. I just wanted out of the marriage and out of Memphis. Well, you don't want to hear this."

You're right, Angela almost said. But before those words slipped out, she said, "So how did you wind up at Du Pres, Hanley, and Hampton?"

"My cousin Missy is a Du Pres, and she's married to Mercer Hanley."

He said that as if it were an explanation for how he was hired by the premier local firm. In the Forest, it was.

"Welcome home."

Angela was grateful that their server arrived with two sizzling platters of fajitas. Good. Preparing the perfect fajita took time. She built hers slowly, spreading a little guacamole on the warm flour tortilla, next a thin layer of sour cream, then the fried red-and-green peppers, onions, and chicken strips. She arranged the contents carefully. If she overloaded her tortilla, it would squirt grease and sauce on her dress.

Ken fixed his with the same meticulous care, then took a bite. "Mm. Even better than I remembered. So tell me, how did you become a death investigator?"

She gave Ken her standard answer: "I enjoy forensics."

"You must see some awful sights."

Shane Mathrews, the headless motorcyclist, flashed before her eyes. "The Forest is a small place, and I'd rather not discuss people's loved ones. What I really enjoy is visiting the retired racehorses at Reggie Du Pres's stables."

"Fast company." Ken had a gentle, genuine laugh. Angela told him about shaking American Hero's tongue and feeding Eecie carrots. She covertly checked her watch and saw it was 1:12. She could leave anytime, but Angela was beginning to enjoy her lunch. It felt good to forget the stress and sadness of yesterday.

The server cleared away their plates, and Ken asked, "Would you like coffee?"

"Coffee would be fine."

Ken looked absurdly happy, as if she'd given him a gift. "Two coffees," he told the server.

When he returned with the coffee, the server said, "Eduardo sent this flan for you. On the house."

"Wonderful." Ken grinned like a kid at a birthday party. "Okay with you, Angela?"

"Sure." But she felt uneasy. Eduardo liked matchmaking. Did Katie tip him off about this lunch?

After the first spoonful, Ken said, "This flan is amazing. Light and sweet with the right amount of cinnamon."

Angela nodded agreement. Her mouth was full. Then she heard the words she'd dreaded. "Roses. Roses. Roses for your pretty lady."

Rosa the rose lady was a fixture at the Forest restaurants. A plump, white-haired woman of sixtysomething, she sold long-stemmed red roses for three dollars each. Why did she have to show up now? Red roses were Angela's special flower. Donegan always gave her red roses. She tried to duck into the bathroom, but it was too late. Rosa was heading straight for their table. Her round, unwrinkled face was lit with a smile. Her white hair was softly waved, and she wore a bright-red blouse and black pants.

"Hello, sir."

Go away, Angela thought. Shoo!

"Hello, miss." Rosa held up her plastic bucket, decorated with heart decals and brimming with dark-red roses.

"Would you like to give the pretty lady a red rose as a memento of your lovely lunch? Only three dollars."

Angela hated the woman's sticky-sweet smile. She wished she could make her go away. No! she shrieked. The sound was so loud in her mind she was sure Ken and Rosa could hear it.

"Yes. Angela is a lovely lady, and she was gracious enough to have lunch with me today." He handed Rosa a five, and she picked out the freshest red rose.

She smiled at the handsome couple as Ken gallantly presented Angela the red rose. A rose the color of blood. The same color as the rose she'd tossed on Donegan's coffin. The walls of the alcove closed in on her and sucked the air out of the small space. She fought to breathe. She struggled to speak.

Ken looked at her with concern. "Angela? What's wrong?"

Panic strangled her. She managed one word. "No!"

She stood up, stumbled against the table in her too-high heels, and ran for the door.

CHAPTER 26

Day nine

Angela couldn't think. She couldn't breathe. She had to get away from the restaurant, the roses, and Ken Rushman. As she raced toward the door, she glimpsed his stunned face and heard a bewildered Eduardo. "Angela! Angela! What's wrong?"

She couldn't explain. She stumbled in the doorway, unsteady without her cane, and kicked off her crippling heels. At last, she was outside. The warm spring sun was a blessing. She hurried to her car, chirped it open, and collapsed in the seat, her head buried in the steering wheel. Please, she thought. Leave me alone. Everyone leave me alone.

But when she looked up, Ken was rushing toward her, his handsome face puzzled and concerned. No! Don't make me explain! She started her car and squealed out of the parking lot, turning left, then right, then right again, blindly picking streets and crying so hard she could barely see. After several turns, Angela had no idea where she was or how fast she was going. At last her heart stopped racing, and she could see through her tears. She slowed the Charger to the speed limit, wiped her eyes, and drove home, relieved the early-afternoon roads were nearly empty.

She turned into her desolate driveway. Three days ago, it had been lined with spring color. Then the sleet storm froze its beauty. Now the brown blooms and ice-burned stalks rotted in the warm sun. Angela stayed inside her car, her heart pounding. What should she do next? Where could she go? She checked her phone for messages, but there was only one from Katie, her voice cheerful and confident.

"Hey, it's me. How was lunch? Is he a great guy or what?"

He's a terrific guy, Angela thought, and lunch was a disaster.

Katie was still delivering her message. *"I want to hear all about it."*

You will, Katie. By now, Eduardo and Ken have probably both called you. Ken is wondering why you fixed him up with a flaming wacko, and Eduardo is asking why he had yet another scene in his restaurant. Oh lord! The restaurant! Did the customers whip out their cell phones and video her overreaction to poor Rosa the rose lady? Was Angela recorded stumbling out of Gringo Daze, wild-eyed and crazy? Damned cell phones were everywhere. And in this attention-getting outfit, the video of the Forest's Gone Girl would go viral. Eduardo and Lourdes's restaurant would become the local soap-opera headquarters, a scene for lovers' quarrels and juicy breakups. The Forest grandees would see Angela fleeing a quiet lunch with a lawyer from a premier Forest firm as if she were running from a terrorist attack. She'd be marked as unstable. Maybe too unstable to keep her job.

Katie's message was still jabbering on: *"So that's it! Call me when you can. I have news."*

"I have news." That meant something was going on with Kendra's case. Angela couldn't call Katie at the office, and she was in no shape to talk. The answer was in her conversation with Ken. Horse therapy, she decided. I need horse therapy.

Angela slipped her high heels back on her blistered feet and hobbled up the drive to her home. Her cane was just inside the door. She used it and the stair rail to get up to her bedroom, where she fell into an exhausted sleep.

Angela woke up at three thirty, the warm sun on her face, her exquisite makeup now muddy smears on her pillowcase. One sticky fake eyelash flapped loose. In the bathroom, she peeled off both false eyelashes and creamed her face twice. She still couldn't remove Mario's makeup job. After four tries, her face was clean and slightly red from the vigorous scrubbing. Now the darkness around her eyes was natural. She pulled her smart hairstyle into a practical ponytail, then put on her jeans, a plaid cotton shirt, and boots. There. Now she felt like her old self.

Downstairs, she dug out another bag of peppermints and caned her way to the Du Pres stables. She felt safer walking with the cane. It was a nuisance at times, but she wasn't ready to give up its protection. She also wasn't ready to return Katie's call and confess her failure. She'd deal with that after horse therapy.

Bud was unloading bags of feed into the shed by the stables when she arrived. He wiped his long, tanned face with a red bandanna, then stuck it in his back pocket. He waved her over. "Thank God you just missed him." He picked up his soda-can spittoon.

"Who?" Angela averted her eyes while he squirted tobacco juice.

"Reggie. The old man's madder than a wet hen at Monty—and since the lawyer's seeing Katie, and he's friends with you, Reggie's mad at all three of you. He was stomping around here with his cell phone, waving his hands and screaming at his lawyers."

"Reggie discussed his personal business in front of you?"

Bud's laugh was like a whinny. He'd been around horses so long, he was starting to sound like them. "Hell, I don't exist for that old man. I'm an employee. He cares more about the stained glass and brass in his fancy stables than he cares about me. I like the job, the money's decent, and I stay out of his way. Today, the way he was ranting, he woulda taken a horsewhip to you."

Angela doubted that Old Reggie, who was way north of eighty, could even lift a horsewhip, but he was powerful enough to run her off his property. And he could evict her. When he'd sold the guest house to Angela's family, there was a loophole. They didn't own the land the house was on, and Reggie could buy the house back for the same price he'd sold it for—$25,000. If he went into a total rage, she could wind up homeless.

"Don't let him catch you here," Bud warned.

"I'll stay away until he calms down."

"That may be a while. Besides, the horses like you. Tell you what— if he's here, I'll give you a red alert. I'll hang my bandanna on this nail where you can see it, and you'll know to keep on walking."

"What's got Reggie so upset?"

"He can't control things the way he wants. He's furious that the judge ruled in favor of Monty and against his cousin Priscilla and allowed a second autopsy."

"But Kendra's paying for that."

"Using Du Pres money she earned on her back." Reggie must have seen Angela's shocked look. "Those aren't my words. That's how the old man sees it. He feels Kendra's fighting the Du Pres family with their own money."

"But he's richer than Kendra. She has only two million."

Did I just say "only two million?" she thought.

"Unencumbered," Bud said. "Her money isn't tied up in real estate, and she doesn't have half a dozen relatives living off her. By Reggie's standards, she's free and clear."

A snorting, stamping sound interrupted them. "That's Hero, impatient for his peppermints. He's at home. Go see him."

American Hero looked like he was posing for a portrait in his splendid mahogany stall. His muscular body was sleek and shiny, his legs long and powerful, his noble head held high. Angela hurried over to him, and the racehorse stuck out his huge pink-gray tongue. She gravely shook it, then hugged the horse while he blew kisses into her hair.

She fed him nearly half a bag of peppermints and felt the tensions of the past few days slip into the stable's soft shadows. She forgot about Jackie Soran and the tragic drug death of her doomed son. Even her wretched, panicked lunch with Ken didn't seem so bad. Hero licked the last of the sticky peppermints off her hands. She patted his nose, hugged him good-bye, and said, "I have to see Eecie now."

East Coast Express was in her stall, demanding Angela's attention. The racehorse's little white goat slept in the corner. Angela rubbed the tiny white star on the big bay's forehead, hugged her neck, and covered her with kisses until Eecie nickered.

"Okay, you can't live on love alone. How about some peppermints?"

The goat jumped up at the word *peppermints* and made its rusty demand. Angela fed Little Bit a treat, and Eecie nudged her hand. Angela nearly spilled the bag of candy. "Hey! Eecie! You have to share." She gave the rest of the bag to Eecie, one candy at a time. As the horse gobbled each treat, it seemed to take a bite out of Angela's sorrow and despair. She was down to a dozen peppermints when her cell phone rang. Katie. She shoved the candy in her pocket. This time, Angela took the call.

"I know where you are. I'm parking outside now." She sounded angry.

Katie stomped into the stable before Angela had even stashed her cell phone, trailing bursts of rage. She hadn't bothered changing out of her gray suit and flat shoes. "What the hell happened? You're the most talked-about woman since Kendra got her ass slapped by Luther and he wound up dead. All you had to do was eat lunch! Just lunch! How did a plate of fajitas turn into a fuckin' drama?"

"I'm sorry."

"Don't apologize to me. Save that for Ken." Then Katie's eyes narrowed. "Or maybe he doesn't deserve your apology. Did he say something? Insult you? Hit on you? I swear, Angela, if he did anything, I'll break his ass." She looked ready to grab a pitchfork and march to Ken's office.

"It wasn't Ken's fault. It was mine. He was a perfect gentleman. Eduardo decided this was some kind of date and put us in the alcove by the fountain, then lit a candle. You didn't tip him off, did you?"

"Of course not. Quit stalling and start talking."

"The conversation was a little stilted at first, but Ken and I were getting along fine. I was actually enjoying the lunch—so much that I decided to stay for dessert. And then . . . then . . ."

Her voice broke and filled with tears. Katie's was soft. "Angela, honey, what happened? You can tell me."

"Rosa came along. Rosa the rose lady. Eduardo sent her to our table, and she started in with her 'roses for the pretty lady' routine, and Ken bought me a rose. A red rose. Donegan always gave me red roses, and a red rose was the last thing I put on his coffin at the . . . at the cemetery." Angela was crying now, aching sobs that wouldn't stop. Eecie moved closer, and Angela threw her arms around the horse's muscular neck and bristly mane. The horse blew her a kiss. Katie rubbed Angela's back.

"There's nothing wrong with Ken," Angela said. "Except it's too soon. If it wasn't for that rose, I might have lasted the lunch."

Katie looked contrite, her bluster and swear words gone. "I'm sorry, Angela. I'm so, so sorry. Donegan is gone, but you don't have to bury yourself with him."

"I'm not dead!" Angela was suddenly angry. "I'm alive. I'm working. But I'll live on my terms."

CHAPTER 27

Day nine

Angela was calm enough to ask Katie, "What's your news?"

"Monty texted me this morning. The forensic experts are flying in this week. We talked about it last night. He's worried. Kendra's salvation depends on their findings."

"So that's why you called me." Now Angela was embarrassed by her tearful outburst. What the hell was wrong with her, carrying on like that? Angela stayed by Eecie, petting her soft nose and feeding her more peppermints. The racehorse's quiet strength calmed her, and she was amused by the powerful animal's childish greed for sweets. "Which experts, and when are they coming?"

"Carol Berman, the big-deal pathologist, is first. She'll be here tomorrow. She's doing the second autopsy on Luther. Evarts ordered me to be there."

"That's good."

"I guess. But you know what he's like. I'm walking a tightrope. Evarts is mad as hell that Monty questioned his judgment. He thinks Judge Boareman betrayed him when he ruled that the defense could have an independent autopsy. I thought he'd bust an artery when the judge said Evarts could attend the second autopsy. Chauncey meant it as a courtesy, but that's not how Evarts saw it. He's sending me in his place. I'm supposed to report on Carol's findings. I have no freakin' idea how I'm going to tell Evarts he screwed up Luther's autopsy."

"Maybe he got it right."

"And maybe I'm Beyoncé in disguise. There's a two percent chance he got it right—and I'm being generous."

"He's not that incompetent?"

Katie shrugged. "He does a decent job. But we both know he hates posting burn victims. It's a good thing we don't get many. The man lives on red meat and doesn't want any reminders that we're all roast on the hoof. Greiman told him what he and the fire investigator had found before Evarts even looked at Luther. He did a quick post, then wrote his report. By his lights, he did everything right: he consulted the experts and came to the conclusion he was supposed to. He made the blue bloods happy. Now this upstart lawyer is questioning him. When Carol Berman says he's wrong, I'll be the messenger, and you know what happens to the ones who bring bad news."

"Is Carol Berman doing the autopsy at SOS?"

"No. That's one break I get. Luther will be transported to the East Missouri State Medical Center in Franklin County. I won't have Evarts stalking the hall, waiting for the news. It will give me time to prepare something to soften the blow. Luther's family is furious that he's going to be posted a second time. They say it's disrespectful."

"And cremating a man who burned to death isn't?"

"I'm just saying. The day after Carol Berman gets here, the other two experts arrive—Mo Heedles and Laurie Hartig. They're looking at the fire evidence. That will be at an independent lab here in the Forest. The next day, we're all meeting at Lin Kalomeris's law office in Saint Louis—Monty, Mo, Laurie, Carol Berman, and you, if you want to come."

"Wouldn't miss it. I'm guessing this meeting is also secret."

"Top secret if we want to keep our jobs. That's why it's at six a.m."

Angela winced at the early hour. She'd have to get up at four thirty to make it.

"Sorry about the time. Lin's arranged for a breakfast buffet. All you need is enough coffee to get you to downtown Saint Louis. After the meeting, Monty will drive all three experts straight to the Saint Louis airport. I can be back in time for work. Are you working?"

"I'm off, unless there's some kind of disaster."

"Good. If for some reason you can't make the meeting, leave me a message that breakfast is off. I'll know what you mean."

"Are you going to show Carol around the Forest?" Angela asked.

"Can't risk it. I can't show her any of the usual courtesies."

"Too bad."

Katie shrugged. "At least we got her for this job. Monty doesn't say much, but he's scared to death for Kendra. Luther's family is doing their best to spread the poison. You wouldn't recognize the old lech from their stories. Priscilla and Eve are carrying on like he was the sweetest, kindest, most generous husband and father until that Mexican she-devil led him astray."

"But Kendra isn't—"

"Mexican," Katie finished. "I know that and so do you. But as far as the Forest is concerned, she just crossed the Rio Grande clinging to a tire. And her enterprising parents are taking good American jobs. Talk is, Jose helped her kill Luther. He could be arrested any day now."

"No wonder Monty's worried."

"He's a good guy. He's fighting for her, but he's worried."

"For good reason. At least Kendra has enough money for her defense. As soon as you know what Carol concluded, will you call me?"

"Better wait until the meeting. What are you doing for the next two days?"

"Sitting in doctors' offices. I have an MRI scheduled for tomorrow. If it shows the veins in my neck are open, I can get off Coumadin, and Doc Bartlett will quit sticking me with needles. Did you autopsy Zander yet?"

"This morning. It made me sick. I'm still waiting for the tox results. It looks like he died of a heroin overdose, but he didn't shoot up. He snorted it. I found a powdery residue in his nasal passages. Someone stuck that needle in his arm in a clumsy attempt to make it look like he used a spike."

"So he died during the party, and his rich friends abandoned him."

"Looks that way. You were right about the livor mortis. The blood pooled on his right side and leg. He was lying on his side when he died, and he stayed in that position for several hours after his death. Then he was moved."

"They left him lying dead at the party? I've seen it before, especially if everyone else was too stoned to do anything. But that's so cold-blooded. No one tried to resuscitate him or call 911?"

"There's no record of any call for help," Katie said. "Whatever killed Zander, his friends were more interested in saving their own asses. I'm guessing after he died, they carried him to his car and dropped him in the trunk. The tech report says traces of feces were found in Zander's BMW, along with some hair. Tests show those were his hairs and body fluids. It wouldn't be unusual for Zander's hair to be in his own car trunk, but I doubt that he would take a dump in his beloved Beemer. Butch thinks Zander's body was hidden in his trunk, and then his car was moved a couple of hours later to Du Pont Close, and someone staged him so it looked like he'd OD'd with the needle. There's unknown DNA on the syringe. The techs found an unknown print in the car trunk."

"Which makes that person the last one who drove Zander's car."

"Looks like it. We have to find him, though."

"Or her," Angela said. "Zander's death will be big news in the Forest."

"Evarts is doing his best to make it bigger. He called a press conference at three this afternoon."

"So it will be splashed all over the evening news tonight."

"He didn't have to wait till tonight, Angela. It's already a 'special report' on two stations. Take a look at my iPad."

On the small screen, Dr. Evarts Evans looked like one of the kindly, white-haired "nine out of ten doctors" who made TV recommendations. Camera-ready in a blue shirt, red tie, and starched lab coat, he delivered sound bites that were crisp and easy to edit.

"Heroin abuse is a growing concern in our country," he said. "More young people are dying from this drug than ever before. Yesterday, a teenager died of a heroin overdose here in Chouteau County. Out of respect for his family, I will not release his name, but he was disadvantaged."

"Disadvantaged?" Angela said.

"Poor white trash," Katie said. "Zander was a Toonerville kid."

Evarts cleared his throat. "This young person was also a dealer. Police found a felony quantity of heroin in his vehicle as well as drug paraphernalia. These included the so-called love roses, which are used as pipes to smoke heroin and crack."

Video of a love-rose pipe with a chunk of copper scrubber appeared on the screen.

"Earlier this week, we had another death in the area that could be attributed to possible heroin use—a sixteen-year-old male who had a high level of opiates in his blood when he collided with a truck on Bodman Road in southwest Chouteau County. The driver of the truck was not charged. The victim lived in Jefferson County."

Angela said, "Evarts is using all the code words to let the locals know the two dead heroin users weren't Forest blue bloods."

"He can't say the flower of the Forest aristocracy is using smack."

Evarts looked straight into the camera. "Since 2007, heroin overdose deaths have shot up."

"That was a poor choice of words," Angela said.

Evarts erupted with a flow of statistics. "Heroin is one of the most addictive drugs in the world. The Centers for Disease Control and Prevention counted nearly ten thousand six hundred heroin overdose deaths in 2014. That's five times the heroin death rate in the twelve years from 2002 to 2014. Five times.

"Prescription painkillers are a major factor in heroin use. They are the gateway drugs. Young people get them from their family or friends or use their own prescriptions. But prescription painkillers are expensive, and the supply is drying up since authorities have cracked down on the so-called pain centers that dispensed them with little or no medical supervision. People have turned to heroin, which is cheaper and more available.

"Authorities believe that the deceased drug dealer got his heroin in Saint Louis. That city has a significant drug problem. The Mexican cartels are bringing cheap heroin into Saint Louis. Sometimes the Mexicans give it away free to hook their customers."

"There's your Mexican connection," Angela said.

"Easy drug money is a temptation to our poorer youth," Evarts said. "I'm asking parents to check their children for signs of drug use. Children as young as ten years old have been known to use heroin. Common signs of drug abuse include poor personal hygiene, reckless behavior, and withdrawal from friends, family, and activities."

"He's just described your average teenager," Angela said.

Evarts continued, "Additional signs of heroin abuse include a runny nose or constant sniffing, needle marks on arms or even legs, slurred speech, poor motivation, hostility, and possession of drug paraphernalia. Some of these may sound like normal adolescent behavior, but if you see three or more of these signs, it's time to find out what the problem is. Even if your child isn't abusing heroin, it could be some other important issue that needs to be addressed."

"Nice save," Katie said.

"I keep thinking about poor Zander's mother," Angela said. "She saw the signs and couldn't do anything to save her boy."

"That bastard Evarts. Not only is that boy dead, he's labeled a dealer and 'disadvantaged.' That's fuckin' heartless. At least he didn't use Zander's name."

"Did you notice anything odd about that press conference?"

"It was all odd," Katie said. "And self-serving."

"But there was no mention of the burns on Zander's hands or the homemade fire starters in his car. Is Evarts covering up the fact that Zander may be the Forest arsonist?"

"Evarts does whatever will advance his career. We both know that. Clearing Kendra would upset a lot of powerful people."

CHAPTER 28

Days ten, eleven

KEEP OUR CHILDREN SAFE AT HOME, screamed the headline in the *Chouteau Forest Chronicle*. The self-anointed "Voice of the Forest" shouted its disapproval of Saint Louis in the editorial, spouting statistics on the city's "drug problem" and trotting out the murder rate. The editorial said:

> Saint Louis is one of the ten most dangerous cities in the nation. Mexican cartels are selling cheap heroin at prices as low as five dollars for each button, which is about one-tenth of a gram of powdered heroin. Officials say the Mexican gangs give away free samples to hook our unsuspecting young people.

The editorial said that as if the Forest had gates and moats to keep outsiders away.

> We must keep them away from the Mexican menace. Saint Louis is a bad influence on our young

people. There is no reason to leave the Forest for
that dirty, dangerous city. We have everything here
at home in Chouteau County.

Right, Angela thought. Including our own homegrown arsonists
and drug dealers. That editorial was a prime example of Forest thinking:
Crime didn't happen in the enchanted enclave of Chouteau County,
which was filled with decent, upstanding rich people. Except when it
was committed by "Mexican" outsiders like Kendra Salvato and "disadvantaged" teens like Zander Soran—and they didn't belong.

Angela was disgusted with the rag's insular view. Free and worth
every penny, she thought. That's what I get for not bringing a book to
Doc Bartlett's office. She flung the paper on the empty plastic chair next
to her. The liver-spotted old man leaning on his cane raised his bushy
eyebrows in surprise. Angela tried to give him a reassuring smile.

She was tired of waiting in yet another doctor's office. Yesterday,
she'd had her MRI at eight in the morning, then she'd been poked,
picked at, and probed by a neurologist, a hematologist, and a cardiolo-
gist. This morning, she'd cleaned house. Now it was two thirty, and she'd
been waiting half an hour for her two o'clock appointment. Dr. Bartlett
was going to give her the test results and the final verdict. Angela had
been taking Coumadin—the main ingredient in rat poison—for more
than a year after the strokes, and the ugly gray pills had to be monitored
carefully. So did her food. Even a spinach salad could throw off the
delicate balance she'd worked to achieve. Her arms were covered with
bruises, old and new, from as many as four blood draws a week.

If this MRI showed that her carotid arteries were open, she could
switch to another, simpler medication. That would give her an additional two to six hours a week free. Since she'd started her stroke recovery, she'd pushed hard to get off Coumadin.

At two forty-five, a grumpy Angela was finally called into Doc
Bartlett's office, then left to brood in an examination room for another

fifteen minutes. At least she didn't have to change into a paper gown. After the nurse took her blood pressure, Angela studied a photo of orange-and-red autumn leaves on the wall. The doctor was a better-than-average nature photographer and decorated her office with photos of sunsets, leaves, trees, and even leaping trout.

Finally, the short, sturdy doctor breezed in, all smiles, holding Angela's thick chart. "Good news! Your test results were excellent. Your carotids are open. No more Coumadin."

"Wonderful!" Angela's pique was forgotten.

"You'll have to take an aspirin every day, but that's it."

Angela nearly floated out of the doctor's office, she was so happy. She was sure she could abandon the cane soon. The day was a perfect match to her mood—sunny and warm with a light breeze. She'd settled herself into her car when her cell phone rang, and she checked the display: J. Salvato.

Why was Kendra's father calling her?

Jose sounded rushed and frightened. "Miss Richman, it's Jose. I'm in trouble. I can't find Mr. Bryant, the lawyer. He doesn't answer his cell phone, and his office line is busy."

"Monty's at Luther's autopsy. His phone is probably turned off. What's wrong?"

"I've done something terrible. I hit a police officer."

"Who? What happened?"

"That Detective Greiman."

I've wanted to hit him myself, Angela thought, then remembered that was the old Ray Greiman. She was supposed to be working with the new, improved Greiman.

"He said something terrible about Kendra. No father would stand for it. I have a temper, and I hit him. Then I ran."

"You slugged a cop and fled the scene? Where are you?"

"In the storage shed behind the gas station on McKenzie Road. Next to the machine to fill your tires with air."

"That's about two blocks from where I am. Hang on and I'll get you. You can tell me what's wrong after I pick you up."

"Hurry, Miss Richman. The police are everywhere."

Angela peeled out of the doctor's parking lot, then slowed down. She couldn't risk getting stopped now. If she was caught with a fugitive, she'd lose her job. At the gas station, she parked around the back by the storage shed. The door was partly open, and Jose was crouched behind a stack of cardboard boxes, sweat running down his face. He was grass-stained and stank of sweat and fear.

"Jose, get in the back of my car and keep your head down. I'll be right back."

She caned her way into the gas station, bought a bottle of water so her stop wouldn't look suspicious, then opened her car trunk and pulled out a white cotton sheet, the kind used for a body actualization.

Jose was crouching in the foot well behind the passenger seat. She handed him the water. "I'm covering you with this sheet, just to be safe, and taking you to Monty's office. Tell me what happened on the way over. It will only take a few minutes."

Jose took a long, thirsty drink as the sheet settled over him. "Will Mr. Bryant still represent me after what I did?"

"If he represents accused murderers, I'm sure he'll take on a cop slugger. But he'll answer that question. Tell me what happened."

Jose's voice was steady and only slightly muffled by the sheet. At first, his accent was thicker than usual, and he stumbled over his words, but as he grew confident, those issues disappeared.

"My crew and I were working at the Stockton Apartments. Detective Greiman called my office and asked my receptionist where I was. She told him, and he stopped by the apartments. He said he had a few questions for me. I told the crew to finish mowing the lawn while I talked to him. He asked me lots of questions—many of them the same one, over and over. I didn't like their tone.

"He asked if the Porter Gravois estate still owed me money. I said they owed me two thousand dollars, but I'd written that off as a bad debt. Dr. Gravois is dead, and his widow has no money. There was no point in pursuing any action against her or the estate.

"He didn't believe me. He said two thousand dollars was a lot of money. I agreed, but if someone doesn't have it, then you have to let it go. He kept repeating that it was a lot of money, over and over. I couldn't convince him that I wasn't pursuing the money.

"Then he said if I couldn't have money, I could have revenge. I could burn down the Gravois estate, and then Mrs. Gravois would get nothing, just like I got. I said I wouldn't do that to a widow going through hard times. I began to think I should call Mr. Bryant, because Detective Greiman refused to believe me. He said I had a grudge against the 'first families'—that's what he called them, the important people of the Forest—because they looked down on me, and that's why I started the fires. He said I had access to the Hobarts' property because my company did their yard work, so I knew their keypad code. I do, but I wouldn't burn down their pool house. That family has had enough tragedy.

"Then he said I cut the grass around the old barn that Mr. Du Pres owns. That's also true, but why would I burn it down? If it was sold and became a restaurant, I'd have more work, putting in the landscaping and maintaining it.

"I said I couldn't have burned down the Gravois house. I wasn't in town that night. He said, 'Prove it,' but I couldn't.

"Now I was worried and starting to get angry. I'm a good worker and a good businessman. Then he said Kendra and I were in it together. He said I killed Luther, too—I told my daughter to put on a sexy outfit and have her 'lead on the old man'—those were his words—and 'after the old boy was too tired to move' I warned her to get out and then started the fire that killed Luther, and I ran. He said she 'ran around in that skeevy outfit to distract the firefighters.' He made my daughter sound like a prostitute. I reminded him that Kendra was Luther's fian-cée. He laughed at me and said, 'Fi-*nan*-cee is more like it. Now that Luther's dead, she's landed ass down in a tub of butter. She can give you and Mamacita back that two thousand dollars and more.'

"That's when I lost it, Miss Richman. My temper was worse when I was younger, but it's still bad. I punched him. In the jaw. He said, 'Congratulations! You've assaulted a police officer. You've won a free stay in jail. You're in big trouble now. I'm gonna roast your beaner ass.' Then he reached for his gun. I thought he was going to shoot me. I ran. I panicked and I ran."

"Did he fire his weapon?" Angela asked.

"Two shots. Both missed. Renaldo was using the leaf blower, and he couldn't hear anything over the roar. He walked in front of the detective, and that kept him from firing a third time. While the detective was distracted, I took off and ran and ran until I got to the gas station. Then I hid inside the shed and tried to catch my breath. About ten minutes later, Greiman stopped here. It's a pickup spot for day laborers. He asked the girl at the counter if she'd seen a Mexican at the station. She said, 'You're kidding, right? This place is overrun with spics. They're worse than cockroaches.'"

"I'm sorry you had to hear that, Jose."

"I'm used to it. I was glad she didn't notice me. What's going to happen to me, Miss Richman? I know I need to turn myself in, but people like me have a habit of getting shot or beat up. I've hit a cop. They'll beat me up, too. They may even say I tried to escape and kill me."

"That's why I'm taking you to Monty's office," Angela said. "He'll tell the police you're going to surrender, and then he'll escort you to the police station. But first he'll video you from head to toe. That way, if you wind up with any new bruises, he'll be able to prove the police are responsible for them."

Angela saw Monty's office—a long, one-story, dark-brown building with impressive brass double doors. "We're here." She parked in a space near the side door, then called Monty's office.

Jinny Gender, his redheaded receptionist, answered, and Angela put the phone on speaker so Jose could hear the conversation. "Hi, it's Angela Richman. We have a problem. Jose Salvato is going to need Monty's services as soon as he returns."

"I'm sorry, Ms. Richman, but Mr. Bryant is away from the office."

"Is he in Farmington at Luther's autopsy?"

"Yes. He'll be gone until late afternoon."

"We have a problem. Jose hit Ray Greiman, and he could wind up dead. Will you unlock the side door? I'll bring him in. He can stay with you until Monty returns."

"I'll be right down. I'll give him some lunch, too."

After she hung up, Jose said, "Thank you, Miss Richman. Thank you so much. You've saved my life."

"Can I ask another question? Where were you on the night of the Porter Gravois fire?"

"I would do anything for you, Miss Richman. But I can't tell you that. I have an alibi, but telling it would cost me my marriage."

CHAPTER 29

Days eleven, twelve

"Showtime!" Katie said into her phone that night. "Are you ready?"

"Popcorn popped," Angela said. "Drinks ready. Two minutes to six o'clock, the zero hour."

The two friends were camped in front of their home TVs, a few miles apart. They were about to watch something so sensitive, they couldn't be seen meeting in the Forest—or even risk a cell-phone conversation. The Forest had eyes everywhere. Katie and Angela kept their landlines for times like these.

"Three, two, one!" Katie said. "There it is."

The Chouteau County Sheriff's Office, the state's prettiest cop shop, was on the screen. TV and news reporters roiled around the sheriff's office, which looked like a boutique hotel.

"Monty really produced the press," Katie said.

Angela could hear her friend's pride. "He looks photogenic."

"He looks damn good. And Jose cleaned up nicely, too."

Montgomery Bryant and Jose Maria Salvato shouldered their way through the media crowd. "Monty's wearing his serious blue trial suit and red power tie," Katie said.

Jose looked like the businessman he was in a similar suit with a silver striped tie. "Did Jose shower at Monty's office?"

"Yes, and Gracie brought over his suit."

Both men ignored the press's shouted questions: "Jose! Did you help Kendra kill Luther Delor?" "Did you kill the old man to avenge your daughter?" "Why did you beat up the cop and run?"

"Do the reporters actually think anyone will answer those inane questions?" Angela said.

"Sh! Monty's talking."

"Good evening. I'm Montgomery Bryant, and this is my client, Mr. Jose Salvato. He's also the father of Kendra Salvato. Ms. Salvato has been charged in the death of her fiancé, Luther Delor. Now Chouteau Forest detective Ray Greiman has made a similar accusation against Kendra's father. Mr. Salvato is a respected businessman in Chouteau County, owner of the Proud American Lawn Service. Let me emphasize—Mr. Salvato, his wife, Graciela Salvato, and their daughter, Kendra Salvato—are all proud Americans. Mrs. Salvato is also an entrepreneur. She owns the Chouteau Forest Deluxe Cleaning Service. Mr. and Mrs. Salvato are naturalized American citizens. Kendra Salvato was born in the Forest at Sisters of Sorrow Hospital, and she graduated from the Chouteau Forest Academy. She went to high school there with many of the Forest first families. Her class photo is displayed in the school hall."

"I wonder if the school administration is rushing to take down that photo," Angela said.

"Quiet!" Katie commanded.

"Now Mr. Salvato is accused of assaulting Greiman," Monty said. "This detective deliberately provoked Mr. Salvato, fired three shots at him, and made racist remarks. Greiman claims that Mr. Salvato acted in conjunction with his daughter, Kendra Salvato, to murder Luther Delor. All these charges are false, the result of poor reasoning and shoddy investigating by the Chouteau Forest Police Department. Mr. Salvato is an innocent man, and he has agreed to voluntarily turn himself in. If he is charged with murder or anything else, I will defend him vigorously. Let me repeat: Jose Salvato is innocent, and his actions today are those of an innocent man. I believe the Chouteau Forest Police Department has targeted the Salvato family because of political pressure and racial prejudice and that both my clients will be vindicated."

"Damn, he's good." Katie was lost in admiration for Monty.

So was Angela. "That took guts. He painted a target on his back when he said Jose and Kendra were targeted because of political pressure and prejudice."

"Everyone knows it. But Monty has the balls to say it."

"I wonder how Jose's and Gracie's businesses are doing," Angela said.

"Jose's lost most of his private homes. But the business accounts are sticking with him. He's reliable, and his prices are good. Gracie's losing customers right and left. She's had to lay off two of her cleaners, but she's still paying them. Monty doesn't know how much longer she can afford to do that, now that Jose's been arrested."

"Who's doing the cleaning? I can't see the Forest ladies scrubbing their own floors."

"Oh, this is great gossip. I got it from Butch Chetkin, whose wife knows the woman. Old Reggie Du Pres tried to get his housekeeper to take over the job, and she flat-out refused. He had to hire Nancy, a Saint Louis County woman who charges double what Gracie does. Old Reggie shrieked like Nancy had stuck bamboo stakes under his fingernails when she told him her rates. 'How difficult is it to scrub floors?' Nancy didn't take any guff off the old boy. She told him, 'You can find out for yourself if you don't hire me.' He hired Nancy, but he doesn't like her smart mouth."

"He must really be upset at the Salvatos if he's willing to part with cold, hard cash. I have good news, too. I'm off Coumadin. I can take aspirin instead," Angela said.

"About fuckin' time. The cane is next, and then you're good as new. I'll see you tomorrow at the lawyer's office in Saint Louis, bright and early."

"Early, definitely. I don't know how bright I'm going to be at six in the morning."

When the alarm rang at four thirty the next morning, Angela slapped the clock like it had insulted her, then dragged herself out of bed. She dressed, gave herself a shot of coffee, and caned her way into the chilly morning darkness.

The highway was nearly clear at that hour. Angela loved the feel of the road under her Charger, and it unspooled like a great gray ribbon. She kept a wary eye out for speed traps on I-55 on the long drive into Saint Louis and listened to *The Jenny Carter Show*, one of her favorite radio talk shows. Fortunately for Angela, the show was also rebroadcast at the more reasonable hour of 7:00 p.m.

Jenny was thirtysomething, short and cute, with long brown hair and a terrific smile. The one time Angela had met her, the popular talk-show host barely came up to her shoulders—and Jenny was wearing high heels.

This morning, Jenny was discussing what she called "the Jose Salvato incident" with retired homicide detective René Sabatini. The detective had a deep, resonant voice. Before each answer, he paused to consider it thoughtfully.

"What do you think of Mr. Salvato's reaction?" Jenny asked. "Was he justified in running away?"

"First, let me make clear that I'm only going by the facts as reported in the news media, Ms. Carter," the detective said. "I wasn't there, and I don't know the officer personally. If the detective was only punched, as reported, then he had no right to use lethal force. Firing three shots at a fleeing suspect was excessive. In my opinion—and I know a lot of people won't agree with me—that detective should be disciplined and fired."

Fat chance, Angela thought. Ray Greiman will probably be given a raise and a medal.

"But Mr. Salvato did hit the detective," Jenny said.

"He did. He—or rather his lawyer—admits that Mr. Salvato punched the detective in the jaw. Obviously the detective was not seriously injured, as he was able to talk and ambulate."

"But shouldn't Mr. Salvato be charged with assault? The officer believed Mr. Salvato had committed arson and homicide," Jenny said.

"Whose side are you on?" Angela said to the radio.

The detective answered, "Any charges brought against Mr. Salvato for punching the detective would be a misdemeanor battery on an LEO—that's a law-enforcement officer. Even if the detective was going to arrest Mr. Salvato for arson or homicide, I do not believe that warranted shooting at a fleeing suspect. Mr. Salvato's identity was known. He is a respected local businessman. He was not suspected of random acts of violence, just a specific act related to his daughter's love life. It's not likely anyone else was at risk."

"If Mr. Salvato is charged with assault on a law-enforcement officer, will his lawyer be able to argue there are mitigating circumstances?" Jenny asked.

"As for mitigating circumstances . . . hm . . . the detective's comments exhibited racism, but I don't see that as being sufficient to excuse assaulting an LEO. One could argue that the detective should have known that pushing racist buttons like that could result in a strong emotional response. In fact, wasn't that actually why the detective was questioning Mr. Salvato the way he was? If I were a defense attorney representing Mr. Salvato on a battery LEO charge, that's what I would tell the jury. The detective was trying to evoke an emotional response, and that's exactly what he got. Keep in mind, Mr. Salvato went straight to his attorney and turned himself in on the same day. That should count in his favor, too."

"You tell 'em, detective," Angela said to the radio. She was proud of her part in this drama, even if most people didn't know about it.

Detective Sabatini wasn't finished. "The incident is odd. My LE contacts told me the detective wasn't trying to elicit more details of the crime—he seemed to be trying to offend Mr. Salvato. That would be counterproductive and further evidence of racism. Unless there are further details that haven't come to light yet, I cannot at this time defend these actions."

"Thank you, retired detective René Sabatini," Jenny said. "Let's go to our callers. Here's Donald from Chouteau Forest. You're on the air, Donald. What's your question?"

"I want to comment on what this so-called detective said. He should be defending his brother officer, who puts his life on the line every day he goes to work. Too many of our police officers are shot and killed, and this Jose dude is a Mexican. They don't have the same respect for the law as regular Americans. If he was in his country, he would have been shot, no questions asked. He's lucky he's in America."

"Thank you, Donald," the retired detective said. "I agree there are too many police deaths, but Mr. Salvato was not armed, and he was not threatening the officer. I'm not trying to excuse Mr. Salvato. He did hit an LEO. But the officer should not have made the racist comments."

Jenny's show had made the time pass quickly. Angela could see the Gateway Arch shimmering in the early-morning light, and she was entering the spaghetti tangle of downtown highways. The traffic had thickened.

She would need all her concentration now. She switched off the radio, turned off the highway, and threaded her way through the maze of one-way streets to Lin Kalomeris's law office.

Soon she'd know what the experts had found—and if there was any hope for Kendra Salvato and her father.

CHAPTER 30

Day twelve

The Salvato defense team was in a larger conference room today at Brandt, Bosman, and Kalomeris, with an even more stunning view of the sun-gilded Arch and the powerful brown Mississippi. How does Lin Kalomeris get any work done in this law office? Angela wondered.

Lin looked fresh and alert in a charcoal suit with a blue blouse, her makeup perfect, her blonde hair in a neat twist. Katie wore a gray pantsuit and no makeup. She seemed attentive and thoughtful. Monty was annoyingly cheerful and energetic at this early hour. He introduced everyone to Carol Berman, the noted forensic pathologist from Delray Beach, Florida.

Carol was a fiftysomething brunette with large, brown, inquisitive eyes. The pathologist was so petite, Angela suspected she might buy her clothes in the children's department. Her navy suit was expertly tailored to her slight, curvy figure.

"I just moved to Delray from Oklahoma City so my friends and family would visit me more often. Every time I talked someone into coming to Oklahoma, we'd have another tornado."

"Are you married?" Angela asked.

"Still looking to meet Mr. Right." Carol smiled at Monty. Angela noticed Katie stepped slightly closer to her man.

"And these are our two fire investigators, Laurie Hartig and Mo Heedles," Monty said. "Laurie is from Las Vegas."

Laurie was about five feet six, slim, and serious. Angela was amused to see she wore an eye-catching power suit in fire-engine red, with matching lipstick and nail polish. Angela guessed her age at late thirties. Mo was in her early sixties, with a clipped Eastern accent and short white hair. An avid baseball fan, Mo was the only one disappointed with the view. "If we were in an office on the other side, I could have seen Busch Stadium."

"Maybe next time you're in town, the Cardinals will be, too," Lin said.

Mo lit up like a stadium scoreboard.

"Now, everyone, please help yourself to the buffet," Lin said. "We have a lot of work to do in a short time."

A generous buffet was spread out on a long table: Hot scrambled eggs, and ham and sausages in silver chafing dishes. Trays of muffins and croissants. A rainbow of melon, blueberries, and strawberries. Angela loaded her plate, refilled her coffee cup, then sat at the long conference table next to Katie.

Carol took the seat next to Monty. She didn't flirt with him exactly, but she asked a lot of questions about his work. Katie watched the two, and her fingers twitched on her fork. Angela wasn't sure if her friend wanted to stab Carol or Monty. Finally, Katie said, "Carol, tell us how you broke the Howe murder-for-hire arson."

Carol said, "Uriah Jonas Howe was an unemployed veteran with PTSD accused of setting fire to a trailer. A twenty-two-year-old mother and her two children died in that fire. The prosecution said Uriah Howe had been promised half of the victim's two-hundred-thousand-dollar life-insurance policy by her almost-ex-husband. Uriah's friends swore he wasn't a killer. I examined the evidence and discovered the culprit was a faulty water heater. Uriah was exonerated, and so was the victim's estranged husband."

"Incredible," Lin said. "Let's start with our two fire investigators, Laurie and Mo."

The women spoke as a team. Laurie was precise and factual. Mo provided technical translations and comedy relief.

Mo began. "The prosecution said that Ms. Kendra Salvato poured gasoline on a sleeping Luther Delor, then lit it. The intense fire created a fireball that roared up to the ceiling, then bounced down, killing Mr. Delor and leaving Ms. Salvato covered with soot and blistering her fingers. Now that Mr. Jose Salvato has been arrested, he's considered an accomplice. We don't believe the facts support that theory."

Laurie said, "The investigators came with preconceived conclusions, what we call expectation bias."

Definitely described Jose and Kendra's case, Angela thought.

Mo jumped in. "The detective and the fire investigator had their minds already made up: there was a gasoline container at the scene, they found some evidence that looked like gasoline had started the fire, they saw that video of Luther Delor acting like a drunken fool, and bingo—the Salvatos were guilty."

Laurie continued the tag-team presentation. "The investigator did an excellent job of documenting the fire while it was active and then during the investigation. The evidence appeared to be properly collected and stored. He took samples and control samples of the carpet, bedding, and wall hanging."

"It was flagged, tagged, and bagged," Mo said. "It will stand up in court—and that's important for your case."

"About the fire itself," Laurie said. "The victim's house is of fairly new construction—less than five years old. It has concrete floors and cinder-block walls. Ms. Salvato said the bedroom door was closed at the time of the fire, and so was the master-bath door. This helped keep most of the fire contained in the master bedroom. The fire started slowly. Ms. Salvato said she woke up and saw some white smoke and a few flames on the polyurethane mattress. The fabrics on the bed and the hangings behind it were highly flammable silk. Ms. Salvato tried to wake up the victim but couldn't. The fire spread quickly. When most people see small flames, they don't think the fire is dangerous yet. They don't realize how quickly the fire can grow and release its toxic gases."

"Same with smoke," Mo said. "People think white smoke isn't as dangerous as black smoke. Not true."

Laurie smiled at her colleague. "We estimate that within three to five minutes, there was flashover. The flames and smoke shot straight up the curtains behind the bed and hit the ceiling, where the temperatures reached about eleven hundred degrees Fahrenheit."

"That's hot," Mo said. "Bodies are cremated at fourteen hundred degrees."

"Everything started burning," Laurie said. "By that time, Ms. Salvato had fled the room and made her way outside."

Mo said, "The fire may have left Ms. Salvato's brain deprived of oxygen. It consumes the oxygen in a room, and that can affect people's motor skills—it makes them clumsy. It also affects their judgment. Plus, the burning mattress and other items can release toxic gases. Several witnesses said she didn't tell anyone to save Luther right away and seemed hysterical or didn't make sense. They believed she waited until it was too late to save Mr. Delor. But she may not have been clearheaded enough to say anything."

Both lawyers—Lin and Monty—were smiling. Kendra's defense improved with each sentence.

Laurie said, "As the report stated, the batteries were removed from the smoke detectors. Six detectors were recovered. We found fingerprints on the inside of three that match the prints on file for the victim."

"Wait a minute," Angela said. "Where did you get Luther's prints? His hands were burned to the bone."

"The techs recovered the victim's prints from objects in his office," Laurie said. "The victim had a history of careless smoking. We can't prove that Ms. Salvato did not remove the batteries, but we can say the victim's prints were the only ones found inside the smoke detectors."

"Now we're getting to the good part," Mo said.

Laurie said, "The investigator found significant areas of large, shiny char blisters—what's known as alligator char—on parts of the wood bed frame. In the past, fire investigators believed that alligator char meant an ignitable liquid had been used. But newer tests say there is no scientific evidence to support this."

"You've seen alligator char in your fireplace," Mo said. "When the investigator concluded that the alligator char was a sign gasoline had been used as an accelerant, he was using old, discredited science. That new research has overturned a lot of misconceptions."

Except in the Forest, Angela thought, where misconceptions grow and thrive.

"The fire investigator found irregularly shaped patterns—pour patterns—on the burned carpet by the bed," Laurie said. "He concluded that those patterns were the result of ignitable liquids.

"We also examined the remains of what appear to be a silver metal belt buckle by victim's side of the bed. The buckle had his initials, LRD, on it.

"We examined samples of the burned carpet and unburned samples from the bedroom closet and concluded the patterns were caused by debris—in this case, the victim's clothing on the floor in the area where the belt buckle was recovered. Also, the glue was improperly applied to the wall-to-wall carpeting, which created what looked like a pour pattern. The investigator also took samples of the burned mattress and bedding. We found no gasoline on any samples.

"Ms. Salvato was covered with soot, and her hair was singed because she tried—and failed—to wake the victim. She suffered smoke inhalation when she tried to run back into the burning house to save the victim.

"The investigator's fatal fireball theory is ridiculous. If there really had been a fireball in that bedroom, it would have melted Ms. Salvato's lace outfit, which was not made of fire-resistant fabric. She would have had life-threatening or even fatal burns over a substantial part of her body.

"We found no evidence of gasoline or other accelerant, and no evidence that this was an incendiary fire. Luther's death was an unfortunate accident."

"Then how did he die?" Angela asked. "Did he burn to death? Or did the smoke kill him first?"

Mo and Laurie smiled.

"Carol can answer that question," Mo said.

Who killed Luther Delor?

Just when Angela thought she'd find out, Lin said, "Okay, everybody, let's take a break and resume in fifteen minutes."

The group scattered. When Angela returned from the bathroom, Mo Heedles was the only person in the conference room. Angela joined the fire investigator at the coffee urn. They drifted to the tall window.

"Did Carol tell you who killed Luther?"

"I didn't see her last night." Mo took a long drink of coffee.

"I'm glad you and Laurie found the evidence that she and Jose didn't murder Luther in his bed."

"Don't get too excited," Mo said. "Kendra still could have murdered him in bed. But she didn't set it on fire. There's always the old pillow over the face for a final exit. It would be easy to asphyxiate a drunk old man."

"And nearly impossible to prove," Angela said. "The evidence would be too delicate to survive a fire."

"You mean the pillow burned up," Mo said, "so there's no DNA."

"Right, but there's also petechial hemorrhage. If Luther was smothered, he'd have tiny red spots from the burst blood vessels in his eyes and maybe on his face. Petechiae are hard to see under the best circumstances—and these are the worst. I didn't see any when I did the body actualization."

"At least the lawyers can create reasonable doubt," Mo said.

Angela realized everyone was back seated at the table, with full coffee cups and refilled plates, waiting for the pathologist's presentation. Both women sat down. Carol smiled, then said, "I'll give you the highlights. The first autopsy concluded that Luther Delor's blood alcohol level was 0.30. He'd had at least six drinks. His weight was estimated at about one hundred sixty pounds, based on his medical records. His exact weight is not known because parts of his hands and feet were partially consumed by fire, and the body mass shrinks in the heat. The victim also had advanced cirrhosis of the liver."

"So if the fire didn't kill him," Mo said, "the alcohol would."

"In my opinion, yes. Eventually."

Wouldn't the Forest love that information, Angela thought. "Our Luther" was a raging alcoholic.

"I do not dispute any of those autopsy findings," Carol said. "We did not find any evidence that the victim had been using illicit drugs, though we did find significant levels of sildenafil. That's Viagra." She gave Monty a dazzling smile that faded slightly when she aimed it in Katie's direction.

"Again, witnesses say—and the video shows—the victim took that drug before his death. According to his internist, Dr. Carmen Bartlett, she specifically forbade him to take Viagra. He was taking a number of drugs for his heart problem, including lisinopril, digoxin, and simvastatin. That last drug is for high cholesterol.

"The victim was wearing only underpants at the time of his death, and they were partially burned. My forensic colleagues tested but did not find any ignitable liquid residue. I did not find any on the body, which was badly burned."

Come on, Angela thought. The fire investigators told us there was no gasoline on Luther. Let's get to the news.

"We did not find any evidence of high levels of carbon monoxide in the blood or tissue. And no soot or smoke in various areas of the body, including the lungs, trachea, and bronchi, or in the victim's stomach. Nor did we find any black soot deposits in the internal airways, which is often consistent with the victim breathing in a smoky environment."

Which means what? Angela thought. Before she could ask, Carol skipped on. "We also tested for other toxic compounds which can be present. We found none."

Katie looked pointedly at her watch. She was as impatient as Angela. Carol said, "The victim suffered second-, third-, and fourth-degree burns over a significant area of his body. Only parts of his pelvis and buttocks on his right side, which were in contact with the mattress, were not burned. In my opinion, the victim's burns were not survivable."

Angela felt her heart sink. Luther's injuries were so horrible that the jury wouldn't just give Kendra and her father the death penalty. They would burn them at the stake.

"However," Carol said before pausing. "Luther Ridley Delor did not—I repeat, did not—die of his burns."

This was news. Katie sat up straighter at the table. Mo and Laurie leaned forward.

"The victim had a massive myocardial infarction and was dead of a heart attack before the fire started. Ms. Salvato was unable to rescue him because he was dead by the time the fire started. The victim's heart was significantly weakened by heart disease, by taking Viagra against his doctor's orders, and by a high alcoholic intake. We believe he died while smoking, and his cigar set the mattress on fire."

Mo said, "He was dead when the fire started?"

"That's right," Carol said. "No one killed Luther Delor. He had a massive heart attack, possibly from the Viagra, and he set his bed on fire when he dropped his cigar. His death is accidental, not murder."

CHAPTER 31

Day twelve

"You can't kill a dead man," Angela said. "Kendra and Jose are innocent. The prosecutor will have to drop the charges, right?"

The defense team was at the conference table, which was littered with empty coffee cups and plates of half-eaten muffins. Lin had the chair at the head of the table.

Monty leaned forward. "Charges can be dropped by the prosecutor, but Mick's a political animal running for reelection. Some powerful people want the Salvatos on death row. Who knows what he'll do?"

"Both Salvatos are in jail," Angela said. "Once Mick finds out Luther was dead when the fire started, can't he just let them go? There's no case." She reached for her coffee, but the cup was empty. It would be rude to get more now.

"I'm not sure he'll give up without a fight," Lin said. "The charges can also be dismissed by the judge up until the jury announces its verdict. How does Mick get along with Judge Boareman? Does Chauncey toe the party line?"

"Boareman's retiring soon, so he's getting more independent," Monty said. "He'll be moving to Boca Raton this summer."

"That's far away from his cronies in the Forest," Lin said. "Why not ask Boareman for a motion to dismiss?"

"On what grounds?" Monty said.

"Prosecutorial corruption," Lin said. "You have a lot of corruption here. The defendants are clearly not guilty, and you have the forensic evidence to back this up."

"And if the charges aren't dismissed?"

"I think they will be. I'll help you," Lin said. "We can do a run-through here."

All three experts—Carol, Mo, and Laurie—checked their watches. "Will we still have time to make our flights?" Laurie asked.

"This won't take long," Lin said. "Let's get going. These motions are done *in camera*—in the judge's chambers. This room is now Judge Boareman's chambers, and he has his favorite court reporter present."

"That's Valerie Cannata," Monty said. "She calls him 'Judgie.'"

Katie snorted.

"I'm the judge," Lin said. "Angela, you're the prosecutor."

"But I don't know anything."

"Perfect," Lin said. "You've got the same qualifications as Mick. You and Monty will argue the motion in front of me and my court reporter. You don't need witnesses.

"Now, Mr. Defense Attorney, do you have a motion before this court?"

Monty stood up, straightened his shoulders, and adjusted his tie: an actor getting into his role. "Basically, Your Honor, my investigators will testify that the fire that killed Luther Ridley Delor was started by the victim's cigar that fell on his bed after he died. The fire was not arson. The conclusions of the prosecution's witness—that my client poured gasoline on the deceased—are based on erroneous and outdated science. If she had actually done that, she would have been burned to a crisp. My experts will also prove the victim was already dead of a heart attack when his cigar started the fire. I've got an autopsy that shows that there was no smoke in the victim's lungs from the fire. Both my clients are innocent. They did not start the fire, and they did not kill the victim. Furthermore, the prosecution has no evidence that my clients set the other three arson fires, except that Mr. Salvato and his wife, Graciela Salvato, knew the gate codes at two of three of the properties, through their businesses. These gate codes are available to numerous friends of the property owners, as well as workers, including mail carriers and UPS drivers. We ask the court that all charges against my clients be dismissed—murder in the first degree as well as the three arson fires—and save the State of Missouri the cost of these trials."

Lin turned to Angela. "Madam Prosecutor, what do you have to say?"

"Your Honor, Dr. Evarts Evans is a respected medical examiner, and fire investigator Douglas Hachette did a thorough job of collecting the evidence. Their conclusions should stand. As for saving the county the cost of the trials, those are necessary for the public safety and in the interests of justice."

Lin addressed the imaginary court reporter. "Let's go off the record."

"Now, Madam Prosecutor, you are going to waste a lot of the State of Missouri's time and the State of Missouri's money, not to mention a hell of lot of my time, on this case. Don't you have an election coming up? How would it look if you brought this case to trial?"

Lin's scowl was so realistic, Angela bit her lip to keep from laughing. "How about if you, Madam Prosecutor, file a motion dismissing both these cases with prejudice due to the finding of new evidence? Then you, Mr. Defense Attorney, sign the motion, agreeing to it. You might even make a report to the newspaper that you are proud of the prosecutor for being fair and honest in this case, blah, blah, blah. You know. Similar to other bullshit articles you've snuck into the paper."

Monty hid a grin. "Thank you, Your Honor."

"Both cases are dismissed!" Lin stood up, too. The mock hearing was over.

"Monty, keep in mind that the prosecution can appeal the court's granting of the motion to dismiss," Lin said. "The judge can do lots of stuff—unless it's illegal or unethical—that may or may not be approved of by the court of appeals later on. But I think you stand a good chance of getting dismissals."

"Can that really happen?" Angela asked.

"If we're lucky," Monty said. "And the judge grants both motions."

"How soon can you have the hearing?" Angela said.

"As soon as the prosecutor and judge agree. This afternoon, if I'm lucky. After I deliver our experts to the airport, I'll start the process."

Katie was throwing notes and papers into a leather case. "I'd better beat feet to the ME's office to tell Evarts. If he hears the news first from the clerk, he'll rip me a new one. There's no way I can soft-pedal this."

"You worry too much, Katie," Monty said. "If the motion is granted, Evarts will be too busy trying to spin his screwup. Priscilla, Eve, and the Du Pres family will be outside his office with torches and pitchforks."

Lin shook Monty's hand. "Good luck, Monty, and let me know what happens. If he dismisses the murder charges, I'm off the case. You know how I feel about the death penalty."

The three experts started to stand, too, but Angela said, "Wait! Before everyone leaves, I have a quick question for our fire experts." Lin stopped at the door to listen. "Chouteau County has been hit with a series of incendiary fires—arson fires."

"What are they using to start them?" Mo asked.

"Shortening smeared on the walls, toilet paper, potato chips, and gasoline. The fire investigator and the police think Kendra and her father set the fires to get revenge. I think they're set by teenagers."

Laurie jumped in. "Those fires sound more like teen work to me, but I haven't seen the reports. Usually, teen arsonists are between fourteen and seventeen, and the fires are not set at their homes. The kids are stressed, angry, anxious, or have some other emotional problem. They often come from broken homes or a poor social environment, or act out with disruptive behavior."

"That's half the teens in the Forest," Angela said, "if a poor social environment means neglect."

"Where are these fires?" Laurie asked. "Any in vacant buildings?"

"One fire was in a historic barn, another at an empty mansion, and one at a pool house. The pool house wasn't abandoned, but no one stayed there full-time."

"Adolescent fire starters like vacant buildings and empty lots," Laurie said. "They also go after schools and churches."

"No churches or schools," Angela said.

"Yet," Laurie said. "This is serious. Here's my card. Call if I can help."

"And here's mine." Mo produced her card. "Keep in touch. Looks like I won't be back for the trial, but I'll see a game at Busch Stadium sooner or later."

CHAPTER 32

Day twelve

Lin waved good-bye and left. The three defense experts gulped down a final cup of coffee, then wheeled their suitcases toward the door. Angela gathered her things and had almost made it out of the room when Monty stepped in front of her. He was so close she could smell his spicy aftershave.

"Angela, I need a favor. Would you go to the Chouteau County Jail this morning?" His voice was light but commanding.

"Sure. What do you need?"

They were near the huge windows, but both ignored the million-dollar view.

"I want you to see Kendra. I think Judge Boareman may split the decision—dismiss the murder case but deny the motion to dismiss the arson cases. If that happens, I'm worried about Jose. He says he has an alibi for the Gravois estate fire, but he refuses to tell me where he was. I've begged him. He's looking at three life sentences if we can't establish where he was that night."

"Aren't life sentences rare—and given out only when someone dies in the fire?"

"Freveletti will play up the Mexican angle," Monty said. "He always has. They'll throw the book at Jose. He says if his wife finds out about his alibi, she'll divorce him. Gracie hates this person."

"A woman? Is Jose having an affair?"

"He says no, but Gracie made him promise that he'd never see the person again."

"Is Jose gay?" Angela asked.

"He denies it. He'll go to prison before he tells anyone where he was. Personally, I think he'd rather be convicted of arson so Kendra can go free. Jose would sacrifice his life for his daughter."

Angela felt a flash of anger. "That's noble, but useless. The Forest arsonists are still free, and they'll start more fires. What happens if they hit a church next—or a school? You know Zander wasn't acting alone. That boy's body was dumped in his car trunk, then he was staged to look like he OD'd in his car. That's cold. It would take at least two people to pull that off."

"That's why I need you. We can't waste time. Talk to Kendra as soon as you get back."

"Should I tell her what the experts said?"

"No, I don't want to raise false hope. I'll tell her as soon as I know if we'll get a hearing."

"Can I take her anything in jail?" Angela asked. "Chocolate? Lunch? A cake with a file inside?"

Monty laughed. The morning sun gilded his strong features and the crow's-feet stamped at the corners of his eyes. Why did crow's-feet look good on men? It wasn't fair.

"You're not allowed to bring prisoners anything. Just find out what her father is afraid to tell me."

Once Angela got out of downtown Saint Louis and back on the highway, traffic was light. She was home by nine thirty. She stopped by her home and checked her messages. She had a text from Monty. **Hearing set for three today.**

She texted back: Good luck. Text me when you want to meet @ your office. On my way to see Kendra.

Next she texted Katie: Are you okay?

Katie texted back: Survived. Fearless Leader covering his ass like a nun in a hospital gown.

Angela laughed, then called Butch Chetkin. "I've got news, but it's not public yet. Luther died of a heart attack, and he started the fire when his cigar fell on the mattress. He was already dead by then. Monty filed a motion to dismiss both cases, the murder and the felony arson charges."

"Well, well. I wondered why Greiman's been in Mick's office for so long. This should be interesting."

After Butch hung up, Angela left to see Kendra. The Chouteau County Jail looked almost like a junior college, if you overlooked the tall fence topped with razor wire. Inside, the genteel appearance gave way to institutional grunge: cinder-block walls and scuffed tile.

At ten that morning, the line for the metal detector was surprisingly long. Angela saw a half dozen tired older women, a white-haired man, and four or five women in their twenties, some with energetic toddlers and others holding crying babies. Many of the young women violated the Jail Visitors Dress Code posted on the wall: "Visitors wearing suggestive clothing, transparent fabric, short shorts, or miniskirts will not be permitted to visit."

Angela was behind a large young woman whose wobbling tube top threatened to roll down her substantial chest. In front of her, a scrawny woman in a skirt not much bigger than a belt wore a fur jacket that looked like it was made from cocker spaniels. Her toddler clung to her knee-high boots and practiced earsplitting shrieks.

At last, Angela put her purse on the conveyor belt, walked through the metal detector, and was cleared.

At eleven o'clock, Kendra was seated at a booth behind a Plexiglas barrier. She looked younger and prettier without makeup, though

Angela could see dark circles under her eyes. Her hands had healed from the burns, and her nails were short and polish-free.

She picked up the phone and managed a worried smile. "Angela! So glad you came to see me."

"I've been worried about you," Angela said. "You must be so frightened."

"I am. And I feel so guilty that I couldn't save Luther. I tried, Angela. I really tried."

"I know you did." Angela wished she could tell Kendra about the experts' findings and relieve her mind. But that was Monty's job. "Monty's on the case. Soon you'll be back working at Killer Cuts."

"I don't think so. I haven't told anyone, not even my parents, Aunt Connie, or Monty—but I was planning to leave Luther, and that night at Gringo Daze was the last straw. I was sick of the drinking and groping. When I first started dating him, I was too dumb to realize he was an alcoholic. When I get out of here, I'm moving to Austin."

When, Angela thought, not if. Kendra is looking forward to the future. "You need a fresh start."

"Exactly." Kendra's sad smile made her seem suddenly older. "Even if I'm acquitted, I will always be the Mexican bitch who killed Luther."

"Kendra! That isn't true."

"I know those people, Angela!" Suddenly, she sounded angry. "I was never Luther's fiancée. To them, I'm a slutty husband stealer. Austin is young and fun, with an amazing music scene. It's okay to be Mexican American there. I have cousins in Austin, and my parents can visit me."

Angela saw this as the perfect opening. "Kendra, I'm glad you're making plans for the future, but your father can't visit you if he's still in jail."

"He's a good man. He knew Mrs. Gravois didn't have any money. He didn't even turn that debt over to a collection agency. He didn't burn down her house."

"He needs an alibi for the Gravois fire. He won't tell Monty where he was that night. Please, Kendra, tell me."

Kendra was silent for a long time. She stared at the shelf in front of her, tracing her fingers over the words scratched in the scarred wood. Karim 4 Ever. Tiffany luvs Jerrod. Denise is a hoor.

"Kendra? Please. Who was your father with?"

A long sigh. "He met Maria, an ex-girlfriend from a long time ago before I was born. She's nothing but trouble. Maria wanted to marry my father. She said she was pregnant and tried to blackmail him, but he married Mama instead."

"Is she trying to get money for the child?"

"What child? She may have had a miscarriage, or maybe she wasn't even pregnant. She hasn't done as well in the United States as my father. She shows up from time to time and asks for money, and he gives it to her, which pisses off Mama, who says she's a mooch. Last time, he gave her five hundred dollars, and Mama made him promise he'd never see her again. But two days before the Gravois fire, Maria called my cell phone when she couldn't find my father. I was in jail then and she couldn't reach me, but she left a message. Then she called my Aunt Connie. Maria said it was an emergency. That's the only reason Connie would talk to her—she has no use for the woman. Maria said she needed rent money or she'd be evicted. Her landlord sent her a five-day notice for failure to pay rent, and she needed two hundred dollars. She threatened to call my mother next, and that's the only reason why Connie told my father. He went up to give it to her."

"Up where?" Angela asked.

"North. Chicago. He told Mama he had to look at a used commercial mower at a dealer in Chicago. He could have bought the same thing in Saint Louis, but he needed an excuse to leave town. My mother watches the money like a hawk. He drove to Chicago, gave Maria two hundred dollars in cash, and drove home. He can prove he took the trip—he bought gas and stayed at a hotel. But there is no Chicago dealer. He's terrified Mama will find out and leave him."

"What's Maria's last name?"

"Garcia."

"Oh."

"Yeah, the Latino Smith. Chicago is the fifth-largest Hispanic community in the United States."

"What's her address?"

Kendra's burst of optimism vanished. "I don't know, and my father won't say. All I know is this woman with the anonymous name lives three hundred miles away in a city with nearly two million Hispanics."

CHAPTER 33

Day twelve

Angela left the Chouteau County Jail feeling like she'd escaped. How did Kendra stand being shut up in that grim place? She was a remarkably strong woman. It was noon. Angela had been there only two hours, but she felt like she'd spent a week.

Her cell phone chimed, and she checked the display. Ann Burris, one of the few Forest dwellers who believed that teenagers were behind the arson fires, was calling.

"Angela, any news about Kendra and Jose?"

"Nothing." Angela wished she could tell Ann the experts' findings. She hated keeping this secret from the woman who wanted to help.

"That poor family," Ann said. "Gracie must be beside herself."

Gracie? Angela hadn't given Kendra's mother a thought. She didn't even ask about her when she talked to Kendra at the jail. "We have to find the Forest arsonists, Ann, or Kendra and Jose will be locked up for good. Kendra's only twenty years old."

"Then what I have to tell you is even more important. So much is happening lately. Bryan and I heard about that poor boy's death—the one they're saying was a drug dealer. We've heard through the grapevine that police found materials to start a fire in his car trunk, but they aren't saying he's the arsonist."

"No, they're not. They're keeping that information quiet. The dead boy is Zander. Alexander Soran. Seventeen years old."

"That's the one. Listen, he wasn't acting alone."

"We know that."

"Did you know that two other Forest teenagers were with him?"

"No." Angela felt her heart beating faster. "Do you know their names?"

"No. But a young man who goes to school with Zander told me."

"What's his name?"

"I'm not sure," Ann said. "I can picture what he looks like—big guy, taller than me. Brown hair. Nice face. Where did I talk with him? Was it at the hardware store? A restaurant? I can't remember. But I talked with him for quite a while, and I think he could help."

"Oh." Damn, for a moment it sounded like a real lead. "I'll check with Monty, but we need his name, or at least the place where this young man works. It's not like you to be so distracted."

"I'm going crazy at work. I'll find him, Angela. I promise. Bryan will help me. I wish I could remember his name and where he worked."

"Me, too." Angela hoped her annoyance didn't show. Ann must really be under pressure. "Please keep trying. Your information could set Kendra and her father free."

Ann's tantalizing phone call left Angela restless and disappointed. At home, she forced herself to eat a peanut-butter sandwich, then threw in a load of laundry. The kitchen clock's hands refused to move. They seemed stuck at three o'clock. What was happening? Would Judge Boareman defy the Forest powers and grant both motions to dismiss? Or would he go the way Monty predicted and dismiss the murder charges? That would get Kendra and her father off death row. Or would he play it safe and subject the Salvatos to two trials?

When the mail carrier arrived, Angela rushed out like she'd been expecting a check. The mail was the usual dull collection of medical bills and a circular for a shoe sale. When her text chime sounded, she leaped on her phone as if it might run away. Monty had texted: J granted one motion. Murder charges dropped. Gave Kendra the news. Meet me at my office @ 5 p.m.

Angela's heart leaped. Kendra and her father were no longer facing death. The arson charges seemed a small hurdle after the threat of lethal injection. She wondered how Katie was but didn't dare call her friend. Their boss would be furious at this news. She hoped she wouldn't have to go into the office until Evarts cooled down.

By the time she was driving to Monty's office, the spin had started. The Forest powers had skillfully smoothed over Dr. Evarts Evans's slipshod autopsy. The medical examiner's careless errors that could have sent two innocent people to death row—including a young woman— were never mentioned. They would be quietly forgotten.

Angela was stunned by how quickly the cover-up was completed. She flipped on her car radio at four thirty and heard the announcer say, "Chouteau County prosecuting attorney Mick Freveletti called a press conference at four o'clock today to discuss the death of business leader Luther Ridley Delor. The county prosecutor held the conference outside the Chouteau County Courthouse."

Angela heard the crush of reporters, the mob's confusion, the motorized cameras snapping like popcorn. The prosecutor's pronouncement rose above the noise. Mick had a politician's voice: steady, sincere, and calming. The kind of voice that made voters want to believe the most outrageous lies. Mick could say them without hesitation.

"Good morning." He gave the unruly media a moment to settle down. When there was silence he said, "Recently, charges for murder in the first degree were filed against Mexican American Kendra Salvato and her father, Jose Salvato, a naturalized citizen, in the burning death of Mr. Luther Ridley Delor, a prominent Chouteau Forest financier."

No mention that Jose was also a successful businessman, or of the name of Luther's sleazy business. The lines were clearly drawn: Luther was a powerful insider. Kendra and her father were Mexicans—foreigners. Only Luther had the respectful title. He was "Mister."

Mick's words smoothly rolled on. "New evidence has come to light that reveals Mr. Delor was deceased at the time of the fire that destroyed his home in Olympia Forest Estates. The deceased had died of natural causes. He had been smoking in bed, and his cigar set fire to the mattress. The fire that we believed had been set by Mr. Delor's fiancée, Kendra Salvato, and her father, Jose Salvato, was accidentally set by the late Mr. Delor. Therefore, in the interests of justice, the charges of murder in the first degree against Kendra and her father, Jose Salvato, have been dismissed." No mention of Judge Boareman or Monty's motion to dismiss.

The media erupted into frenzied questions: "Does this mean Kendra Salvato goes free?" "Will she sue the county for wrongful arrest?" "Where did you get the new evidence?" "Why did you change your mind?"

Mick ignored the questions and pushed on. "Neither Kendra nor her father, Jose, will be released at this time. We are not dropping the charges against them for the three counts of felony arson. The historic Du Pres barn was destroyed, as was the Gravois family mansion and the Hobart pool house. These fires were a substantial danger to the lives and property of the people of this county, and the Salvatos will be prosecuted to the fullest extent of the law. Drug-dealing Mexicans have spread to Saint Louis, and now we have more in Chouteau County. They must be stopped. They have damaged not only our property but our peace of mind—the reason we live in Chouteau County. We cannot and will not show mercy to this Mexican menace. Upon their conviction for these crimes, we will request the maximum penalty: three life sentences."

Mick paused dramatically. He was reassuring the Forest's first families that the interlopers would never see the light of day—and Kendra would never enjoy Luther's $2 million.

Angela felt sick. Kendra and Jose had escaped death row for a living death. Mick was asking for a "pine box sentence"—Kendra and her father would leave prison in pine boxes.

Mick ended with this dramatic statement: "I pledge that these two dangerous criminals will spend the rest of their lives behind bars, and I will continue to protect the property, peace, and safety of Chouteau County."

More media questions battered Mick: "What evidence do you have?" "Will you accept a plea bargain?" "When is the trial?"

He ignored the pack of reporters. "Thank you. No questions. Thank you."

Angela's elation was gone. Mick had turned the defense's victory into a life of misery for Kendra and Jose. Angela couldn't bear to listen to the gleeful analysis. She switched off the radio and saw the setting sun reflected on the massive brass doors of Monty's law office. She parked in front of the long, low one-story building.

Once inside, she didn't have time to admire Monty's collection of horse paintings or men's-club decor of leather wing chairs and Oriental rugs. His redheaded receptionist, Jinny Gender, greeted her. "Mr. Bryant is waiting for you. I'm supposed to take you straight back to his office. Would you like something to drink: coffee, tea?"

"No, thanks." She'd had a week's worth of coffee this morning.

Monty was tapping at the computer in his book-lined office. She could see the lush Missouri hills through the huge window. She took the chair in front of his carved mahogany desk, and he gave her a welcoming smile.

"You were right," she said. "The judge split the decision."

"At least Kendra and her father are off death row."

"And locked up for the rest of their lives," Angela said. "Mick is already spinning Evarts's failure into another success for his office. Did you hear his press conference?"

"Just finished looking it up online. Then I called Gracie to reassure her. That poor woman is on a roller coaster. First, I told her the good news after the hearing. Next, she hears this saber-rattling press conference. I told her it's not as bad as it sounds."

"Why not?"

"The evidence—if you can call it that—is Jose and Kendra knew the gate codes to the Hobart estate and the Du Pres barn property. But so do UPS and FedEx drivers. And pizza drivers, and the security guards—and sadly, some of those are wacko wannabes. Not to mention the Du Pres's friends, family members, and staff. It would be hard to find someone who doesn't know those gate codes. A jury will never convict." Monty spoke with an easy confidence, as if he knew the world would do things his way.

"Not even a Forest jury, whipped into a frenzy about Jose the Mexican and his predatory daughter?"

Monty looked a shade less confident. "Juries have been known to do strange things." That was as much as he'd admit.

Angela finally broke the silence. "How is Gracie?"

"Holding together. She's closed her business until this is sorted out, and she has her staff on half pay. She's paying them out of her own pocket."

"That's really generous."

"Did Kendra tell you why her father won't tell me his alibi?"

"Jose was in Chicago seeing a former girlfriend." Angela gave him the details and said, "Can we get Butch to track down Maria Garcia?"

"Technically he can. The Forest PD is a tiny department, so the detectives are called upon to be generalists. So, yes, Butch could go to Chicago. But police politics are tricky. He may not be too popular with his coworkers if he makes Greiman look bad. I'd rather not put him between a rock and a hard place. My investigator, KJ Lakker, should be back from vacation by now. I can send him to Chicago."

"How's KJ going to track down a woman with a name like Maria Garcia? It's impossible."

"Kendra gave us a good place to start. Maria's number is on Kendra's cell phone. I'll get her phone from her mother, and KJ can find Maria. Anything else?"

"We almost got a lead from Ann Burris, who called me this afternoon. She says she met a boy who went to school with Zander, and he told her there are two other arsonists—both Forest teenagers."

"Wonderful." Monty's blue eyes were lit with a smile. He sat up and put his elbows on his massive desk.

"Not really. Ann can't remember the kid's name or where she talked to him. I told her it's important that we find him."

"Important?" Monty said. "It will save two people from a living death."

CHAPTER 34

Days twelve, thirteen

Angela was at home and brooding, her dinner untouched. Twelve hours ago, she'd been in Lin Kalomeris's downtown law office, convinced Kendra and Jose would soon be free.

Tonight, those hopes were dashed. The Forest grandees were determined to punish the Salvatos. Kendra's life would be over before it had begun. Angela had watched the press conference on TV that night. Mick Freveletti had looked positively gleeful at the prospect of putting the Salvatos in prison for life. Angela wanted to slap that smug smile off his campaign-poster face. She'd turned off the television before the so-called news analysis and tried to read, but she couldn't concentrate.

She was asleep on the couch when her cell phone rang. She leaped on it.

"Angela! I've got him!" Ann Burris was so excited the words tumbled out. "I've found the mystery man! He saw the arsonists who burned down the Gravois estate. He has their names! He has proof! He videoed them!"

"He has video? Fantastic! I'll be right over with Monty and Detective Butch Chetkin."

"No!" Angela heard real panic in her voice. "You can't bring them. Not yet."

"Why not?"

"It's—it's—the situation is sensitive. I think the three of us can persuade him to talk, but he's afraid, and for good reason. He's so young, and they could ruin him. He could lose his job, and he needs it. But we can talk him into speaking up. I know we can. Bryan has a plan."

"Is he at your house?"

"Not right now. He's coming back as soon as he gets off work at twelve thirty tonight."

"That late? Who is he? What's he do?"

"You'll never guess. I'll tell you when you get here. I know it's late—it's eleven thirty. But he'll be here shortly. We can have a drink and wait for him."

Angela had to force herself to drive the speed limit, or close to it. She wanted to floor the Charger and roar through the Forest streets to Ann's home. Many Forest mansions were grandiose hulks, but Ann's was pretty: a white marble mansion with clean lines. The windows and doorways were frosted with creamy baroque designs. The courtyard was a sculpture garden with Greek and Roman statues collected by Ann's great-grandfather. The marble gods and goddesses were softly timeworn.

Ann's house was impressive on the outside but warm and homey inside. Ann answered her door in a gold-brown sheath that brought out the highlights in her hair. Bryan, right behind her, wore gray slacks and a blue-and-white striped long-sleeved shirt that Angela guessed was a Thomas Pink.

"Come in," Ann said.

Angela followed the couple into a room with plush brown sofas and chairs that begged you to sink into them, thick Oriental rugs, and comfortable pillows in restful honey-gold tones. While Bryan fixed Angela a club soda with lime, she joined Ann on the sofa. "How did you find him?"

"We ordered pizza from the Forest Coal-Fired Pizza," Ann said. "As soon as I saw him at the door with the two pizzas, I recognized him. Our source is Big Al the Pizza Dude."

"You're kidding. I know him. Big guy—about six two, lots of curly, dark hair. Looks like a giant-economy-size all-American boy."

"That's him. I needed to get cash for his tip, and he stepped in here to talk to Bryan. The TV news was on, and Big Al saw the story where the prosecutor talked about putting Jose and Kendra away for the Forest arson fires."

"I couldn't believe that press conference. I was so angry I switched off the TV."

"Then you missed the station commentary afterward. That was worse. Al heard the announcer speculate that 'the Mexican'—that's what he called Jose—burned down the Gravois estate because the family owed him money."

Bryan returned with Angela's soda and said, "Big Al said to me, 'Jose didn't do it.' Just like that. I asked, 'How do you know?' and he said, 'I was delivering pizza to Du Barry Circle the night of the fire, and I saw Zander parked in front of the Gravois estate, along with two other kids.'"

"Was Al friends with Zander?" Angela asked.

"Big Al knew Zander, but they weren't friends. He says Zander was a drug dealer and ran with a wild crowd of Forest kids who went to the Academy. Zander acted like they were his friends, but they weren't. Zander was their dealer and errand boy. Al avoided them. They made fun of Big Al because he delivered pizza."

"So then what happened?"

Ann checked her gold watch and grinned. "He can tell you when he gets inside."

They saw headlights swing into the circular drive and heard a rumble. Ann said, "I bet that's Big Al in his old Subaru Outback."

It was. Big Al wore his red, white, and green polyester uniform and smelled like pepperoni. He seemed awkward and a little shy. Ann offered to fix him dinner. "No, thanks, but I'd like a Diet Coke," he said.

Ann brought him a Diet Coke in a crystal glass, and he drank it down thirstily. She brought him another. "Delivering pizzas must be dry work. We were telling Ms. Richman what you saw the night of the fire."

Al shifted uncomfortably in the soft chair. "I'm sorry. I shouldn't have said anything. I could lose my job. Those people have friends here."

"So do we," Ann said. "We can protect you. If you lose your job, Bryan and I will try to find you another. Bryan thinks he knows of a job that pays more than you're making now. Why don't we talk for a little bit, and then you can decide what to tell us? You're famous in the Forest as Big Al, but I don't know your last name."

Al's pale face flushed. "Most people can't pronounce it. It's Shlesinger."

"Fine old German name. Is Al short for Alan?"

"Albert. Albert Shlesinger was my great-great-grandfather on my mother's side. He served in the army during the Spanish-American War. I'm named for him. My great-grandfather served in World War I, and my uncle in Vietnam."

"So you have heroes in your family," Ann said. "Courage is in your genes. Tell us about the night of the fire. You were delivering a pizza on Du Barry Circle, right?"

He nodded. Ann's slow, skillful questioning was drawing him out. "And you saw Zander parked in front of the Gravois estate, along with two other kids."

"Right. One was Judge Charbonneau's son, Marlon. They call him Duke. The other was Jeremy Raclette, the hedge funder's kid. He goes by Kip. His red Beemer was there, too. His father bought it for him when he turned sixteen last year. Someone had thrown a blanket over the top of the estate's spiked fence, and Kip and Duke had climbed over it. Zander was on the other side, tossing big bags over the fence."

"What kind of bags?" Angela asked.

"Plastic. From Cheap and Easy. Some of the bags seemed very light. Others were heavier. One bag broke open, and a twelve-pack of TP fell out."

"Toilet paper?" Ann asked. "What did you make of that?"

"I decided they were going to party and maybe TP the estate. I really didn't spend that much time thinking about it. I had to deliver the pizza."

"Do kids still TP houses?" Angela asked.

"It's rare, thanks to security cameras. I see it maybe a few times a year, usually around homecoming. But everyone knew the Gravois estate didn't have security cameras anymore. I thought Zander and his friends were going to have some old-school fun like Grandpa used to and TP the house."

"Did you deliver the pizza okay?"

"I did, but that customer doesn't tip like you, Ms. Burris. His order was nineteen eighty-eight. He gave me a twenty and said to keep the change."

"That's an outrage," Ann said.

Big Al shrugged. "Happens all the time. People don't understand how little we're paid. I left. When I passed the Gravois estate again, the two Beemers were still there, but I didn't see anyone. I didn't think anything about it until Zander was found dead."

"Did you know Zander used heroin?" Angela asked.

"Sure. His whole crowd uses it. Most of them use needles, like Kip and Duke. Zander snorted it. He thought needles were for junkies, and he wasn't hard-core if he snorted heroin."

"After Zander died, what did you do?"

"Nothing. It's not like he was a friend or anything. I mean, I felt bad he was dead, and his mom is a nice lady, but I didn't see him snort the heroin or anything. But now, on TV, they're trying to blame the fires on Mr. Salvato and Kendra, just because Mr. Salvato has some gate code. The pizza restaurant has the gate codes for every subdivision and most houses, but that doesn't make me an arsonist. I saw Zander, Kip, and Duke at the estate the night of the fire—and I can prove it."

Big Al looked startled, as if those last words had slipped out. Ann acted as if he hadn't said anything out of the ordinary. "How can you prove it?" she said softly.

"I have a dash cam on my car. I have it here." He held up his backpack.

"I have a dash cam on my racing Porsche," Bryan said.

Bryan and Big Al lapsed into tech talk that was way over Angela's head, but it seemed to relax Al. He called up a video on a small screen about the size of a cell phone's. Now Angela could see the whole episode.

The video was time-stamped 3:47 p.m., as Al's car headed toward the Gravois estate. She could see the fence, and in the distance, part of the kitchen addition on the Gravois mansion and the dead topiary and trees—trees that a few hours later would burst into flames like torches. Now the fence was visible—dark metal with a spiked top. Al slowed the video. "That's Zander in the plaid shirt tossing the bags over the fence. One. Two. Three. They're yellow Cheap and Easy bags. That white stuff there is the twelve-pack of TP. And see the blanket over the top of the fence? On the other side, those two dudes are Kip and Duke. Duke is on the right, slightly behind Kip. Kip is short and stocky. Duke is taller and skinnier than Kip."

Both boys wore khaki shorts and polo shirts—Duke's was washed-out blue, and Kip's was yellow. As the car and the camera rounded the curve, Angela saw two Beemers parked on the side of the road. "The black one is Zander's," Al said. "The red one is Kip's. You can see the license plates."

Bingo! Angela thought, but she didn't dare say it out loud. All the police had to do was check the plates and they could place Zander and Duke at the scene.

"That's amazing," Ann said.

"I also have a pizza-run sheet. It shows the date, every time I leave the store, where I'm going, and when I got back. It also shows the order. We're supposed to put down our tips, but I don't put down the really big ones."

"This is incredible," Angela said. "It places those boys at the scene the night of the fire, with materials that were used to start the fire. The fires were set in several places in the house, including the kitchen. You can see a bit of it on your video. The kitchen didn't burn completely, and the fire investigator found potato chips and toilet paper, as well as vegetable shortening, plastered on the walls, along with some fingerprints. All those are fire-starting materials. The police found a receipt from Cheap and Easy for both those things in Zander's car. This could set Jose and Kendra free."

"All you have to do is tell the police," Bryan said. "You have your great-great-grandfather's courage."

Big Al looked very young and uneasy. "I wish I did. But I can't lose this job. I need the money. I'm going to college. Kip's dad is part owner of the Forest Coal-Fired Pizza. I'm also worried about what will happen if I testify. I'll have old man Du Pres after me. Everyone knows he wants the arson case to go away. If he can pin it on Jose and Kendra, he'll be happy."

"You know Kendra and Jose are innocent," Angela said.

Al said nothing.

"They're good, hardworking people, Al. You can set them free. They'll die in jail if Reggie Du Pres gets his way. That's not right."

Silence.

"And those boys—Kip and Duke—killed your friend Zander, or at least let him die."

"Zander wasn't my friend. I don't think it's right that he died, but I live in Toonerville. I have to work to make it through school."

"You like cars?" Bryan knew the answer to his question before Al nodded yes.

"I race vintage Porsche 911s. I can't guarantee you a job, but I know some people at the South County Speedway in Chesterfield. The Forest has no influence there. There's supposed to be a weekend job opening up. I could put in your name and give you a good reference. Ann would, too. No promises, of course. But think about it. Eighteen dollars an hour."

"Eighteen," Al repeated reverently.

"And you don't have to worry about twelve-cent tips."

"Please, Al," Angela said. "You know Kendra and Jose didn't set that fire. You can set them free—if you'll talk to Detective Butch Chetkin and show him the video and your run sheet."

"Well . . ."

"It's the right thing to do." Ann looked incredibly glamorous.

"Uh."

"And no more nickel-and dime tips," Bryan said.

"I'll do it!" Al said.

CHAPTER 35

Day thirteen

Angela called Butch Chetkin at six the next morning with the news about Big Al. "I'm sorry to call you so early, but I have a witness who can place Zander and two other seventeen-year-olds at the Gravois estate the night of the fire. I have their names and a video."

Butch sounded wide-awake. "I'm up and drinking coffee. If you're giving me a witness with a video, you can call any hour. Who is he? Do I know him?"

"Probably. He's Big Al the Pizza Dude. Last name Shlesinger. Goes to Chouteau Forest High School in Toonerville." She told him what Al said last night.

"And he's how old?"

"Seventeen," Angela said.

"He has to be eighteen if he's delivering pizza. That's federal law. I'll pull him out of class and have a talk with him today."

"Please don't. Not unless you want word to get back to Kip and Duke. They don't go to the same school, but you know how news spreads in the Forest."

"Okay, I'll talk to him this morning. He can go to school late. You have his address and home phone, right?"

"Yes. The family lives in Toonerville. His mother's name is Debra, and she's a librarian at the main Chouteau County Library. His father is an insurance agent."

"Big Al's technically an adult, so I could interview him alone. Do you think his parents will encourage him to be cooperative?"

"My guess is yes, and he may be more comfortable talking with his parents there."

"I'll call them now and tell them nothing's wrong—quite the opposite, in fact," Butch said. "I'll ask if we can interview Al before school."

"Can I be there? I won't say anything, but he sorta knows me."

"Sure. See you there."

By 7:00 a.m., Angela, Butch, Big Al, and his mother, Debra, were in the coffee-scented kitchen of the Shlesinger home, a one-story brick rambler with neat white trim. This was definitely a librarian's house—books and bookshelves were everywhere: the living room, the hall, even the kitchen. The four sat at the big wooden kitchen table with blue mugs of coffee. The polished table's centerpiece was a bowl of fresh fruit. Debra, a slender woman with dark hair and small, manicured hands, was seated next to her son. This morning, Al was freshly showered and wore a checked shirt and jeans. She bet he set the girls' hearts fluttering.

Debra Shlesinger fidgeted with the ceramic salt-and-pepper shakers. "I hope I'm doing the right thing, Detective. My husband's in Atlanta today on business, and I couldn't reach him. I don't like my son mixed up with arson and murder."

"I understand, Mrs. Shlesinger."

"Debra."

"Your son has the evidence that can put two arsonists at the scene of the fire," Butch said, "and then we can take them off the streets."

"Yes, I know. But I also know Kip's and Duke's parents are rich and important. My son works hard, but he needs his job. Kip's father is part owner of the pizza place where Al works, and my boy could lose his job."

"Dr. Bryan Berry may be able to get him another one that pays more—eighteen dollars an hour."

"What about college? Al's grades are good. We're hoping for a scholarship, but Reggie Du Pres and Duke's dad, Judge Charbonneau, are on several college boards. They could deny my son a scholarship."

"I can't make any promises, but I can tell you that Dr. Berry and Ann Burris are on college boards for schools locally and in other states. They also have money and influence, and they're in your son's corner."

"But what about my husband and me? Albert could lose some referrals—he'll survive, but it could cost us money—and I could lose my job."

"You're a county librarian, correct? How are your yearly job evaluations?" Butch asked.

"I always get the highest possible ratings."

"You're protected by civil service. If you're fired, you're looking at a substantial lawsuit. Look, Debra, I know you're worried. But I'm worried, too. If your son is right, these two young men are running around setting fires and shooting up heroin. They're dangers to themselves and to the whole community. The third member of that group, who was also a dealer, OD'd later the same night your son saw him. So far, no one has died in the fires they've set, but that's only a matter of time. Big Al says he was named for his great-great-grandfather, a war hero. Please let him continue the family tradition of bravery. We will do our best to protect him, and now he has powerful friends, too. They can help him."

"Come on, Mom. These dudes are dangerous." They were, but Angela wondered just how civic-minded Al was. Did he want the rich kids who treated him as invisible to finally know who he was? "And I am an adult."

"Still living in this household," Debra reminded him, and sighed. "All right. I hope you know what you're doing." Once again, Al told his story and then showed Butch his video and pizza-run sheet.

"So I've got them stone-cold, right?" Al said.

"You've got them at the scene *before* the fire and *before* Zander OD'd," Butch said. "It's a start. Right now, all we have them for is trespassing. Toilet paper was used to help start the fire, but it's not illegal to possess TP—or throw it over a fence."

"Oh." Al looked disappointed. "So I wasn't any help at all."

"I didn't say that. You've come forward. You've given me a place to start. Now it's up to me. I have to get some warrants and check with some people. Do you know if Kip, Zander, and Duke had Facebook accounts?"

"Facebook? That's for old—" Al skidded to a stop. "I mean, high school kids don't really use it. They use Snapchat mostly."

"Do you know their account names?"

"You need their usernames," Al said. "That's how you find a Snapchat account. You also have what's called a vanity name, but there would be a million Zanders, Kips, and Dukes on Snapchat. Most photos are shared in a closed group of friends, and I'm definitely not a friend of those three. No way I'd get a Snap from them. What are you looking for?"

"I'm hoping they took a selfie that places them at the Gravois mansion."

"They could have. We like Snapchat because photos and videos aren't around forever, like on Facebook. Once a Snap is opened, you get to decide how long it will last—anywhere from one to ten seconds. Then, unless you save it or screen-capture it, it's gone—sort of. Most people think Snaps are erased once they're read. That's not quite how it works. Snapchat usually stores chats and images for thirty days."

"Any way to stop Snapchat from destroying the photos?"

"Snapchat is tough. That's why kids use it for sexting and stuff." He looked at his mother. "Not that I'm into sexting." His ears were bright red, and Angela wondered if some girls had sent him racy photos. Al seemed to know a lot about this subject.

"You better not be." His mother sounded maternal, playful—and clueless.

"Do you have any of their cell phones?" Al asked.

"Not yet. We haven't approached Kip or Duke," Butch said. "What if we find Zander's phone?"

"Unopened Snaps sent to a group chat are deleted by default after twenty-four hours. But if Kip or Duke saved it, you could still see it—if you find the phone and username within thirty days."

Debra was getting restless with the tech talk. She glanced at the kitchen clock and asked, "Is there anything else? Al should be going to school."

"Nothing else. You've been a big help, Al. Right now, the best thing you can do is go to school, go to work, and keep quiet."

"No problem there," Al said.

"He's smart," Debra said. "He knows what to do." She gave her son a proud smile. "I e-mailed the school that you were going to be tardy. Looks like you're going to miss your first class. I'll write you a note and drive you to school."

Angela and Butch thanked them both and left. "Want to get breakfast at the Forest Salade Shoppe?" he asked. "They make a mean chocolate-chip pancake."

"Deal." Angela got into her car. "See you there."

She arrived first at the restaurant and asked for a booth. To humor Butch, she took the seat with her back to the door. After they ordered coffee and pancakes, Angela asked, "Before we start, what are you going to do about Greiman? Isn't this his case?"

"It is, and he's done nothing with it. In a department as small as ours, the lines of responsibility can be easily adjusted."

"Will the chief go along with that?"

"He may not like it, but it's better to ask forgiveness than permission. If I present him with a solid case, he can't do anything about it. As for Greiman, I don't care what he thinks. I've kept quiet, but I've seen him bungle one investigation after another and somehow come out smelling like a rose. I'm not afraid to go against the grain. My father was a former chief in Peerless Grove, Kansas, so I guess you could say policing is in my blood."

"I didn't know that. Where's Peerless Grove?"

"About eighty miles south of Kansas City. Old man's retired now and still lives there with Mom. He's sixty-eight."

The server arrived with two stacks of chocolate-chip pancakes, butter, and warm maple syrup. There was a respectful silence while Butch and Angela dug into their warm, chocolatey pancakes. After nearly half a stack and another coffee refill, Angela asked, "What will you have to do to solve this case?"

"The pizza driver can put the boys at the scene. Al saw them, he saw their cars, and his video got the tag numbers. But what's to say they started the fire? The fact that they had TP? Like I told Al, it's not illegal to possess toilet paper or throw a twelve-pack over the fence. I need to get a warrant for all their cell-phone records to show they were at the fire scene. I also need the security-camera footage on the five other Du Barry Circle estates, and another warrant for the boy's car—Kip, I think his name is. Will they lie about being at the scene? Probably. If they lie but were seen trespassing at the Gravois mansion before the fire and if they had TP, chips, and shortening, that might be enough for an arrest."

"What about a conviction?"

"Not with the kind of lawyers their parents can afford. We do have that unidentified print inside the car trunk—and the unknown DNA on the syringe stuck in Zander's arm. The fire investigator found prints and DNA where they partied in the Gravois's kitchen, and an unknown print on the TP wrapper and on the can of shortening at the scene.

None of that burned when the fire went out in the kitchen. I can get Cheap and Easy video footage that will show them at the register buying the TP and other supplies."

"If Duke and Kip were in the store with Zander," Angela said. "He was their errand boy. They may have let him go in alone and buy the fire fixings. The receipt was in his car."

"But if their fingerprints are on those items, we've got them at the fire." Butch took another forkful of pancake.

"They're seventeen," Angela said. "Will they be charged as juveniles or adults?"

"Adults, although their lawyers will fight it. Too bad the dead kid's a nobody—I don't mean to be harsh, but if Zander's mom had any influence, she might swing more weight than the killers' parents."

"If they killed Zander. His mother said he wasn't a user, but the autopsy said otherwise." She took a long drink of her coffee.

"You know what would be really nice?" Butch said. "If we got Kip's or Duke's phone, got their Snapchat account, and saw selfies of them at the fire scene."

"Can't the lawyers for Kip and Duke block you from seeing those Snaps?"

"Nope, these kids like to brag. They may share their story with everyone, so there's no expectation of privacy. I'm going to pay a visit to the SROs at the Forest Academy and Chouteau Forest High School."

"What's an SRO? I don't think you mean standing room only."

Butch laughed and signaled for the check. "SROs are school resource officers, police officers who work in a school. They're pretty cooperative. They don't even have to see the actual post. They hear things. I'll start with Peter Simonetti at Chouteau Forest High and see if he's heard anything. Then I'll check with the Academy's SRO. You'd be surprised how quickly it will unravel. Once you start following someone online, he'll let something slip in a publicly accessible space. Then it's warrants and proof. As soon as I get an account username, I'm filing a request to preserve the data."

"When the boys are charged, will they be jailed or released to their parents?"

"I see them going to detention or jail and not getting out anytime soon. Which is why I'm not going to say anything until I have those warrants. But don't worry, Angela. We'll get 'em."

"You may find them, Butch, but those kids will never do jail time. Meanwhile, Kendra and her father are facing life in prison on flimsy evidence."

"Don't be so sure it's over for Kendra and Jose, Angela. Monty is a good lawyer. At the very least, the arrests will end the fires."

The server arrived with the check, and Butch grabbed it. "My treat. You working today?"

"Nope. Just another doctor's appointment. But those are running down."

Angela wanted to visit the Du Pres stables for some horse therapy before she saw Doc Bartlett, but when she got home, she saw Bud's beat-up pickup bouncing down the gravel road leading to the horse farm. He signaled her to stop, and she pointed to her driveway. Bud parked behind her car and climbed out of his truck holding his soda-can spittoon. He wore old, saggy-seated jeans, a blue work shirt, nearly transparent with age, and a straw cowboy hat.

"Glad you didn't go up to the stables. Old Reggie's there right now. He's getting another OTTB horse from Kentucky. I'm leaving this afternoon to pick her up. I'll be gone two days. Wait till you see her," he said. Angela heard real enthusiasm in his voice and a softness he never used for people. "She's a beauty. Her name is Valerie's Spirit. She's dark brown with a white star and a black mane and tail. A very sweet horse. I got her picture here." Bud brought out his cell phone. Where other people had photos of their families and pets, Bud had horse pictures.

"She's a lovely shade of brown," Angela said. Bud looked pleased at the praise and wiped his forehead with his red bandanna. The morning was hot.

"Reggie's going to be around the stables most of today, but then he has some fancy-Dan thing at his club for the next two days, and you'll have the stables to yourself."

"Good. I'll bring extra carrots and peppermints for Eecie and Hero."

"They'd like that." Bud's face creased into a sun-wrinkled smile. Angela thought he'd leave, but he hung back. "You can see the stables from your bedroom window, right?"

"I have a clear view."

"Good. If you get up in the middle of the night, keep an eye on them, will you?"

"Of course. What's wrong, Bud?"

"I saw that performance the county prosecutor put on yesterday, saying Jose and Kendra are the Forest arsonists, but I don't buy it. I think the real arsonists are still out there, and they're still starting fires."

"I think you're right, Bud. Reggie spares no expense for those horses. Doesn't he have a sprinkler system in the stables?"

"Can't have one. He has fire extinguishers and fire alarms, but that horse barn is what they call 'old mill construction.' They used heavier timbers back then, which are slower to burn, but they don't have sprinklers. Sprinkler systems can only be used in heated areas. Most barns aren't heated well enough. The horses are warm from being sheltered, their winter coats keep them warm, and they wear blankets. I've done what I could to protect them from fire, Angela. I even talked Old Reggie into new security cameras for the stables, and he bought them. The guard shack has the new monitors, and there's a set in my rooms at the stables, but I'm not going to be there to watch them. And the night guard is way too interested in texting his girlfriend."

"I'll keep an eye on your horses, Bud, and we can swap cell-phone numbers. Here's my information. Call me if you want me to check something, or even if you have a bad feeling."

She waved good-bye.

Her appointment at Doc Bartlett's went smoothly and quickly. "Your blood-test results are excellent," the short, energetic internist told Angela. "Keep doing what you're doing."

"Can I quit using the cane? I'm always forgetting it."

"Let's check your balance and reflexes."

Doc Bartlett put Angela through her paces: "Stand on your right leg. Now your left. On your toes." After five minutes, she said, "Okay, toss the cane."

Angela paid her co-pay with a smile, then checked her voice messages in her car: Butch had called.

She called him right back. "What's happening, Butch?"

"I'm in a hurry, Angela. Mom called. Dad's had a heart attack and I'm on my way to Peerless Grove. I'll be gone for a couple of days. But I have good news. Pete, the Chouteau High SRO, says there's a picture from the fire. Kip is seeing Trina, a girl who goes to Chouteau High, and she's part of Kip's Snapchat friends. She Snapped a photo of the ruined mansion and said, 'It was a really HOT time at the Gravois house.' She hinted she knew someone who had set the fire. Her friend Charlotte didn't believe her. Trina said, 'I saw the pics.' The word traveled, and Pete heard it. Now we have a name. We'll see if she kept a screenshot or knows the usernames, and then warrants are on the way. When I get back, we'll wrap this up."

"You aren't worried Greiman will catch them first?" Angela said.

"Man couldn't catch a cold," Butch said.

CHAPTER 36

Day thirteen

Angela walked for hours, finally free of her cane. She went barefoot, feeling the sun-warmed grass under her feet. That night, she was stretched out on the couch reading when Ann Burris called.

"Angela, we have an emergency." Ann sounded breathless and worried. "I know it's eight o'clock, long after working hours, but how do we get in touch with Detective Chetkin?"

"He had to go out of town. What's wrong?"

"Big Al was just here. He's heard something disturbing. You need to hear it."

"Does he want to meet again after work?"

"That may be too late. This is urgent, Angela. Bryan and I are taking a late flight for San Francisco. We have to be at the airport by ten o'clock tonight. Bryan's giving the keynote speech at a conference tomorrow night." Her pride was touching.

"How about if I order a pizza?" Angela said. "Big Al will have an excuse to talk to us. Come to my house. What do you and Bryan want?"

"Nothing, thanks. We've eaten. We'll be right over, ready for our trip with our bags in the car. We can go straight from your place to the airport."

Angela called in her pizza order, then raced around the living room, tidying up. She fluffed the couch pillows, threw out the pile of old mail, dusted the coffee table and end tables, then gave the guest bathroom a quick cleaning. She moved much faster without that cane.

Bryan and Ann arrived soon after Angela finished her chores. They made a stylish couple: Ann was dressed in a striking beige pantsuit, and Bryan in a charcoal sports coat, blue shirt, and gray pants. By the time Angela had given Bryan a beer and Ann a glass of white wine, Big Al arrived with her pizza. He looked harried and once again smelled like pepperoni. Angela thought it would make a great aftershave. She paid him and gave him a tip that made him smile, then left the pizza on the coffee table.

"I don't have much time." Al refused to sit down. "Kip and Duke, the guys setting the fires, are planning something for tonight. Something bad. I delivered six pizzas to Duke's house earlier tonight—he's Judge Charbonneau's son. The judge and his wife weren't home. They won't be back for two days. Duke and his sister, Carlie, were having a party. They were both drunk and high. So was everyone at the party. Carlie—she's fourteen—answered the door in her underwear."

"You're kidding. At fourteen?" Ann looked shocked.

"Happens all the time." Big Al paced Angela's living room. "She's really hot, but come on—she's way too young. I didn't want to look, but I couldn't help it. I mean, she was practically naked. Her beige bra and bikini panties were the same color as her skin, and it looked like she had on nothing at all."

He was blushing furiously. "Carlie was coming on to me. Not because I'm a hunk or anything, but because, you know, she can."

"I doubt that," Angela said, then regretted it. Poor Al was almost speechless with embarrassment.

"Please tell us what happened next," Ann prompted. "Time's running out and you have to get back to work."

"Right. Work." Al quit pacing. "Carlie had fifty dollars. She said I could keep twenty for a tip and she'd give me thirty. That's like really generous. More than fifteen dollars is good on an order like that. All Carlie had was one-dollar bills, and she kept dropping the bills and then losing count. She was rubbing up against me, dropping more bills and she'd have to start over. Every time she bent over to pick up a bill, she'd drop them again. She thought it was funny.

"All the while this was going on, I could hear the party in the great room. They were playing beer pong. The music was so loud I could feel the bass. The walls were vibrating. Duke and Kip were talking in a little room near the front door. I don't know what you call rooms like that in a rich person's house—it was sort of a waiting room. They had to talk loud to be heard over the music. Kip said, 'We'll do Old Reggie's stables. When we finish, *Equus* will look like *Bambi*.' You know *Equus*?"

"Sure," Bryan said. "The Peter Shaffer play about a psychiatrist who treats a young man with a sick fascination with horses. He blinds them. The boy's seventeen . . ."

He stopped as they all realized that Kip, Duke, and the late Zander were seventeen.

"They're going to blind Reggie Du Pres's horses?" Angela's heart froze with fear. She saw her favorite racehorses—powerful, imperious East Coast Express with her pretty white star, and the darkly magnificent American Hero—with mutilated eyes. Her stomach turned, and she tried to push away that horrible thought.

"No," Big Al said. "They're gonna set fire to the barn."

"Fire!" Angela said. "No! Horses are terrified by fire. Why would they do that?"

"Kip said burning the stables with live horses inside would be way cooler than just burning down an empty old house. He said horses go insane in fires."

"They do," Angela said.

"That's incredibly cruel," Ann said.

"I don't think they care," Al said. "Duke agreed it was cool—'like a movie, only for real. Burning down the Du Pres's stables would give the old dude something else to think about besides getting rid of my father. He's mad at him.' They're going to set fire to the stables after eleven o'clock tonight."

"Tonight? For sure?" Angela said.

"That's what they said. Cheap and Easy is open until eleven. They're going to buy what Kip called 'supplies' and then go to the stables."

"That's where they bought the supplies to start the Gravois estate fire," Angela said. "They got TP, potato chips, and shortening and used them as fire starters."

"Duke said if anyone at the party sees them leave, 'We can say we're going on a beer run. They'll be too stoned to know when we left the party and when we got back. We're here right now and nobody knows it.'"

"The barn has sprinklers to put out the fire, doesn't it?" Ann asked.

"Not according to Bud," Angela said. "It has fire detectors and extinguishers, but the old building can't have a sprinkler system. I hang around the stables a lot—I love being with the horses. Du Pres's security staff watches the stables and the rest of the property. Bud had new cameras installed so security can watch them in the guard shack—and Bud can watch them from his room. Except Bud's in Kentucky tonight, and the security guard spends his time texting his girlfriend."

"Kip knows about the cameras," Big Al said. "They've scoped out the place. Kip will stand by the junction box with the box door open while Duke is just out of camera range. When Duke gives the all clear, Kip will yank the camera cables, then Duke runs in and does his thing with the matches, and they video the fire. He said the loser night guard won't notice anything's wrong until he 'sees the burning horses running by.'"

Angela's stomach lurched.

"Those racehorses will die in the fire." Ann looked sick.

Bryan asked, "Al, did either Kip or Duke see you at their house? I'm asking for your safety. If Duke saw you with his sister and she wasn't wearing any clothes . . ."

Al interrupted him. *"You don't get it!"* He was almost shouting. "You just don't get it. Duke didn't see me. Kip didn't see me. Carlie didn't see me. I was standing right in their house, but I'm invisible. I'm the pizza dude in a polyester uniform that stinks of pepperoni."

"So you're a ghost," Angela said.

"No!" Al was pacing again. "I'm not a ghost. A ghost used to be human. I don't exist in their world. They can say whatever they want around me. That's why Carlie parades around naked in front of me. She gets to tease the nobody, the nothing, and I can't do anything about it. If I tried to grab her, I'd be in jail. If I said anything, they'd beat me senseless. They can do what they want because I'm not a person. They don't care what they say in front of me, any more than you care what you say in front of your couch. I'm not a person. I'm a thing."

Angela had never heard a sadder—or more accurate—explanation of the Forest social structure.

"We have to act fast," Bryan said. "It's almost nine o'clock. Angela, if Butch Chetkin isn't available, who would you call? What about the stableman?"

"Bud's in Kentucky, picking up another horse. Calling him won't do any good. We need help now. I'd better call 911."

"They'd know," Al said. "They have the police-scanner app. All the kids do."

"What's that?" Ann asked.

"You can download it free on your phone," Al said. "Lets you tap into live police, fire department, and other emergency radios. Drug dealers love those apps. They always know when the cops are coming. If you call 911, as soon as a car's dispatched, Kip and Duke will scatter."

"I can call Detective Greiman." Angela wondered if the new, improved Greiman would take her seriously.

"Call him now, while Al is still here," Bryan said. "Put your phone on speaker so we can all hear."

Angela did and got Greiman's voice mail. She left a message. "I hope he'll call me back. But when Ray's off duty, he usually doesn't pick up his phone."

"I'd better leave. I gotta get back." Al looked uneasy.

The three thanked him for his courage. They heard his old Subaru rattling down the drive. After Al left, Angela said, "Those boys are monsters. What are their parents like?"

"Absent," Ann said. "The judge spends his free time politicking. Duke's mother is too busy in the Forest Women's Club to have much interest in her son. He's been raised by nannies and housekeepers. Kip's family isn't much better. His father's verbally abusive, and his mother drinks."

"That doesn't excuse their cruelty," Bryan said.

"No, it doesn't. But they're a couple of sad cases." Ann looked at Bryan. "It's nine thirty. Should we cancel our trip? We can't let anything happen to those beautiful horses."

Bryan hesitated, and Ann said, "I can't ask you to miss your conference. You need to be rested for your speech tomorrow night. Why don't you go ahead and I'll join you later?"

Ann seemed torn: she wanted to save the horses, but she didn't want to miss the trip to San Francisco.

"Don't cancel your flight," Angela said. "I'll call Reggie Du Pres myself and warn him. I live on his property."

"Would you?" Ann was all smiles. "That would be super. There's no point in either of us talking to Reggie. He knows we think the arsonists are local kids, and he's not happy with us. This would prove we're right and he's wrong—rub salt into his wounds."

"I can handle it," Angela said. "You two go to the airport."

The two scattered gratefully, and Angela called the Du Pres home, hoping Old Reggie was awake and would talk to her. She knew he didn't like her, either. Reggie himself answered the phone. "Miss Richman." His patrician voice was imperious. "Why are you calling at this uncivilized hour? You should know you don't ring a household after nine p.m."

"I'm sorry to disturb you, Mr. Du Pres, but this is an emergency. May I come talk to you about it?"

"Come here? To my home? You may not! I'm preparing for bed. Anything you have to say can be said on the telephone. What is this so-called emergency?"

"It's a real emergency, Mr. Du Pres. Three teenagers have been setting fires in the Forest. They burned down your barn, set fire to the Hobart pool house, burned the Gravois estate, and tonight they want to set fire to your stables."

"Ridiculous! Who would do that? Give me their names at once!"

Angela hesitated, then figured Kip and Duke were going to be arrested anyway. "Duke Charbonneau and Kip Raclette."

"You mean Judge Charbonneau's son, Marlon, and Jeremy Raclette."

"Yes."

"When you had those strokes, Miss Richman, you had mental problems. You talked to dead people and people who didn't exist, didn't you?"

"I'd just come out of a coma."

"I fear your mind still isn't functioning properly. Marlon is the son of Judge Charbonneau, and his father is a respected member of our local judiciary. It's true Jeremy's father is a hedge funder, but his mother is a Mintern. Neither one of those families would commit such a despicable crime. The Forest arsonists have been arrested and are in custody, Miss Richman. Jose and Kendra Salvato set fire to those buildings. Because I knew your parents, I will do you a favor and not mention this to the

Raclettes and Charbonneaus. But what you're saying is actionable. You could be sued for slander, for destroying the reputations of those fine young men. In the meantime, you are barred from my stables. Do you understand? You are not to set foot near my stables or touch my horses for any reason. Good night, Miss Richman!"

CHAPTER 37

Days thirteen, fourteen

Barred. Angela was stunned. Barred from the Du Pres stables? This couldn't be happening. Two junkies wanted to torch the Du Pres stables and watch the horses run burning through the night. East Coast Express, with her sly sense of humor, and the peppermint-loving American Hero would die for their twisted entertainment. Reggie could sue her if he wanted. She had to save those horses.

But Angela couldn't save two horses by herself—not to mention the pet goat and the pony. She needed help. Someone who could handle half a ton of crazed racehorse. Angela had never even ridden a horse.

Katie. Katie rode. And Monty owned a horse farm. They both knew horses. They were her last chance. Angela prayed they were home—and together—as she called Katie's cell phone.

Her friend answered, sounding relaxed and carefree. "Angela, you just caught Monty and me leaving. We're going out for a late dinner. Want to join us?"

"No. I need you here. Now."

Katie heard her fear in those sharp, short sentences, and her mood switched to serious. "What's wrong? What happened? Are you sick?"

"It's not me. It's the Forest arsonists. They're going to set the Du Pres stables on fire after eleven tonight. Reggie won't believe me."

"Holy shit. It's ten o'clock."

"Right. Get over here. Do you have old boots and jeans?"

"In my truck."

"Get them. Make sure Monty wears his. Tell Monty to bring whatever we need to get the horses out of the stables in a fire. And hurry!"

Katie didn't ask questions. "We'll be there in fifteen."

"Make it ten." Angela hung up, then raced upstairs and changed into jeans, a long-sleeve shirt, and boots. She found some unwrapped peppermints in the jeans pocket and felt a pang. Would she be able to give her favorites their treats again?

Next, she put the untouched pizza, paper napkins, and bottled water on the cedar chest at the foot of her bed, the biggest free space in the room. She flicked off the bedroom lights except for the night-light. Downstairs, she left one light burning in the living room. Her home wouldn't attract attention if Kip and Duke drove past it.

When she saw the headlights of Katie's truck in her driveway, she ran outside. Katie hit the brakes, and a worried-looking Monty climbed out of the passenger seat. Both wore sturdy boots and old jeans. "Tell us what's happening," he said.

She did. Quickly and concisely, she told them about Big Al, Kip and Duke, and the conversation Al heard tonight about the two fire setters who wanted to watch the horses burn.

"And you told Reggie this," Monty said.

"He refused to believe me. He said that the arsonists were already in jail, and Kip and Duke came from fine families. They'd never commit such a despicable crime."

"Stubborn old fool," Monty said. "Did you contact anyone else?"

"There is no one else. Butch is in Kansas, and Bud is picking up a racehorse in Kentucky. Greiman's not answering his phone, and if I call 911, the kids have the police-scanner app. All we can do is wait for them."

"Then let's go to the stables and keep watch," Katie said.

"Can't. Not with Reggie on the warpath. But we can see the stables from my bedroom. It's the best view."

"I'll turn my truck around and leave the keys in it so we can drive there if we have to," Katie said.

While Katie backed up the truck so it was facing out of the drive, Monty said, "This is bad, Angela. Horses are terrified of fire, and racehorses are already skittish. If the barn catches fire, these won't be the gentle horses you know. They'll be insane with fear. Racehorses weigh thirteen hundred pounds. They can kill with a single kick. They won't mean it, but they can't help themselves. This is primal fear. I brought flashlights in case the lights go off during the fire. There are leads and halters in the back of the truck, extra fire extinguishers from my barn, and horse blankets. They're good for putting out small fires."

Katie rejoined them, holding a tangle of rope and leather. "What time is it?"

Monty looked at his iPhone. "Ten forty-two. We should take our posts."

Upstairs in Angela's bedroom, the three sat on the bed, where they had a clear view of the stables and the moonlit paddock. Angela opened the window. The night was warm and clear, the black sky spread with stars like diamonds on jeweler's velvet. It was so quiet, they heard a horse whinny.

"How many horses are in the barn?" Monty asked. For some reason, he dropped his voice to a conspiratorial whisper.

"I don't see anyone in the paddock," Angela said. "Eecie has the stall closest to the main door. Her goat stays in there with her. American Hero has the next stall. If his pony isn't with him, it's next door. That's all."

"Good," Monty said. "Katie will lead Eecie. I'll go for Hero. You handle the fire extinguishers, Angela. You know how to use one?"

"Yep. My father taught me the code—PASS: Pull the pin. Aim the nozzle. Squeeze the handle. Sweep the base of the fire."

"Right. And if the fire is bigger than you, don't try to put it out. Let the stables burn. The important thing is to save the horses."

"I hope you don't have to lead a horse, but I'll give you a short lesson," Katie said. "This"—she held up a long leather cage studded with buckles—"is the halter. And this rope is the lead. You're going to be in a hurry, but try to stay calm. Hold the halter in your *right* hand and use your left arm and hand to gently hold the horse's muzzle. That's important. Walk to the horse's *left* side. So you're standing on the left, but holding the halter in the right hand when you slip it on. Keep it slow. Don't throw the halter on instantly, or you'll spook the horse and be stuck in the stall with a bucking animal. Pat the horse on the shoulder and talk to it the whole time. Try to sound calm. Horses will pick up your fear. Hold the halter in the same direction as the horse's head."

She took Monty's arm and said, "If his arm is the horse's head, and his fist is the nose, the halter goes on like this. Got it? The halter has to face the same direction as the horse's head."

Angela nodded and prayed she'd never have to use this information.

"Slip the halter over the horse's nose and ears and keep talking to it. Fasten this top buckle—the crown piece. Don't let the halter touch the horse's eyes. This is the lead line. It's already clipped on the halter. I'll attach this gear to your belt with another clip, and if you need it, you'll have it ready."

"I hope I don't," Angela said.

"We all do. But you'll be fine. Remember, keep left, and hold the halter with your right hand, and whatever you do, don't get backed into a corner in the stall or in the barn. A panicked horse can kill you with one kick. Fire is their greatest fear."

"I should know more about the barn," Monty said. "Does Bud store hay in the stables?"

"I don't know," Angela said.

"He doesn't," Katie said. "The hay and feed are in a tin shed about a hundred yards away."

"Good. Hay will add fuel to the fire."

"Bud keeps a clean barn and a safe one," Katie said. "It has less dust than my house and no cobwebs, trash, oily tack, hoof-cleaning rags, or dirty paper towels. He's a fanatic about smoking. Visitors have to put out their cigarettes in a sand bucket."

They heard a rumble outside. "What's that?" Monty asked. A battered SUV passed on the road in front of Angela's house.

She looked out the window. "Just a Range Rover. It's heading toward his house. We should eat this pizza while we wait. If there is a fire, we'll need fuel."

After they polished off the pizza, Angela asked, "What time is it?"

"Eleven fifteen," Katie said.

Angela felt hope blooming in her chest. "They're not coming. I was wrong. Big Al was wrong—there won't be a fire tonight."

"Don't pack it in yet," Katie said. "Those two birds are drunk and high and at a party. They said 'after eleven.' In junkie time that could mean anything from now until daylight."

They sat in silence for a while longer. "What happens if we see someone heading for the barn?" Angela asked.

"Call the Du Pres security and then call 911," Monty said. "If it's a false alarm, that's the least of our problems."

"There's a car coming up the road with no lights," Katie said.

"It's a red Beemer," Angela said. "I think Kip has a Beemer."

"How'd they get through security?" Monty asked.

"The night guard isn't the sharpest knife in the drawer, according to Bud," Angela said. "And the boys know Reggie. The first families get a free pass."

"The Beemer's not going toward Reggie's house," Katie said. "It's taking the road to the stables."

"Do I call security or 911?" Angela asked.

"Not yet," Katie said. "The boys can say they stopped to pet the horses. They're parked by the hay shed. They're getting out of the car . . ."

"Now what?" Monty asked.

"They've got bags of something. Yellow bags."

"Cheap and Easy bags," Angela said. "We'd better go."

"Get in the truck," Monty said. "If we see them starting a fire on the drive there, we'll make the calls."

They ran outside and squeezed into the front seat of Katie's truck. She roared out of Angela's drive, lights off, gravel spraying and pinging against the truck's body. When they got to the top of the hill, Katie said, "What the fuck! The shed's on fire, and there are burning bales piled at the entrance to the barn."

Angela hit 9-1-1 and punched "Send." The operator answered, "9-1-1. What's your—"

Angela interrupted her. "Fire! Help! The Du Pres stables!"

Katie slammed on the brakes, and the three leaped out. Angela could hear the horses screaming and the goat's frantic, rusty bleat. "Angela! You put out that bale," Monty shouted. "We'll go around back and get the horses out that way."

Angela grabbed two fire extinguishers from the back of the truck, pulled the pin on one, and squeezed the handle.

Nothing happened.

Black smoke stung her eyes. The orange-red flames were almost as tall as she was. She squeezed the handle again, and white foam spurted out. Angela aimed her extinguisher at the crackling, swirling fire. The foam smothered most of the hay bale, but now flames were dancing on the stable doorway. Angela pulled the pin on the second fire extinguisher, and the bale was a smoking, blackened mess. Behind her, geysers of flame shot up from the hay shed, and sparks exploded.

Where were Monty and Katie? Why weren't the horses in the paddock? Angela could hear a horse's hooves thudding and a terrible, almost human screaming. She ran to the back entrance and saw Eecie rearing up on her back legs, white showing around her eyes, foam streaming from her mouth. Monty could barely hang onto her lead and avoid getting trampled.

"Where's Katie?" she shouted over the roar of the fire.

"Her ankle's broken!" he yelled over Eecie's screams. The horse thudded back down on all fours. Monty tried to pat the Thoroughbred's neck, and she snapped at him with big yellow teeth. "Easy, girl," he said. She screamed again.

Monty regained control of the lead, wrapping it around his hand. "The bastards put a rope across the rear entrance, then opened the stall doors, hoping to break the horses' legs if they ran out. Katie ran into the rope first and fell over it. She can't walk, but she's safe under a tree. The goat's outside now, and so's the pony. You're going to have to get Hero out. He's still in there. His stable door is open, but he won't leave."

Eecie rose up on her back legs again, and Monty fought to hold onto her, muscles bulging in his arms.

Angela couldn't see into the smoky stable, but she could hear Hero's screams. She ripped off her shirt and dunked it in the horse trough, then wrapped it around her mouth and nose. There would be more oxygen at floor level. Her father had taught her that. She dropped down to the stable floor and felt her way along the walls, trying not to breathe in the smoke. Her lungs burned. Kip and Duke must have scattered straw through the stable. It burst like fireworks.

Hero's kicks and thuds were louder. She was almost at his stall. The smoke cleared and she saw him—eyes wide, foam flying, teeth showing. "Easy, boy. It's me, Hero. You know me." She stood up, and the heat slammed her body.

Try not to show fear, Katie had said. Angela unclipped the halter and lead from her belt and approached Hero on the left. She held out her hand with the peppermint. Hero sniffed it. He had no interest in the treat, but he seemed to recognize it—and her. She crooned soft words as she slipped the halter over his head, buckled the crown piece, and grabbed the lead.

Hero calmed slightly, and she kept crooning nonsense and pulling him out of the stall. She found another peppermint. He took that one. Now they were in the smoky barn. She moved as quickly as she could, patting and talking to the horse. She was choking on the smoke, but it parted for a moment. She could see the exit up ahead and flashing emergency lights. The fire department was here.

"Almost free," she said to Hero. The smoke seared her lungs. The horse tried to turn around, but she wrapped the lead around her hand and pulled him toward her. She'd be dragged into the fire with him he if he didn't follow her out of the barn.

But he did. She crooned and talked, though her lungs burned and her throat was on fire. She emerged from that fiery barn with Hero and felt strong hands grab her and unwrap the lead from her hand.

"He's safe," she said, though those two words scorched her tortured lungs. Someone mercifully clapped an oxygen mask over her face, and the world went black.

CHAPTER 38

Day fourteen

"What the fuck do you mean, I have to stay another day for observation?" Was that Katie? Angela thought she recognized her friend's voice but couldn't see her. Angela was in a fog—or maybe it was smoke—and heard Katie in her room. Weird. Why was Katie at her house?

Angela's head felt like it was stuffed with cotton. She heard a man say, "I'll take care of her. She can go home with me." Angela recognized Monty's voice.

Then she saw the bandages on her right hand and the IV line stuck in her left. Some machine was clipped onto her finger. She had a cannula stuck in her nostrils, and it felt uncomfortable. Why am I wearing this?

Oxygen, her slow brain told her. I got oxygen last night, and now I'm in the hospital getting more. She shifted in the lumpy bed and coughed. It hurt her chest to breathe.

Now she was awake enough to figure out that the woman on the other side of the privacy curtain was Katie, her hospital roommate. Angela heard Katie telling someone—a nurse?—"I'm fine. My vitals are fine. I was here for observation. You've seen me. I've seen you. We've both seen enough of each other. I need to go." Katie sounded angry and impatient.

"Doctors make the worst patients," the nurse said.

"This one does. I've seen what happens to patients who spend too long in the hospital. They wind up being *my* patients!"

"Katie!" Monty said. "I know you don't feel good with a broken ankle, but you owe the nurse an apology."

Silence. Then Katie said, "I'm sorry. I really am. I'm worried about my roommate, Angela. She still hasn't come to."

"Katie!" Angela called. "I'm behind the curtain. I'm awake. I'm fine." She erupted into a series of raspy coughs. The nurse came running over. "Good morning."

"This is Sisters of Sorrow Hospital," Angela said. "I was admitted last night after the fire at the Du Pres stables."

"That's right." The nurse sounded as if Angela were an unusually bright third grader. "Let me check your vitals." She stuck a thermometer in Angela's ear and a blood-pressure cuff on her arm.

"Very good. Would you like breakfast?"

"I guess so," Angela said. "Everything tastes like smoke."

The nurse bustled out. Monty, who looked and smelled like he'd spent the night in a fireplace, pulled back the privacy curtain. "Morning, Angela." He smiled at her. "Glad to see you awake. You had us worried last night. Now that you're okay, I badly need some coffee and breakfast. Then I have to make some phone calls. I'm going to the cafeteria. You and Katie can talk."

Katie's hair was flat and matted, and she had dark circles under her smoke-reddened eyes. Her face was chalk white and her splinted, swollen ankle was propped on a pillow. Even her foot looked resentful.

"How did we get in the same room?" Angela said. "Why aren't you in the orthopedic ward?"

"No room. After the ER X-rayed my ankle and determined I had a hairline fracture, they put me in this splint and told me to keep the weight off it until it was pain-free. Two freaking weeks at least. I asked for one of those knee walkers so I can get around and go to work. Still two weeks, but after that I get a walking boot for another freakin' month. Meanwhile, it's rest, ice, compression, and elevation. They kept me overnight in the telemetry ward for observation, where they observed I'm a pain in the ass."

"The telemetry ward? Isn't that the ward where the Angel of Death killed all those people?"

"Now you know why I want the hell out of here. Do those blisters on your hand hurt?"

Angela looked at her wrapped paw. "Not really. I just noticed them. Are the horses safe?"

"Yes, thanks to you and Monty. The fire department put the fire out before it did too much damage. The investigator thinks the old stables can be repaired. The horses are safe but spooked and skittish—even the goat's off its feed. They're all at Monty's stables for R & R. Bud's bringing the new racehorse to board there until the Du Pres stables are repaired."

"Bud must be beside himself," Angela said.

"Monty said he's never heard the man so upset. Bud wanted to leave the racehorse in Kentucky and fly straight home, but Old Reggie insisted he drive the horse home ASAP."

"How did you break your ankle?"

"Fracture," Katie corrected. "It's only a hairline fracture. That was thanks to Kip and Duke, those boys from so-called good families. They decided to make their own movie, and they had a plan to make it more exciting. They put a burning bale of hay at one entrance to the stables."

"That's the fire I put out."

"The little shits also strung a rope across the other entrance. They started the fire and opened the stall doors, hoping the horses would run full tilt at the rope and break a leg."

"Except the horses panicked and didn't leave their stalls."

"Right. And I ran full tilt into the fucking rope and fractured my ankle. Glad I wore lace-up boots. Otherwise, the ER would have had to cut off the boot. When I fell, it hurt so bad I couldn't stand up."

"I can imagine what you must have said."

"I guess I was pretty bad. But cussing saved my life. Monty followed the trail of F-bombs into the smoke, carried me out, and set me under a tree away from the fire."

"Rescued by a handsome prince, Snow White," Angela said.

Katie snorted. "Yeah, I'm Snow White—except I drifted. I hated sitting on my ass while Monty went back inside the barn to rescue Eecie and the other animals. He swatted the goat, and it ran through the barn and outside. He shooed the pony out of the stable. Then he put a halter on Eecie to lead her out, and she went nuts."

"I saw."

"So did I. And I couldn't do a fucking thing. Not even stand up. I found my cell phone in my pocket and called 911 again. Then I called Old Reggie. He got the staff up there and directed the fire department. Told them where they could find the fire hydrants. He'd spared no expense installing hydrants up near that barn, and it paid off. His stables were saved."

"Did they catch Duke and Kip?"

"Duke, the judge's son, is dead. They found him in the tack room. He was badly burned."

"Oh. Those horses never hurt him." Some small part of Angela felt sorry for Duke. She wasn't sure how she felt about that.

"Doug Hachette, the fire investigator, thinks Duke went back to get a trophy or something that belonged to one of Reggie's horses," Katie said. "He died with his cell phone in his hand. Doug thinks Kip, the hedge funder's kid, was either helping his friend steal something or trying to save him. They found Kip passed out on the threshold of the tack room. He's here in SOS with smoke inhalation and burns on thirty percent of his body. He'll probably make it, but he'll need skin grafts. His ass is cooked."

"So he's going to jail," Angela said.

"I hope so, but I mean his rear end really is cooked. He fell on his face, and his pants were on fire—liar, liar."

"You don't have much sympathy for him."

"I'd like to autopsy him while he's alive. Those two planned a cruel, senseless death for those gorgeous animals."

"Did Kip confess?"

"Hell, no. He went into a coma after he passed out. The firefighters found him and loaded him into an ambulance. His rich daddy's lawyer got to the hospital before Mummy and Daddy arrived from Vail and camped out next to the kid. Greiman and Hachette actually figured this part out: They impounded Kip's Beemer at the scene and got a warrant for it. Inside, they found a Cheap and Easy receipt for potato chips, shortening, nylon rope, and five gallons of gasoline."

"The same fire starters used for the other fires," Angela said.

"Right. The gasoline container was tossed in the trunk—empty. They also found two cell phones. One belongs to Kip."

"Did they find Zander's phone?" Angela asked.

"They're not sure, but they're pretty sure they'll get both Kip and Duke for the rope in the stables. The busted ends were wrapped in black electrical tape to keep them from unraveling."

"That tape is sticky," Angela said.

"Sticky enough—I think they can make those animal-abuse charges stick. Greiman's having the lab test the rope for prints with some process using Super Glue fumes. He's hoping it has both sets. They're also testing the rope for DNA. The morons videoed each other buying everything at Cheap and Easy and also their stable prep and fire starting. Video with running commentary. Definitely on Kip's cell phone. Duke's may be too fire damaged."

"But they've got them," Angela said.

"Fucked themselves good and proper." Angela heard her friend's satisfaction. "Duke's going to have to answer to a higher court, but Kip's facing the music down here—along with the wrath of Reggie Du Pres. Personally, I think Duke gets off easy dealing with God. Reggie's going to make Kip's life hell on earth."

"And now Kendra and Jose will go free."

There was an awkward silence.

"What? They're not free?"

"Old Reggie and his puppet, the county prosecutor, still say the Salvatos set the other three fires."

"No!" Angela was shocked.

"Wait, wait. It's not over. One reason Monty was so eager to start making calls is Butch said he was coming back to work today. And KJ, the private investigator, left Monty a message late last night that he'd located Maria Garcia, Jose's alibi and old girlfriend, in Chicago. Monty didn't get a chance to call either one back. So we may still be able to get them off the hook."

"How's the Forest reacting to the scandal?"

"Shattered." Katie grinned. "All their precious assumptions are as shattered as if someone dropped them off a skyscraper. Two sons of first families set fire to the Du Pres stables—blue-blood crime. Once again, it's a media circus here. Reporters are rolling in from all over the country—no, the world. Even the BBC News is covering this."

"You're kidding."

"I shit you not. Saw it this morning. Let's see what's on now."

While Katie turned on her TV, an aide arrived with Angela's breakfast tray. Angela examined the prefab pancakes, lumps of scrambled eggs, and gluey oatmeal and wondered which one would taste best with the smoke flavor in her mouth and nose. She opted for the eggs.

On the TV screen over Katie's bed, Angela saw a bubble-haired blonde reporter interviewing Ollie Champlain, Luther's crusty hanger-on. Ollie looked like he'd been left outdoors in a bad rain this morning, as he pontificated on the two boys who burned the Du Pres stables.

"I don't understand it," he said. "Those boys had everything: good family, good upbringing, good education. It's not like they were Toonerville kids. But they did hang around with that Toonerville boy who OD'd. Like that Mexican gal that Luther *bleep*. The one in jail. It's them outsiders causing the problems. Not us. Not ours."

"And there, in a nutshell, is the Forest philosophy," Katie said.

"Actually, Ollie does look like a walnut," Angela said. "And he's cracked."

Before Katie could answer, Monty dashed into the room, a smile on his face. "I think we're going to do it. We're going to have the evidence to free the Salvatos."

"Spill," Angela said. Katie was too dazzled by her man to say anything.

"First, Butch Chetkin's father is okay. He was sent home from the hospital yesterday with orders to lose forty pounds and eat a low-salt, low-fat diet. Butch got him settled at his house. He arrived back in the Forest late last night, and he's at work this morning.

"He says the unidentified print on the syringe in Zander's arm and the print inside Zander's BMW trunk, plus the unknown prints the fire investigator found on the TP wrapper and the can of shortening at the Gravois fire, are being processed. So is the unknown DNA on the syringe that was stuck in Zander's arm, as well as the DNA and prints in the Gravois estate's unburned kitchen. Oh, and that was Zander's phone found in Kip's car at the fire scene."

"Did Butch get a warrant for it?"

"Doesn't need one. Zander's mother gave him written permission to look at it—she found the password when she was cleaning Zander's room. Butch got a police tech to open the phone. Zander liked to save his Snaps. They show Zander, Kip, and Duke posing with the potato chips and toilet paper in the abandoned kitchen of the Gravois house. Another one shows all three boys rubbing big globs of shortening on the walls and unrolling TP around the kitchen. Zander also saved Snaps of the three partying in the Hobarts' pool house. And one shows Kip pouring gasoline on the walls with TP strung all over the inside."

"What about the historic barn that Reggie wanted to sell?" Angela asked.

"That's the best one yet," Monty said. "The boys piled debris and their usual fire starters in a corner, and Kip set it on fire. Then the three are urinating on the barn's For Sale sign. The text says, 'Three fire hoses.'"

"Caught with their dicks out," Katie said. "What did KJ have to say about Maria Garcia?"

"She said Jose brought her two hundred fifty dollars in cash— enough to cover her rent and a little extra. He refused to stay at her apartment that night and stayed instead at a hotel. KJ has the receipt, and the staff said Jose really did stay there. KJ even talked with the hotel maid, who confirmed the bed had been slept in and the bathroom used."

"She remembered a stay from that far back?" Angela asked.

"Heck, yes. Jose tipped her five dollars. She rarely gets more than a dollar—if anyone even bothers tipping. Jose's generosity saved him."

"From the law," Katie said. "I suspect Gracie's going to give him an epic ass chewing."

"If he's lucky," Angela said.

"So the next step is to march into the prosecutor's office and demand that Kendra and Jose go free," Katie said.

"Not yet," Monty said. "Getting those DNA and fingerprint results may take a little time. Once I have all the proof, then I make my demands. I'll give Mick Freveletti all the evidence that Kendra and Jose are innocent. I'll remind him that the press will still be in town for Duke's funeral, and I'll explain that the media frenzy will be ten times worse unless he accepts the overwhelming evidence that Kendra and Jose are innocent and all charges are dropped."

"And then?" Katie asked.

"We have one heck of a celebration, my love." He swept Katie into his arms.

"I like stories with happy endings," Angela said.

EPILOGUE

One month later and beyond

Angela had been out of the hospital for a month when a letter on Reggie Du Pres's engraved stationery was delivered to her house by one of his staff.

> Dear Miss Richman,
> You have my permission to visit any of my three race-horses, which are currently boarded at Montgomery Bryant's farm, at any time. I also grant you permission to ride the horse of your choice, so long as you are supervised by Bud, the head stableman. I'm enclosing three framed portraits, to wit, Valerie's Spirit, American Hero, and East Coast Express.

The last two horses were photographed in the winner's circle. Angela especially liked the photo of Hero wearing a blanket of roses. That letter was the closest the old man would come to an apology.

Bud and Katie talked Angela into riding American Hero. She was afraid to get on the big, powerful horse. As Bud helped Angela into the saddle, he assured her that Hero was gentle.

"It will be a whole new world," Katie said. She had graduated to a walking boot, and her moods ranged from touchy to outraged.

"It sure is," Angela said. "I'm more than five feet off the ground."

And too scared to move in case she slid off the horse.

Bud gentled her the way he'd talk to a skittish horse. "We'll go for a little walk around the paddock. I'll lead Hero, and I'm here to catch you if anything goes wrong. You hold the reins soft, like this." He arranged her hands. "Thumb up, with three fingers on the rein and your pinkie outside. Good."

Angela felt awkward on the muscular, shiny-coated horse, and her hands seemed oversize and clumsy in that position.

"Stay relaxed," Bud said.

Relaxed, she thought. The one word that guaranteed you felt tense. Hero began a slow walk, led by Bud. Angela's heart beat faster. She was afraid she'd slide off the saddle—or Hero would suddenly remember he was a racehorse, jump the fence, and go galloping across the fields. But he stayed in that slow, steady walk.

"Good," Bud said. "You're doing fine. Let your seat move with your body. Let your legs lightly have contact with Hero's sides. You don't have to freeze your arms. Let your arms follow with his head as it goes up and down, so you're not pulling on the reins. Then you're gentle on his mouth. There, now you're getting a feel for it."

She was, a little. As Hero continued his slow progress, she felt more comfortable on his back. She began to enjoy the view. They made three trips around the paddock, then Bud said, "Are you ready to step up the pace to a trot?"

"Uh, not today, thanks." Angela patted Hero on the neck, and Bud helped her dismount. She hugged the horse and kissed him. He kissed her back. She gravely shook his tongue and gave him peppermints and a carrot.

"How did you like your first ride?" Bud asked.

"It was . . . interesting."

"So you didn't like it." Bud seemed disappointed.

"No, I did. It's just that I'm used to cars. You can't put the pedal to the metal on a horse."

Bud laughed. "Yes, you can. Especially that one. But not right away. You'll have to know him better."

Angela started taking riding lessons with Bud three times a week. She learned how to balance herself, how to use the reins and her legs, how to shift her weight to give the horse direction. It was a warm November day when she tried her first canter and felt the horse's powerful body and the wind in her face. That's when she really relaxed and began to enjoy riding. At Christmas, Katie and Monty gave her a pair of custom-made riding boots. Horses had been Angela's solace since the strokes. Now riding became her escape from the worst part of her job. She grew fit and learned to fight the sadness that sometimes overwhelmed her.

After months of lessons, Angela went for a long afternoon ride on the Du Pres estate. She and Hero ended up on the highest hill. It was spring again, and the Missouri hills were a tender green. She'd been thinking about Donegan, wishing he could be with her. She knew she'd love only one man in her life, but at least she'd had that love, and that was a gift. The red flowers blooming nearby reminded her of the roses Donegan had given her. She patted Hero's neck and thought of the horse's photo in the winner's circle, when Hero was blanketed with roses.

"We've both won the grand prize and stood in the winner's circle," she told the horse as she patted his neck. "That should be enough for both of us."

◆ ◆ ◆

Jeremy "Kip" Raclette spent two weeks in a coma at the hospital. He would need more than a year's worth of painful skin grafts, as well as rehab for heroin addiction. He had to stay on his stomach with his ass in the air. It was humiliating. His friend Duke had died in the fire, and Kip thought Duke got the better deal. Kip never told anyone that he was going to the tack room to help Duke steal the trophies. If people wanted to think he was trying to save his friend, fine with him. The police found his cell phone with the stable video and released parts of it to the media. People were outraged when they saw Duke and Kip, flying high on heroin, setting the hay bale on fire to block the main entrance, and then laughing crazily when they strung the rope at the other entrance. Nobody but the drug-addled Duke and Kip thought the blazing stables and screaming horses were cool. The Forest's anger raged nearly out of control when the dramatic portraits of American Hero and East Coast Express were released, along with an adorable video of Snickers, Hero's pony. Little Bit captured all hearts when she tried to eat a TV reporter's mic.

The police sent out a carefully worded press release that announced seventeen-year-old Kip Raclette had been badly burned, and Duke Charbonneau had died in the fire. The press release said the boys had no legal reason to be at the stable and that the police had recovered video showing the two setting the barn on fire and photos placing them at the scene of the other three fires at the Hobart pool house, the historic barn, and the Gravois estate. Upon Kip's release from the hospital, he would be charged with multiple counts of felony arson, animal cruelty, and felony murder because Duke had died during the commission of a felony.

Kip's father had to hire security to stay outside the boy's hospital room. He was getting so many death threats and so much hate mail over those two stupid racehorses, that pony, and the goat with the dumb name, the hospital said it couldn't be responsible for his safety. The nurses who tended Kip's painful wounds looked at him with contempt, but said nothing.

"You know why the cops are waiting to charge you, shithead?" his father screamed on his one visit to the hospital. "Because I have to pick up all your bills. I have to pay for your rehab and your hospital care. I hope you rot in jail. The state can lock you up and throw away the key for all I care."

They nearly did. Kip felt the full fury of the Forest, led by Reggie Du Pres. The boy was afraid he'd be dragged out of the hospital and lynched before he got to court. He was going to be tried as an adult. His mother used some of her Mintern money for one last favor. The lawyers arranged a plea bargain for thirty years and told him he was lucky to get that.

His parents weren't so lucky. Because Kip was a minor, they were sued by everyone: Reggie Du Pres wanted the money for the restoration of his stables and his historic barn, plus his own mental pain and suffering.

The fire became a gold mine for Monty. Every injured party in the Forest hired him to sue Kip's parents. The Hobart family wanted the money to rebuild and refurnish the pool house that their insurance didn't cover. Angela and Katie sued for their medical bills, lost wages, and pain and suffering.

Judge Charbonneau was also sued, since his son helped commit the crime. The lawsuits quickly ate up his savings and his family trust.

The Raclettes and the Charbonneaus both filed for bankruptcy. The judge didn't bother running for reelection. He and his wife moved to a small apartment in Toonerville. Their daughter, Carlie, is in rehab. The Raclettes moved somewhere back East and cut all ties to the Forest. Kip never sees them in prison.

Luther Ridley Delor was cremated two weeks after the fire, and his ashes were buried in the family plot in the Forest cemetery. After the private funeral, Priscilla Du Pres Delor resigned as president of the Chouteau Forest Women's Club.

Mario Ortega's Killer Cuts Salon eventually regained its former clientele. At first, the customers continued to go to Nikolai of New York. But then the invading hairstylist fried Priscilla's hair the day of Luther's funeral. She was forced to wear a long black veil for the ceremony, and hats and scarves for weeks afterward. Priscilla swallowed her pride and returned to Mario, and the other members of the Forest followed suit. Mario hired the part-time manicurist to take Kendra's place.

Kendra Salvato now goes by her middle name, Graciela—Grace, for short. She and her family moved to Austin, Texas, and she enrolled in the business school at the University of Texas. She's working toward a degree in business administration and plans to help her parents' businesses. She's currently dating a college senior who's also a musician.

Jose Salvato sued Chouteau County for false arrest. His attorney, Monty, pointed out that the prosecutor had no evidence to support the charges of arson. The county settled out of court for an unknown amount, and the charges against Jose for assaulting a police officer were quietly forgotten. Jose sold his Chouteau Forest lawn-care business and moved to Austin to be with his daughter. Because the climate in that part of Texas is hot and dry, Jose has gone back to school to learn xeriscape, the art of landscaping in dry regions. He promised his wife that he will never meet with his ex-girlfriend, Maria Garcia, again. This time, he kept that promise.

Gracie also sold her business, and the Forest dwellers were sorry to see her go. The new owner raised the prices. Gracie started a new cleaning service in Austin. Thanks to shrewd marketing, it's starting to break even. Their daughter is supporting her parents until their businesses succeed.

Big Al the Pizza Dude got a full scholarship to the engineering school at the university of his choice. He went to work at the racetrack and loved that job. On his last night as a pizza driver, he stopped by Angela's house with her favorite pizza: pepperoni and mushroom. It was sunset, and the sky was streaked with gold. Angela heard his beat-up Subaru wheezing and clunking up her drive and opened her door to meet him.

"Al! It's good to see you, but I didn't order a pizza."

He looked uncomfortable. "I know, Ms. Richman, but I thought you might like one. If you don't feel like eating pizza tonight, you can freeze it."

"I always feel like eating pizza. Let me get my purse."

"It's on me. And I don't want a tip, either. I owe you."

"No, we owe you. We wouldn't have saved the horses or caught the arsonists without your help. You saved those innocent animals from a fiery death."

"I'm sorry Duke died," Al said.

"What a waste," Angela said. "Both those boys."

"I didn't just come to give you a pizza. I need a favor. That sweet blue MINI in your garage—do you drive it?"

"No, it belonged to my late husband. I haven't even started it since he died."

"Oh." Al's face fell. "I was hoping I could buy it from you. I mean, if you wanted to sell it. My Subaru's about to keel over."

Angela looked at Al and thought about the car her husband had enjoyed, now rotting in the garage. She needed to put her own car in there. It was time. "I agree it's a sweet car. And locking that car away is killing it. Let's take a look."

Angela got the keys for the car and opened the garage. Inside, it smelled of oil, mold, and dust. She could write her name in the thick dust on the MINI. But she didn't have the urge to run away. She could face this with Al.

She handed him the MINI's key. "Go on, see if it starts."

The driver's door opened with a creak. He turned the key and the car coughed, then roared into life.

"Yes!" Al pumped his fist.

Angela loved the pure delight on his face. "It's not good for a car to sit this long. It needs to be driven. If you like it, I can talk to your mother about transferring the title and the insurance."

"I can pay you a little something each month," he said.

"You deserve a reward for saving the Du Pres stables and capturing the Forest arsonists. If this car runs, consider it your reward."

"Awesome. Are you sure your husband would want this?"

"My husband was a good man. He's beyond wanting or needing anything. But I want it. Do you want to go for a test-drive on the Du Pres estate?"

"Sure."

She climbed in on the passenger side. Al backed the car out of the garage. And off they went, into the bright sunlit future.

THE INSIDER'S GUIDE
TO CHOUTEAU COUNTY
PRONUNCIATION

Missourians have their own way of pronouncing words and names, and you don't tell the Show Me State how to say something. The French were among the first settlers, but we resist Frenchifying.

Chouteau is *SHOW-toe*.

Du Pres is *Duh-PRAY*.

Gravois is *GRA-voy*.

Detective Ray Greiman is GRI-mun.

The state is divided on how to pronounce its own name. The eastern part calls it Missour-ee. In the west, it's Missour-uh. State politicians have mastered the fine art of adjusting their pronunciation to please whichever part of the state they're in.

ACKNOWLEDGMENTS

Fire. It's fascinating, fearsome—and mysterious. We're still learning about fires, their causes and effects, even today. Many experts helped me with *Fire and Ashes*, and I've tried to get their complicated information correct. Any mistakes are mine.

Thanks to Captain Brian Pollack, fire investigator for the City of Delray Beach Fire Rescue Department (IAAI-FIT), who spent many hours helping me with the details in *Fire and Ashes*. He also recommended a useful textbook, *Fire Investigator: Principles and Practice to NFPA 921 and 1033 Fourth Edition*.

Thank you to the following: John Lentini, CFI, D-ABC, Scientific Fire Analysis, LLC, Islamorada, Florida. Retired death investigator Mary Fran Ernst, one of the authors of the training text *Medicolegal Death Investigator*. Death investigator Krysten Addison. Harold R. Messler, retired manager, criminalistics, Saint Louis Police Laboratory. Nurse and mystery writer Gregg Brickman, who helped with the medical information. Bill Hopkins, retired Missouri judge and author of the Judge Rosswell Carew Mysteries, who helped with the legal details. Detective R. C. White, Fort Lauderdale Police Department (retired) and licensed private eye, who provided boundless help about police procedure.

Thank you to my agent, Jill Marr of the Sandra Dijkstra Agency, and to my Thomas & Mercer team, including acquisitions editor Jessica

Tribble, developmental editor Bryon Quertermous, author-relations editor Sarah Shaw, and Dennelle Catlett in Amazon Publishing public relations. I'm particularly grateful to the good catches by copy editors Haley Swan, Jill Kramer, and Elise Marton.

Many thanks to both Molly Portman and Alan Portman—Big Al the Pizza Dude—for their invaluable help on teen customs, pizza delivery, Snapchat, and tech info. Thanks to Will Graham, author *of Spider's Dance*, and Nora E. Saunders of Saunders & Taylor Insurance, Inc., Fort Lauderdale. Joanna Campbell Slan, bestselling mystery author and Daphne du Maurier Award winner, and Jaden Terrell, author of *A Taste of Blood and Ashes*, also helped, as did Marcia Talley, author of the Hannah Ives mysteries, and editor and author Christina Wood.

Randy Rawls, former president of the Florida chapter of the Mystery Writers of America and author of the Beth Bowman and Tom Jeffries mysteries, advised me on drugstore-cowboy gear. Thank you, Donna Mergenhagen, Dr. Robin Waldron, Molly Weston, Dick Richmond, Susan Schlueter, and Mary Alice Gorman and Richard Goldman of revuzeit.com.

Some people gave me their names for this novel. Rene Sabatini is the owner of Azure Realty in Lighthouse Point, Florida. A generous donation to charity was made to have his name in this novel. Lin Kalomeris, a southeast Florida Realtor with Balestreri Real Estate, made a generous donation to have her name in *Fire and Ashes*. Sarah E. C. Byrne also donated to charity. She's a lawyer from Canberra, Australia, and a crime-fiction aficionada. Jenny Carter is a retired computer geek who lives in Fort Lauderdale and, like her character, loves to walk everywhere in really high heels. Carol Berman is the manager of J. McLaughlin in Palm Beach Gardens, Florida. Laurie Hartig is the founder of Spread the Word Nevada, which helps at-risk children get the books they need. Mo Heedles is a mystery fan from New Hampshire. Jinny Gender, Montgomery Bryant's office assistant, is actually a red-haired Saint Louis woman. Ann Burris and Dr. Bryan Berry live in Fort Lauderdale.

Dr. Berry performs complex dental procedures and races Porsches, and the glamorous Ann is involved with a number of charitable organizations, through her own connections and her work in community relations for the Holland America Line. Ann made a generous donation to the Broward Public Library Foundation.

Thanks to Valerie Cannata, a former court reporter and horse lover who was part owner of the Thoroughbreds East Coast Express, American Hero, and Valerie's Spirit. Thanks also to horsewoman Jennifer Christensen for her expertise.

Thank you, Femmes Fatales, for your encouragement and advice. Please read our blog at www.femmesfatales.typepad.com. My fellow bloggers at The Kill Zone have given useful and entertaining writing advice. Read us at killzoneauthors.blogspot.com.

And finally, thank you to my husband, Don Crinklaw, my first reader and true love, for his help and support.

Any questions or comments? I'd love to hear from you. Please e-mail me at eviets@aol.com.

ABOUT THE AUTHOR

Award-winning author Elaine Viets has written thirty-one mysteries in three series, including the bestselling Dead-End Job series, featuring South Florida private detectives Helen Hawthorne and her husband, Phil Sagemont. She also writes the Josie Marcus, Mystery Shopper mystery series and the dark Francesca Vierling mysteries. She has served on the national boards of the Mystery Writers of America and Sisters in Crime. She's a frequent contributor to *Alfred Hitchcock Mystery Magazine* as well as anthologies edited by Charlaine Harris and Lawrence Block. Viets has won the Anthony, Agatha, and Lefty Awards.

The Angela Richman, Death Investigator series returns the prolific author to her hard-boiled roots. *Brain Storm* draws on her personal experiences as a stroke survivor, as well as her studies in the Medicolegal Death Investigators Training Course at Saint Louis University's School of Medicine. *Fire and Ashes* is the second novel in the series following *Brain Storm*.